A GET HAUNTED TALE

THESE WALLS STILL TALK

Brian Paone

Editor: Denise Barker

Graphic Designer: Amy Hunter
Author Photo: Taylor Seyler
Copyeditor: Gerri Rodriguez
Formatter: Kari Holloway

Published by Scout Media

ISBN (print): 978-1-960855-09-1
ISBN (eBook): 978-1-960855-10-7

July 26, 2024 – February 11, 2025
(Jefferson City, MO / Saint Robert, MO / Fort Meade, MD / Fort Belvoir, VA)

For more information on my books and music:
www.BrianPaone.com

MSP MAP

1.
Women's Unit | Lobby |
Housing Unit 1

2.
Gas Chamber

3.
Death Row | 3D |
Housing Unit 3

4.
A-Hall | Dungeon |
Housing Unit 4

CHAPTER 1:

OUTSIDE OF MISSOURI STATE PENITENTIARY

Christian stopped the rental car in front of the ominous stone entrance to the bloodiest forty-seven acres in America—at least dubbed so by Time magazine. The two-glass front doors and an array of windows peered down at the roadway, judging its nightly tour of guests and choosing which of those guests the abandoned prison's disembodied inhabitants will toy with tonight.

Christian leaned over Hannah, who sat in the passenger seat, to get a better view of the two sprawling castle-like towers on either side of the Missouri State Penitentiary entrance. Those towers stretched beyond his vision and looked as if they had suffered and had weathered their own arduous battles—internal and external—and had lost more than they had won.

"I told you that I don't want to talk about it anymore," Hannah said into the phone as Christian found an empty parking spot farther down the road from the prison.

"Looks like a full house. Did you see how many people were already lined up?" he asked.

She flashed him the *hold-on-one-second* symbol with her index finger and scowled at him. She knew Christian had only said that so her boyfriend—if Dollard even *should* be called that anymore—could hear another man's voice in the car with her. A not-so-subtle reminder that Hannah had asked *Christian*, and had *not* asked her boyfriend, to attend this overnight ghost hunt on one of the country's most-haunted properties.

Little did Christian know, Hannah had only asked him to go *to see* if it would make Dollard jealous. She felt like she had literally tried everything else to salvage the relationship. And she was sure her therapist—and her alcoholics anonymous sponsor, for that matter—would have a field day with her intention.

"Fine, Dollard. I'm going now. Talk to you tomorrow. That's if the ghosts don't eat me or anything." Hannah slammed the phone onto her jeaned thigh and released a frustrated scream that ricocheted back to her from the windshield.

She didn't want to look at Christian in the driver's seat. She knew he was glaring at her. She knew he was judging her. She wanted a moment to breathe—or to not breathe. Maybe that would be better for everyone involved.

No. She had worked tirelessly with her sponsor and therapist to expunge those thoughts during the past year of sobriety. Those days were over. Or at least they would be after tonight—after she made the last purge of her demons and returned to the penitentiary what rightfully belonged to it. *Then* she would be free.

She steeled herself and slowly espied Christian. Just as she thought; his brows were furrowed, and the look of disappointment *of her* and the look of longing *by him* were written all over his face.

"I don't know why"—he stopped himself; she assumed it was to prevent him from saying something he would regret—"you put up with him."

She looked away. Didn't want to answer. Wouldn't answer. It was just too hard to explain to someone who hadn't gone through what she had endured over the past fifteen years. Rather, the past fourteen years of being a functional alcoholic, and then a not-so-functional alcoholic.

"He was there when no one else was," she muttered, even surprising herself.

"I'm here for you. I'm here right now to do the most important thing for you. To prove to you that this faceless shadow man with a brimmed hat, who you've been seeing, is just a figment of your imagination and a product of your …" He let his words trail off. Again, probably not to say something he would regret. Christian was both great and terrible at doing that.

She snapped her gaze at him. "And my *what*? You were going to say *alcoholism*. He wasn't a hallucination, Christian."

"Then why the fuck have you not seen him a single time since you've gotten sober?" he yelled.

Hannah quickly stuck the tip of her index finger into her mouth to nervously chew on a cuticle and pushed her black-rimmed glasses farther up her nose with the back of her other hand. She focused on the line of guests lengthening in front of the penitentiary doors.

She slipped her hand into the front pocket of her jeans and slowly removed the rolled-up stolen item from the last time she had visited the penitentiary. She felt the thick and worn fabric between her fingers, the texture reminding her of a karate belt. The dark gray strip of fabric was about eighteen inches long and about two inches wide. From top to bottom, it contained loops made of the same fabric that rested one atop the next. Hannah didn't really know what it was. Maybe she would have an opportunity to ask someone here tonight about what the inmates had used it for.

"Hannah, I want to show you that these demons come from within you from faulty beliefs, not from that object nor from any ghost attached to it." He nodded toward the item in her grip, then sighed. "However, as the supportive friend that I am, you know I'm your biggest cheerleader for this quest of yours to purge your demons by returning that strip to the prison tonight. And, if you doubt that, keep remembering that I am the one here doing this with you and not"—Christian inclined his chin over his shoulder, indicating a boyfriend who had decided to stay one thousand miles away on the East Coast—"*that* guy."

Hannah wiped a single tear from her eye. "It's the final thing I have to do to close that chapter."

Christian sighed heavily and thumbed out the window toward the growing line of people. "I also think it'll be fun to show all those other crazies that all their ghost experiences are just creations in their heads too."

"I just can't anymore." Hannah stuffed the strip of fabric into her pocket and flung open the door. She slammed it, leaned against the car, and folded her arms. She felt the car jerk and heard Christian's door slam on the opposite side.

"C'mon. You know I'm only hard on you because I love you."

She arched an eyebrow at him as he rounded the front bumper, slinging his backpack around one shoulder.

"As a *friend*! Jeez, Louise."

"Yeah, right." She chuckled and pushed herself off the side of the car. She matched Christian's pace toward the end of the line sprawled down the sidewalk toward the entrance of the penitentiary.

When they solidified their place in line, Hannah pulled her phone from her back pocket. "Oh, did you download the ghost-hunting app I told you to?"

Christian flashed her a devilish smirk. "*Maaaayyyybeee.*"

Hannah punched his arm. "You didn't."

He released a full-blown laugh and kneeled to unzip his backpack.

Hannah watched some of the items stuffed inside try to escape, then gasped. "Are you fucking crazy?" she whispered forcefully, bending to meet his gaze.

He narrowed his eyes in confusion. "What?"

Hannah pulled her lips taut, reached into his backpack, and slid a vodka bottle with a blue cap out just an inch so he knew what she meant but so no one else could see. "Not only do they have a strict no-alcohol rule inside the prison, Christian Halifax, but how fucking insensitive are you to bring that? What? You thought you would just get wrecked around me, while we are hunting ghosts?"

"Calm down, Hannah Banana."

"You didn't know me when I was drinking. You've only known Sober Hannah."

"I know. I know. You tell me all the time how meeting me the day after your final bender felt like it was a new beginning." He reached up and tucked a wayward strand of her brown hair behind her ear that had gotten stuck in the frame of her glasses. She knew he had only done that to soften her; she hated herself that sometimes small acts like that usually always worked. "It's just one of those break-in-case-of-emergency liquid-courage things. For me. Not you."

Hannah smiled at him, not because she forgave him for bringing the liquor but because she knew unequivocally that Christian *would be* there for her, through thick and thin.

Christian met her gaze and returned a coveted smile of his own—one that said so many more things than her smile had conveyed. Things she didn't know if she could ever reciprocate. Or at least in the manner he wished for.

Maybe one day. *Maybe.*

"So, what's the app called again?" he asked, breaking her reverie, his phone in hand and his backpack zippered again and slung over his shoulder.

Hannah cleared her throat and tried to rid her brain from the distractions of Christian's energy that he was so good at projecting toward her. "It's called Casper-Capture."

Christian's fingers tapped on the screen as he navigated the app store. "I assume it's this one, with the image of everyone's favorite friendly ghost as the icon?"

She chuckled and smirked as she lowered her gaze. Sometimes his goofiness worked wonders on her mood. "Yeah, that one." She surveyed the cluster of guests in front of them, who clearly were there together, to see how many people were present. She heard another group get in line behind them and said to Christian, "The hunt doesn't start for another thirty minutes, and so many people are here already."

Christian glanced up from his phone. "Can't believe this many people believe in this hocus-pocus."

"Stop being so cynical. And stop using the name of my favorite movie to make something sound juvenile."

"Okay, Hannah Banana, then explain to me how this app is supposed to see ghosts and translate their voices. Through a cellphone." He scrunched his lips, as if to say, *Hmmmm?*

"Taylor-Made Technology designed it. They are paranormal investigators who are at the forefront of ghost-hunting software. Cellphones use, I dunno, frequencies or signals to turn people's voices into words, so …"

Christian's brows knitted together. "You don't really know, do you?"

"I–I don't. I think it's called a magnetometer or something. It detects electromagnetic fields."

"See? Hogwash. I just don't believe a phone app can *see* or *hear* ghosts."

"Sometimes you gotta have some blind faith and just believe. Casper-Capture is world-renowned, and all the most-revered ghost-hunting teams across the world use it exclusively. I bet you more than 75 percent of everyone here tonight will be using the app."

"I'm sure. You know why?"

Hannah put her hands on her hips. "Because it works."

Christian did nothing to hide his scoff. "Because they have a fabulous marketing team, who suck you into believing that it works."

"I think we're moving," she said, more to change the subject than as an announcement.

They shuffled forward as the line ahead ambled through the now-opened glass doors.

"And how do you plan to find what cell you stole that piece of fabric from so you can return it?"

"I don't know." Hannah released a long sigh. "I'm not even sure if that's possible. I mean, I was absolutely shitfaced that night when I was here."

"Nothing like celebrating your twenty-first birthday in style, right? Start day-drinking with your girlfriends, then do an overnight ghost hunt in an abandoned prison."

Hannah swallowed hard. "I feel like you're scolding me, like you want to keep rubbing it in that I used to be that person." She raised her gaze to meet his. "I'm not her anymore. That's why we're here."

Christian adjusted his backpack on his shoulder as they inched toward the door. "No, and I say this with the utmost love, we're here because, in your drunken stupor, you stole something from one of the cells that belonged to an inmate.

Then you started seeing your brimmed-hat man in the shadows in your apartment. And you think if you return it on your one-year anniversary of sobr—"

"That's enough," she said through gritted teeth. "I know the story. It's *my* story, remember?"

"Sorry." Christian glanced away from her.

"Sometimes you go too far," she muttered.

"I don't mean to," he said, refocusing on her. "But remind me why you were all the way out here in Missouri for your twenty-first birthday party? Seems there would be a lot closer places in the, what? One thousand miles from home?"

"Do you really not remember, or are you making me retell the story to guilt-shame me?"

Christian shook his head and playfully made a motion like he was swatting a fly. "Nah, nah. I know you were visiting your friend who went to college here. And the shenanigans were afoot."

Hannah chortled.

"I just wished you had gone somewhere closer to home that weekend so we didn't have to get on a plane and rent a car and book a hotel room just for this crusade you're on." Christian snapped his fingers and pointed at her. "Oh, my goodness. You're like Frodo, and the strip of fabric is the ring, and this place is Mordor. So, you've basically taken your love for *The Lord of the Rings* to create this real-life quest you've brought me along on."

Hannah tapped a foot and folded her arms. "Oh, yeah? If that's the case, I guess that makes you Samwise."

"Or Gollum," he murmured from the corner of his mouth.

Hannah used the back of her hand to push her glasses up her nose by the bottom of the frames. She blamed the unusual late-October Jefferson City humidity and peered around the person in front of her. She asked Christian, "Did you sign the waiver? I think that lady is checking."

"Did it when you asked me. See? I do listen to you."

"Sometimes." Hannah playfully punched his arm. "Then you would have seen the list of prohibited items." She nodded at his backpack to accentuate her verbal jab, then slowly drew her gaze up the colossal structure to their left, reminding her more of a medieval castle than a prison. "I wonder what the walls are made of. They look as if they could withstand the apocalypse."

"Or the Battle of the Five Armies."

"You never know when to quit, do you?" Hannah said lightheartedly. Annoyed with him most of the time? Yes. Could she survive if he ever changed? Probably not.

The petite and spunky-like-a-firecracker woman with short graying hair bounded from the group in front of them and regarded Hannah and Christian. "Did you sign your waivers?"

"Yep." Christian showed the woman his phone screen with his digitally signed document. "Excuse me, my counterpart here wants to know what the walls are made of."

"All the floors are cement, and the ceilings are plaster, but the walls and roofs are limestone. Quarried from on-site. The lower yard was a limestone quarry. The inmates dug it out and used the stone. Makes for a good story but an even creepier experience inside. Especially down in *The Hole*." The woman winked at him. "You'll see."

"*Hmm.* I'm sure the Rock Biter would have a field day in this place."

The woman laughed from deep in her belly and placed a hand on Christian's forearm. "I can't believe you're even old enough to know that movie."

Christian spotted the expression Hannah shot him, and he said to her, "What? You got your *Hocus Pocus* and *The Lord of the Rings* thing going. I've got my *NeverEnding Story* thing. We shall not discuss this further." He cleared his throat and smiled curtly at the woman. "Please, continue. I apologize for my counterpart's inconsiderate interruption of you just doing your job, which you are doing an *amazing* job at, if I do say so myself."

"Oh, you guys will be fun tonight. I like you already." She eyed Hannah. "Boyfriend?"

"She wishes," Christian interjected.

The woman chuckled and stepped backward to loudly yell so most everyone in the line still outside could hear her, "Listen up! If you haven't signed the waiver before you check in at the counter inside, you can't attend tonight's event. If anyone has any questions, my name is Jenny, and I will give the safety briefing in the lobby at eight o'clock sharp."

Christian checked his watch and groaned.

They shuffled forward at a snail's pace, but the end of the line of amateur ghosthunters finally reached the lobby of the beast, with fifteen minutes to spare.

Hannah felt as if the front doors had swallowed her whole as she entered.

CHAPTER 2:
THE LOBBY
(HOUSING UNIT 1)

Hannah wove through the congregation in the lobby. "C'mon. I want to see if Get Haunted have merch. They said they might have a new tee-shirt tonight."

"And you follow these people?"

Hannah stopped to face Christian so fast that he had to skid to a halt to not collide with her. "Are you kidding? *These people* are the ones hosting tonight's event. They are, like, superstars of ghost hunting."

"I am *so* not in my element," Christian said, surveying the guests who had packed the lobby.

Hannah shoulder-sliced through the crowd, comprised of people wearing everything from horror movie shirts to Get Haunted tees. She found the small area between the lobby and the start of the yard, where the four buildings sat that would comprise the ghost hunt. She curiously eyed the two metal doorways they needed to pass through, both with opened sliding bars. Either they had once been painted brown but now turned green from mold or had once been painted green and now turned brown from weather.

She rounded the table and froze.

"You okay? See a ghost?" Christian asked sarcastically.

"That's Rob," she whispered, as if hearing his own name would offend him.

"No clue," Christian said.

But Hannah didn't explain. She scooted toward the slim man behind the merchandise table, sporting a salt-and-pepper goatee and donning a black Get Haunted baseball hat and matching tee-shirt. The company's logo of a skull and their font adorned both items.

"Hi. I'm Hannah." She proffered her hand.

Rob shook it, with a smile. "Nice to meet you, Hannah. First ghost hunt with us?"

"Yes, but not my first hunt here." She felt Christian's judging expression behind her.

"Well, hopefully tonight will far exceed your last experience. We try to bring the goods."

Christian leaned over Hannah's shoulder. "Her first hunt here was on her twenty-first birthday. Let's say, she doesn't remember any of it."

Hannah elbowed Christian in the gut and, from the corner of her mouth, said, "Really?"

Rob chuckled and resumed unpacking tee-shirts from a shipping box. "One could argue that your first experience didn't count, right?"

"Oh, it counted," Christian added.

"Will you *stop*?" Hannah asked, now facing him.

Rob bent to grab more tee-shirts from the box and straightened up to place them in the appropriate shirt-size pile. "Boyfriend?" he asked with a playful smirk.

"He wishes," Hannah said, paying him back.

And this time, it was Christian's turn to jab Hannah in the gut.

Hannah scanned the table and pointed to a pile. "Is that the new design?"

"Sure is." Rob lifted a tee-shirt so it unfolded in midair. "Got them last night. Almost didn't get them in time."

Hannah studied the classic Get Haunted logo, superimposed over wisps of smoke covering the silhouette of an old Victorian house. "Do you have it in medium?"

Rob thumbed through the top few shirts and removed a medium.

Hannah paid for it and handed it to Christian. "Can you put it in your backpack?"

"Oh, sure. *Now* my backpack isn't the topic of an argument."

Hannah rolled her eyes. "I just can't with you sometimes." She flashed Rob an adoring smile. "I'm super-excited for tonight. It's an honor to meet you."

"Likewise." Rob gave Hannah a salutation gesture of exaggeratedly rolling his arm at stomach level while bowing. "And please, have some food." He motioned at the table full of pizza boxes, coffee carafes, and dozens of doughnuts.

"Don't have to tell me twice." Christian readjusted his backpack on his shoulder as he slid toward the food table.

Hannah nodded at Rob and politely excused herself to ensure her friend wouldn't make a fool of her by shoving full slices of pizza into his mouth.

"This shit is good," Christian said when he looked up and noticed her. Traces of pizza sauce dotted each corner of his lips. "And I never took you as one to fangirl over some ghosthunters."

"Fangirl over ghosthunters? Still better than fanboying over Megan Fox."

"Yeah, but I was a kid. You're a grown-ass woman. Plus, it wasn't just Megan. C'mon, it was *Transformers*."

"*Suuuure* it was, fanboy." Hannah giggled at one of her favorite pastimes: giving it right back to him when he dished it out, knowing she got underneath his skin just a bit. She loved Christian for his sense of humor and for not caring what people thought of him, but she also knew it was just armor for deeper feelings swimming below the surface. Maybe one day …

"Look, the five-oh are here." Christian inclined his chin toward the police officer standing atop three small steps that led to a hallway. "What's he gonna do? Shoot at the ghosts?"

Hannah stifled a chuckle; she didn't want to give Christian the satisfaction that she found him at all humorous. Nothing would go to his head more.

"The gift shop is only open before the hunt," said someone who wore a green Missouri State Penitentiary Staff tee-shirt. "If you want to buy anything, you have ten minutes."

"C'mon." Hannah tugged Christian's short sleeve. "Let's check it out."

She climbed the three steps, excusing herself past the uniformed police officer, who smiled politely at her and Christian. The gift shop sign, with a left-facing arrow, stood in front of them, and Hannah led Christian into the small room adorned with multiple designs of tee-shirts, magnets, key chains that mimicked the cell door keys, books about the history of the penitentiary, and a glass shelving unit filled with nothing but round clear balls.

"What are those?" Christian placed his palms on his thighs as he became eye level with the glass shelf.

"Cat toys," said the cashier to the right of them, whose name tag read LILY.

Hannah furrowed her brows at the teenage girl. "Cat toys? For what?"

"Go ahead and touch one," Lily answered.

Christian poked one with his index finger, and the ball flashed a staggered red and blue—one side flashing red, while the other stayed dark, then vice versa. It cycled out and stopped flashing. He picked it up and faced the cashier. "For the ghost cats?"

Hannah backhanded him across his bicep. "Stop it," she said with a twinge of a chuckle. "Do you ever quit?"

"Yeah, like I've never heard that one before." Lily rolled her eyes.

Hannah leaned around Christian's body to see the girl. "Oh, honey, don't encourage him."

"We mostly use them to ask the ghosts if they are with us. You can place one on any level surface and ask that if they can hear you, to touch the toy, which makes it flash. It's basically a low-tech ghost detector."

"Bet you guys make a killing with these." Christian returned the ball to the shelf. The red and blue alternating lights flashed from the movement.

"Okay, people, if I could have everyone come into the lobby," yelled Jenny, the firecracker-of-a-woman, from around the corner.

Hannah and Christian meandered down the short hallway and crammed into the lobby with the rest of the guests, most of them silently waiting for the mandated instructions that would signal the start of the hunt.

"Does everyone know how the cat balls work?" Jenny asked.

The room gave a resounding, "Yes."

"See, Halifax?" Hannah teased Christian. "If we hadn't gone into the gift shop, you would have been the only guest here who was ignorant to the multifunctions of a cat toy."

"For your safety," Jenny continued, "along with all of us guides and the Get Haunted crew, we have Officer Duncan from Jefferson City PD. He's in the back, but you'll see him moving around this evening as well. Might even put him to work to wrangle groups from station to station." Jenny shot a snarky wink at the officer standing at the rear of the lobby. "He has the hardest job of all—keeping you guys safe from other humans."

A few chuckles spread through the crowd.

"So, first question." Jenny spun to face every guest in the lobby. "Who's been here before?"

Hannah was surprised at how few people raised their hands.

"There they are. Okay, got a lot of new people here. We've had a lot of first-time visitors this year, which is awesome. I've lived here my entire life. I've been doing this for nine years. It's a prison, so we've got rules. The first one is, we allow nothing but water to leave this lobby, whether you bought it here or brought it. Nothing else. We have a zero-tolerance alcohol policy too. Don't give Officer Duncan a reason to do a bunch of paperwork tonight."

The crowd chuckled, but Hannah flashed Christian a knowing yet loving smile that belied the anger brewing within her, which grew the more Jenny spoke about prohibited drinks.

"If you brought anything else, it'll have to remain here in the lobby, and you'll need to return to the lobby to eat or to drink it. The reason for that is we've got critters. It's Missouri, and it's nighttime, and it's a rural area. We try to keep the animals from entering the buildings to look for food. So, keep that in mind when you're walking around out here tonight. Second, no smoking or vaping in here at all. If you want to use it, you must go out front, which you can at any time. Just let us know. We'll let you out and let you back in.

One of us is usually out there already, getting our fix or hanging out with the ones who are. Biggest rule tonight is, we want you to have a good time. That's why y'all are here. However, this other rule is very serious. It took over nine hundred keys to operate this prison, and I only have four, okay?"

The guests laughed, but Hannah felt some nervousness resided in those laughs.

"Sounds like a bunch of hyperbole to me," Christian whispered to Hannah.

She side-eyed him with a playful smirk. "Oh? Your secret crush losing some of her allure?"

"It is a *huge* deal." Jenny's stare bored right at Christian, as if she had overheard his comment. "If you start messing around, you'll get locked in somewhere you're not supposed to be. That's why we've got to tell you not to do it, right? It's actually happened twice with me in nine years, and it's not fun. It's not fun for us. It's certainly not fun for you because, most times, we can get you out, but a lot of times we cannot. We have to call OSHA. We are state-owned. We have to call our boss. She has to come in. We also sometimes have to involve locksmiths. The last time, a locksmith had to come to the facility to get a guest out—and to find one who can do it, first thing, is not an easy task. Why? Remember that this is a *prison*."

The guests feigned a laugh and shuffled a bit more, anxious to get this humdrum intro over with so they could ghost hunt.

Jenny continued. "You lock yourself into the cell, and you'll pay that individual for their services. We won't cover that for you. That's on your dime. He charged one hundred dollars per hour. It took him *seven hours*. That was a seven-hundred-dollar, plus the admission price, night for them. That's a really expensive hunt, isn't it? So, I'll make it easy for you. We want you to look around. That's why you're here. Anything you come across tonight in any location that is open—cells, alcoves, hallways, offices, I don't care what it is—if it's open, you have access. Step on in. Don't shut the door on your way inside though, okay? However, if you come across a door that is shut, don't even try turning the handle at all. If we catch you in any shape or fashion trying to do something with doors that you're not supposed to touch, that is the fastest way you'll find yourself back out front, with no refund. We do not mess around with that rule at all. It's just safety. And safety first."

Hannah caught Christian slide his backpack off his shoulder and rest it on the floor at his feet—its known contents weighing on her like an impending thunderstorm.

"This isn't the place to run around screaming and yelling. If that's what you think you can do, you're in the wrong spot. This is a historical location first and foremost, and we need it to remain that way. Don't leave with anything you did not come in here with, okay? Don't put something in your pocket and walk out, or you may take something with you that you didn't want at home."

Hannah pursed her lips when she felt Christian's scolding glare fall upon her like razorblades, and she refused to give him the satisfaction of making eye contact. While they now both had a reason to shame the other with two of Jenny's rules, Hannah was trying to right a wrong here. Yet Christian's reckless decision was not only jeopardizing their entire night but also her pilgrimage.

"People ask us all the time if we take home any ghosts with us from here. I've never had anything attach to me in nine years. I go home and sleep like a baby. Never think about it at all. But that's because I leave their items put. It's *their* items. Not yours—regardless of whether the inmates are still here or not. They know. Trust me that they know.

"I'll also give you a piece of advice. When you are trying to communicate with them, don't ask them what they did to get here. You probably don't want to know. How many of you know about us? Anybody? It's okay. I didn't know anything either, until I started doing this, and I've lived here all my life. We were the most violent penitentiary in the entire United States. Level-five maximum.

"Most of the inmates who resided here were here for life, with no parole. In fact, they even did a sentence that was called *life and fifty*. That meant you'll do your life here. You'll die here. You aren't getting out of it. And, after death, you've got fifty more years of time to serve. That's where that respect thing comes in. They are just humans. They may have done a really terrible thing to get here, but they have repaid their debt to society a long time ago, so leave that alone.

"One last instruction, because I know you guys are chomping at the bit to walk across the yard and get this party started with Get Haunted!"

A cheer rose quickly, until almost everyone in the lobby was clapping, cheering, or whistling.

Jenny pumped her palms toward the floor to get the guests to settle down so she could finish. "If any of you are using Taylor-Made Technology's Casper-Capture app, you must—and I can't express this enough—*must, must* have your phones on Airplane Mode for it to work properly. Any signal—data, cellular, Wi-Fi, etc.—will interfere with the magnetometer."

"Good to know." Hannah flipped over her phone in her hand, went to Settings, and hit the Airplane icon. Then she faced Christian. "See? I told you that it was called a magnetometer."

Christian laughed as she watched him disable his phone's data signal. Hannah double-checked that the orange Airplane symbol was atop his screen. With him, she just couldn't be sure unless she saw it with her own eyes.

Hannah took a breath and released a long exhale. It felt somewhat freeing to know she had just cut herself off from the world, just to enter a different one. Maybe not having the *ping*s of notifications from her social media apps or the assigned chime of Dollard's text messages constantly sounding in her pocket would give her an opportunity to breathe, to center herself, to find her true north, and to accomplish her purging.

That was what she had ultimately come here for, right? Meeting and ghost hunting with Get Haunted was certainly a once-in-a-lifetime experience, one she will treasure forever for sure, but truly she was here to return the ring to Mordor.

She chuckled under her breath when she realized Christian's goofiness sometimes wore off on her. And it was a welcomed goofiness. Most of the time, at least.

"Whatch'ya laughing at, Banana?" he asked.

She bladed herself to face him and put her hands on her hips in feigned aggravation. "What if I told you that I hated your nickname for me, Mr. Halifax?"

Christian took a long pull from his water bottle and screwed the cap back on, then released an exaggerated sound of satisfaction.

She knew he had taken that sip for a dramatic pause; he wasn't so thirsty that he couldn't drink after he had answered her.

"Well, I would make sure I called you *Banana* twice as much. Maybe even add in a *peach*. Or an *apple*. Ooo, a *kiwi*."

"Shut up. You're so stupid." She slapped his arm with the back of her hand.

He flinched and leaned away from her, but she saw in his grin how much he relished any flirtatious interactions between them. But unfortunately, that kept her on guard to not let it get too far or to lead him on too much. There was still a *Dollard* in her life back home, one thousand miles away, right? That still meant something, didn't it?

Hannah pursed her lips and forced herself to become stoic and listen to the guide's final instructions—she would deal with her feelings for Dollard and for Christian later.

"Now, if y'all follow me into A-Hall for Get Haunted's introduction," Jenny continued, interrupting Hannah's internal reverie. "From there, we'll break you into groups for the tour part of the night, where you'll have time to hunt with Get Haunted and use their equipment in all four buildings. After that, it will be free roam."

Christian winked at Hannah. "I know what you're thinking, kiddo. Free roam is when you'll dump that piece of fabric."

"Yeppers. We just need to survive the breakout tours first. You brave enough to survive a few hours with the haunts?" Hannah made a *woooooo* noise as she spookily waved her hands in front of his face.

"Oh, you haven't seen brave yet."

"I'm sure," she said, rolling her eyes, then chuckled.

CHAPTER 3:
A-HALL
(HOUSING UNIT 4)

Hannah and Christian followed the horde of believers, skeptics, and amateur ghosthunters from the lobby. She glanced at the Get Haunted merch table to see no one manning it anymore. The center yard came into view, and, before her, one building on the left and one on the right grew bigger, until they sprawled not only lengthwise but like monoliths trying to escape skyward.

Everyone remained silent as they walked. Only the *crunch, crunch, crunch* of their shoes filled the air as they marched, like prisoners, toward the building on the left. Hannah didn't know why, but her gaze kept flitting toward the building on the right, with the glowing green windows for eyes. Ominous. Like it wanted to say something—as if its walls could speak or scream in frustration and anger. She was thankful that they were not visiting that building first. She wished she could remember, from the last time she had been here, what made her feel that way.

The sounds of the shuffling feet grew too loud—loud enough where she thought maybe if she said something to Christian, it might settle her racing heart. Instead, she reached into her pocket and felt the strip of fabric to remind herself why she was here. Of why she was putting herself through this. Well, that and, according to Christian, to fangirl over Get Haunted. She rolled her eyes at the accusation.

Hannah noticed the front of the line had snaked to the right and disappeared through an archway entrance, affixed with a swinging rusted metal door, like the building expected a full meal tonight.

"You okay, Banana?" Christian asked in just above a whisper.

She nodded and realized she had balled her free hand into a fist.

"Relax. I won't let anything happen to you."

She nodded again but wasn't completely sold on how safe she felt when it was their turn in the line to enter the building—A-Hall.

Rows of metal folding chairs filled the first half of the hall, and ahead Hannah saw Get Haunted, all donning their logo tee-shirts.

"This place is wild," Christian muttered to himself.

Hannah side-eyed him and smirked when she saw his mouth agape, eyes wide, as he scanned the expanse of the interior. Four floors, two rows to a floor on the left and right side of the wide-open middle, outlined the interior like a colosseum, exposing cell after cell after cell. Hannah noticed all the cell doors were slid open, the plaster chipped and flaking, giving it a furnace-like aura. The higher she tried to look to the upper floors, the harder it was to see through the blackness. Nothingness seemed to live from the third level upward—and it was that *nothingness* that the now-erect hairs on the back of her neck told her was spying on her and was judging her as she found a row of chairs toward the rear.

Hannah and Christian plopped into two chairs, and Christian sighed as he set his backpack on the floor at his feet.

"Bored?" she asked him.

"*Hmm*?" He eyed her. "Oh, no. Just deep in thought."

"Ghosts getting to you already?" Hannah poked her index finger into his side and tickled him to lighten the mood.

Even though he angrily swatted away her hand, his smirk and the glistening in his eyes told Hannah that her playfulness was what he needed.

Hannah scanned the four decks of cells that she could see. The insides looked like caves, with most of the arched ceiling's first—and sometimes, at places, second and third—layer of plaster either hanging or stripped away completely.

"I think that's everyone," Rob from Get Haunted said, gazing at the back of the hall.

Hannah turned to look behind her to see the last few visitors, which she surmised to be a total of about seventy-five people, had settled into the metal chairs.

"Good," Rob continued. "Welcome, everybody. My name's Rob, and welcome to Housing Unit 4. Or A-Hall, which we try not to say too fast."

A light chuckle rippled through the guests.

"I notice most of you looking around at what you can see of the cells. Through the years, when the paint peeled, they would just paint over it. So you're seeing years and layers of different-colored paints peeling at the same time, like rings inside a tree trunk."Hannah thought the faded red handrailings and exposed pipes going every which way throughout the hall, add in the spectrum of peeling paints, all made the ambience of the place feel as macabre as Freddy

Krueger's nightmarish boiler room in the bowels of Elm Street.

"I am the founder and co-owner of Get Haunted," Rob continued. "To my left is my best friend in the world and the other owner of Get Haunted. This is Sara."

Hannah found herself raise her hand slightly to give a quick wave, a smirk finding its way across her face with the realization that these people, who had been such a positive force in her life recently, now stood in front of her, in the flesh.

"First of all"—Rob cleared his throat—"thank you all for trusting us with your time and your experience tonight. Welcome to Missouri State Penitentiary."

A resounding cheer erupted from the guests. Hannah watched Rob nod and allow the fanfare to travel through the rows before he spoke again, clearly reveling and basking in the enthusiasm inside A-Hall.

"This is one of the best, one of the coolest, one of the most amazing locations we've ever had the pleasure of investigating. We've been here now probably fifteen or twenty times, and every single time, I learn something new. We hope tonight will be just as amazing for you as it will be for us. However, Sara and I get a lot of shit for not being big on the history of a location. And there's a reason for that. If you frontload—like, if I tell you that in cell 115 in Housing Unit 4, Johnny Appleseed committed suicide—any experience you have in that cell will go into a box that we've already created for the story. When the truth is that it might be your own personal experience."

Sara nodded. "Through the last couple years doing this, and with all the amazing people who have attended each event, what I saw was those people choose those events. And there's always a reason."

"Kinda sounds like you," Christian whispered to Hannah.

Hannah inclined her chin to signal that she was too homed in to Sara's monologue to respond to him.

"We watch people grow at every experience." Sara paused and scanned the audience. "We watch people come together. When we break everybody into groups, we watch strangers discuss each other's experiences. Then they build on their experiences together with what's happening in the moment. I don't know, Rob, if you would agree, but for almost every event we host, I feel somebody has left with something so profound and personal that it changed the way they look at things."

"Admittedly, I like to get scared." Rob chuckled and removed his Get Haunted baseball hat to scratch the back of his head. "I'm not gonna lie. Sometimes when you go to a certain location, you just want to be scared."

"Who would *want* to be scared?" Christian whispered. "That's why I think this is all a bunch of poppycock. It's just sad people, looking for a reason to—"

Hanah squeezed his knee so hard that Christian flinched and grabbed her wrist to alleviate the pressure. "Is that what you think I am? A sad person?"

Hannah heard Sara continue to speak and chose to focus on the blonde woman standing at the head of the rows of guests than to hear what Christian might say to defend his comment.

"I think what we're realizing more and more when we explore the paranormal is that we're exploring a piece of ourselves, and we explore connections. It's really what Get Haunted means. It's a connection."

"A connection to what?" asked an older bald man, with a white beard, sitting in front of Hannah.

"See? He's skeptical too," Christian whispered to her.

"Good question," Sara said. "A connection between the location and yourself. We're in a prison tonight. Maybe you're questioning what could you personally connect with here? But you might be shocked, because certain things and energies will resonate with your energy and where you're at today."

"Hear that, Halifax?" Hannah whispered, then chortled. "Beware. The ghosts in here might take advantage of that charismatic energy you have and exploit where you are in your life."

Christian rolled his eyes. "You sound just as looney as she does."

Sara continued. "Just because you're in a prison doesn't mean an inmate wasn't experiencing something in their personal life that you're going through too, right? Don't just look at the surface experience. Reflect on what you're feeling. Ask yourself a couple deeper questions. Don't just go with, as Rob said, that this was where so-and-so committed suicide in his cell. Go deeper and open yourself up."

"I'll briefly expand on that." Rob checked his watch. "What you bring tonight is very, very important. It is not always about what's here. We tend to give all our power and all our magic to the other side, when, in many cases, it's all about you, right? We are the beacons. I know we feel like we're out there looking for them, but they're also looking for us. Also, what you believe in can shape your experience."

"See?" Christian said, his eyes wider. "He gets it. You guys are all gonna see ghosts tonight because you *believe* in them." He folded his arms and relaxed in his seat, a smug expression of vindication crossing his face. "I'm proud to say that this will be a quiet and boring night for me because I find all of you ridiculous."

"Five of us could be sitting in a room, and something could happen right in front of us," Rob said. "And all five of us may interpret it very, very differently. And we have to ask ourselves: why is that? Is it because of our belief systems? Or is it because we're supposed to get a message? Or is it because of how we interpret things? So don't underestimate your abilities. All my big experiences happened when I was just sitting—just *being*—and when I wasn't looking so hard for it. This equipment is great, and you'll have a lot of it to use tonight, but don't let that be your focus. If you're staring at a K2 meter or at a Rem Pod the whole time, you'll miss all the things happening around you. They are great validation tools, but you already have all the equipment you ever need inside you."

"In case you missed it," Hannah said, leaning her body against Christian's arm, "you just need to open yourself up, get in tuned with the inner-Christian, and maybe you'll connect with something." She winked at him to punctuate her point and couldn't help but notice his grin that threatened to turn into a full-on giggle.

"Another great validation is this." Sara paced the length of the rows of seats, in front of the old blue pew from the chapel that now served as a bench, rubbing her hands together. "If you see something, if you feel something, if you hear something, then say something. We're not asking you to scream things out, by any means, but if you feel or hear or see something, you should speak up, because somebody else might have just seen or heard the same thing, but they're questioning themselves. When you guys work together, somebody else can say they experienced it too. These moments are when we help validate each other. This is why we talk a lot and want you to speak up during these Get Haunted events, because every voice matters and counts. You are adding to the conversation."

"Exactly," Rob said, glancing at his watch again, then stood ramrod straight dead center in front of the rows of guests. "And to take it a step further, we may learn something from you. The whole concept of Get Haunted was to bring teams together and to bring people together to learn and to share. We don't investigate in front of you; we investigate alongside you. We hope you guys have fun tonight. You're gonna be safe. If anything happens, and you feel uncomfortable, just let us know. We'll get you outside. You'll be fine."

"Sounds like he's trying to convince himself and not us," Hannah heard the young man in the row in front of her say to the older bald man next to him.

"Again, thank you all for trusting us with your night. We look forward to whatever happens tonight. As Sara always says, Get Haunted can't promise you a paranormal experience, but we can promise you an experience in the paranormal. So, if it's literally dead quiet tonight, we'll still have fun. And that, to me, is the most important part. Please share your theories, share your thoughts, share your evidence. But most of all, work together tonight."

The youngest member of Get Haunted, who had been standing quietly to the side, cleared his throat obnoxiously loudly and rocked back on his heels. He looked like he wasn't a day out of high school.

"Oh, jeez. Trevor," Sara said. "We almost forgot to introduce y'all to Trevor."

The young man waved and gave a pursed-lip smirk to the guests.

"How could we forget Trevor?" Rob said rhetorically, chuckling. "Trevor is kind of a Get Haunted tagalong."

"But we love him," Sara interjected.

"Sometimes," Rob quipped, and the guests laughed. "No, in all seriousness. Trevor brings a lot to the table—"

"Even if it does feel like yesterday's leftovers," Sara purposefully mumbled loud enough for everyone to hear.

Trevor jokingly glared at her.

"Kidding, kidding. You know we love you, Trevor," Sara said.

"This is like watching a nineties' sit-com," Christian said to Hannah.

"I know. I love it," she replied.

"Why don't you say something to the nice people, Trevor," Rob said. "And you people, no feeding the Trevor after midnight."

A few chuckles rose into A-Hall from the seats, and Trevor opened his mouth to speak. But it seemed the words had gotten stuck somewhere between his vocal cords and his teeth. "I–I–I want to s–s–s–say how privileged I am t–t–to be a part of this team and to b–b–be here with all of you tonight. Sorry for m–m–my stuttering. I promise it w–w–w–won't scare off the ghosts tonight."

"Yeah, it's the other things about you that will scare them off," Rob added, and the guests chuckled. Rob leaned backward on the table placed at the front of the rows of seats. "The first half of the night is semi-structured. You'll go through different rotations and learn different techniques from different investigators. The second half of the night is free roam. And we encourage you to not go off to find your own corner by yourself. Link up with somebody. There might be somebody here who you'll vibe with and could go do your own thing together and make some new friends. Hopefully that's one of the benefits of how we'll do things together tonight. So, thank you again. And who's ready to hunt some ghosts?"

Whoops and cheers filled the normally silent A-Hall. Hannah noticed Christian staring at her from the corner of her eye while she clapped and whistled. She vowed to refuse to let his apathy deter her from soaking in this experience nor from completing her mission of returning the stolen piece of fabric.

Rob raised his hands to chest level, and his voice boomed, "And remember, after tonight, you are *all* part of the Get Haunted family."

"They already are, just by being here." Sara smiled at the congregation. "Does anyone have any questions before we turn it over to the penitentiary's magnificent staff?"

A woman in the front row raised her hand.

Sara pointed at the guest to gesture for her to ask her question.

"How did Get Haunted start?"

Hannah noticed how quickly Sara darted her gaze at Rob, maybe trying to deflect the answer to him?

Rob removed his baseball hat and scratched the back of his head. "We're running short on time. I think that story is best held for our next event." He winked at the guest.

"That's some next-level marketing strategy right there," Christian said to Hannah. "Wanna know our whole story? You gotta come back for the sequel."

"Jenny, would you do the honors to introduce your little band of misfits," Rob concluded.

"Why, I would love to!" the firecracker-of-a-woman said, stepping forward.

Hannah had to crane her neck to peer over the person in front of her or she couldn't see the petite tour guide now talking.

"All right, you got me. I do like this woman," Christian whispered to her. "I feel like she's a cartoon character or something."

Hannah chortled under her breath, never moving her forward-facing gaze.

"Her cartoon prison name would be Jenny from C-Block," Christian said as a full chuckle escaped his lips.

"Behind me are my two most-trusted guides," Jenny introduced. "If they would kindly step forward when I introduce them. First is Reese."

The taller woman with long reddish-purple dyed hair stepped forward.

"And Lisa."

A woman with jet-black hair and a sleeve tattoo depicting the Jordy Verill character from Stephen King's *Creepshow* smiled at the group, and she stepped alongside Reese and Jenny, who now looked like a petite Oompa Loompa next to the other two guides.

"We'll separate you into groups," Rob said. "Lisa will be your host here in A-Hall—or Housing Unit 4—and in the dungeon, which is right behind us, down those stairs." Rob bladed himself so the eager crowd could see the descending staircase behind him, with white LED lights wrapped around the railing so no one would trip into the darkness below. "Jenny will be overseeing the women's unit—or Housing Unit One—while Sara will be happy to spend time with you in the gas chamber. We have a cool exercise set up in there for y'all. Resse and I will cover Housing Unit 3, with her taking the Death Row side, and me and Trevor taking the criminally insane floor below. In case you're wondering, Housing Unit 2 no longer exists. The state demolished it after a tornado left it structurally unsound."

Hannah's heart rate quickened a bit when Rob mentioned Death Row. She didn't know why—or maybe couldn't *remember* why. Maybe it had something to do with an incident from the previous time she was here? She exhaled through gritted teeth in frustration that her only experience in this place was in a drunken stupor. And the truth of the brimmed-hat shadow man lived somewhere in the clouded memories of that night.

"On the Death Row side of Housing Unit 3, the bottom floor is called 3D. Just to give you an idea of the energy down there, even the tour guides refuse to stay on that level any longer than they need to."

Jenny chuckled and, in her raspy voice, said, "Oh, I could write a book of things that have happened to me in just that corridor. I stay down there just long enough during a tour to explain it, then I am out. You won't catch me wandering around down there for fun."

Christian leaned into Hannah's ear. "Jeepers. If a woman who looks like she could scrap with Ivan Drago in *Rocky Part Four* fears three-dee, this is gonna be good."

Hannah shushed him, then chuckled.

"At least I can make you smile, Hannah Banana."

"I have started to refuse to take tours down to 3D," Reese added. "I make my guide assistant take them down there. Seen too many things. Felt too many things. However, if you look at these two rows of cells on this bottom floor"—she gestured along the right and left sides of the expansive hall—"you might catch who we call the peekers. Shadow forms will peek out of the cell to see what's going on, then dip back in quickly, almost always in your peripheral vision. This is one of the most common experiences of our guests. They move fast, so you gotta be—"

The people in the first handful of rows gasped simultaneously. Hannah almost stood from her chair to see what had happened. The tour guides and the Get Haunted crew turned to face the descending staircase into the dungeon—into The Hole. The guests who had reacted to something now whispered among themselves.

"What do you think happened?" Hannah asked Christian.

"What did you guys see?" Jenny asked, still facing away from the rows of people.

A jumble of answers made it almost impossible for Hannah to hear, but she could decipher that everyone had seen some sort of shadow figure exit one of the cells on the far-right side of the staircase and come toward them, then evaporate.

Rob moved from in front of the rows of chairs and ambled along the left side of the rows. "Get used to that kind of activity. What some of you just saw is par for the course here." He pointed to the first three rows. "You guys will start in the gas chamber with Sara." He moved farther down. "You three rows will stay here with Lisa." He slid down some more. "You three rows will head to Death Row with Reese, then down to 3D with me and Trevor." And then Rob reached the final three rows, where Hannah and Christian sat. "And you last three rows will start with Jenny in the women's block."

"Yes," Christian whispered.

"You sure you're not *fanboying* over her?"

"You shush." Christian chuckled. "And, touché."

"After you spend about an hour at your location, you will move to the next place. Officer Duncan will be the master of ceremonies, so to speak, during the guided tours to ensure your group knows where you're supposed to go next." Rob nodded at the police officer who stood at the rear of the room behind the last row of seats. "He gets that honor because he has the energy of a jackrabbit. And Sara and I are too old to be running around, herding you guys. He's still young and sprite."

The audience laughed. Some of it felt to Hannah that it wasn't from truly thinking the joke was funny but to alleviate some building tension from what was to come. She wondered how many people here were actually terrified of doing this hunt and only attended tonight to face their fears.

"*Pain,*" an artificial-sounding voice said.

Hannah looked across her row at someone who stared at their phone, their Casper-Capture app loaded and already regurgitating words it caught from the surrounding electromagnetic fields.

"That's what it sounds like when it translates EMF into words," Hannah said to Christian.

He regarded her with an exaggerated stare. "You don't say, Captain Obvious. Should I turn mine on?"

"Not until the free roam. It might be rude."

"Did Jenny explain about how everyone must have their phones on Airplane Mode, or the Casper-Capture app will get false signals?" Rob asked.

Hannah assumed he added this because they had just heard their first communication from someone's phone.

"Jeez, what type of false signals would we get if we didn't go full-on Airplane Mode?" Christian whispered. "Some ghost would be singing ABBA's 'Dancing Queen'?"

Hannah had to slap her hand over her mouth to stop the burst of laughter trying to escape. Sometimes he took her by surprise with a good one.

A handful of guests murmured an affirmative to Rob's question.

"Good. After everyone cycles through each four stations," Rob announced, "you guys will have free roam for the last hour. But not at the gas chamber, because we won't have a guide down there. Free roam is for the three main buildings only. That will bring us to just around 2:30 a.m., when we can gather in the lobby and spend the last thirty minutes at the gas chamber as a group, if anyone wants photos sitting in the two chairs. There won't be an opportunity for that when we're there doing the guided tour part, and we'll close it during free roam."

"Because all tours end in the gas chamber," Jenny interjected behind Rob.

He laughed and pinched the bridge of his nose as he shook his head. "Yes, Jenny loves saying that. If she didn't tell you during the safety briefing, those are the original and actual chairs where thirty-nine of the forty people executed here sat when they were put to death. So, I say, what a better Christmas card photo for you to send to your loved ones this year than of you sitting in one."

"That's when I think we'll have a chance to get rid of the piece of fabric," Hannah said to Christian.

"Free roam. Right."

Hannah noticed Christian wringing his hands between his knees. "You okay, superstar? Nerves gettin' ya?"

"As if," he said in his best Cher voice from *Clueless*.

"Okay, hunters. Roll out," Rob said.

"It would have been cooler if he had said, 'Autobots, roll out,'" Christian whispered as the guests rose from their seats.

"That's it," Hannah retorted, with a playful glare. "I'm not taking you anywhere ever again, Halifax."

The designated three rows meandered toward their assigned guide to be escorted to their first location.

Christian snatched his backpack from the floor, and he and Hannah filed out of their row to stand next to Jenny, while the other guests and their cohorts huddled into a circle around the guide. Hannah surveyed the people they would be stuck with for the next four hours—two women who seemed to be around her and Christian's age, and a trio of men who appeared to be together.

Hannah's goal was to remain as inconspicuous as possible and to just watch each guide or Get Haunted crew do their magic while she immersed herself in something she should have already experienced once but had no memory of. Then the fun would be over, and she would utilize the rest of her time here to purge the last of her demons.

CHAPTER 4: WOMEN'S BLOCK (HOUSING UNIT 1)

Hannah marveled at the expanse of floors above the building that also housed the lobby. She hadn't looked behind her when they had left the lobby to go to A-Hall, so she didn't know floors were above the space where they had started.

The small line following Jenny passed the Get Haunted merchandise table and took a right down the hallway toward the gift shop. They passed the shop and made a left, then climbed cement stairs.

Hannah tried to see what lay atop the staircase, but the blackness seemed to act more like a curtain than just the absence of light. As she climbed, the walls felt closer. *Suffocating.*

"You okay, Banana?" Christian whispered. "You're white as a, well, as a ghost. Pun intended."

"Yeah. I just … I dunno. Suddenly I feel … heavier." Hannah bit the inside of her cheek and pushed her glasses farther up her nose. "God, this humidity."

The twentysomething guy climbing the stairs in front of her turned and said, "You're telling me. This is awful."

She cowered into herself a notch or two. Sometimes she wished that wasn't her immediate reaction when a stranger spoke to her, but distrusting people had always been her initial response. It had probably saved her some grief in life, but it may also have let some opportunities slip by where she might meet new people. She dug deep and decided that if they would be spending the next four hours with this small cluster of people, maybe she should be polite.

So, she smiled at him.

The man turned to face forward as they hit the top of the stairs, which revealed a hallway that traveled along the outside wall, like a stock-car racetrack, with the cells in the center. Hannah glanced upward and saw multiple floors with more rows of cells.

"This was where they housed the women," Jenny said as they walked.

Hannah's gaze fell into each open cell as they traveled past. Each one identical. Paint and plaster peeling. One metal cot, no mats, a single toilet and sink. She couldn't even tell if they were making progress in their journey as they passed these cells, except for her feet moving forward. The cells reminded her of old *Flintstone* cartoons, where the background pattern never changed as it flew by when Fred drove.

They turned a corner. More of the same two-toned cells. Hannah knew they hadn't been two-toned when in operation, but years of oil from people's hands, sharp objects on people's clothes, inmates graffitiing the plaster, and whatever else the years had brought to the prison had chipped away at its original color and had left something resembling the bottom of a bog covering the walls and the bars.

The group walked in mostly silence, some people whispering to each other. Most kept a suspicious and somewhat nervous eye on each open cell they passed—just in case.

"Having fun yet?" Hannah asked Christian, not that she was interested in the answer but because she wanted to break the monotony of the silence—and the rising anxiety that she wouldn't admit she felt. Not yet anyway.

"Okay, here we are." Jenny stopped at the bottom of the staircase and in front of a room with a normal swinging door, which was completely black inside. A row of cells stretched onward behind them. "Behind me is solitary confinement. Or what they called *the blind cell.* They would place prisoners in here, with no light. When you look inside, you'll see no windows. So"—Jenny clapped her hands together to punctuate her next statement—"let's have some fun, shall we?"

Hannah watched the trio of guys, who were clearly here together, shuffle sideways a few steps to create a distinct separation between them and the rest of the group—which only consisted of her and Christian and a duo of women.

Hannah wondered if anyone else was here to return a stolen keepsake that had conjured an entity in their apartments.

Jenny held up something that resembled a thicker and slightly wider version of a hockey puck, with a small antenna on top and a semicircle of LED lights, not illuminated. "This is called a Rem Pod. It detects changes in electromagnetic fields around it. The stronger the energy, the more lights will turn on. And they go from green to orange to red." She bent to place it in the entrance to the cell across from the pitch-black solitary confinement room. "I'll set it here so we can detect anything coming in or out of that cell or passing down the hallway near it."

Christian folded his arms and leaned into Hannah's ear. "I'm sure it's just gonna pick up the electricity in the walls."

Jenny spun to face Christian. "Oh no, sir." She waggled a finger at him. "The electric current in the building is too far from the Rem Pod for it to detect it."

"Your girlfriend certainly told you, Halifax," Hannah whispered.

"Shut up, Banana."

Jenny backed away from the device and sat on the hallway floor next to the open door of solitary confinement and across from the cell with the Rem Pod in its opening.

"Is it okay if we sit in the blind cell?" asked one of the guys from the trio.

"Absolutely. Better yet, put one of the cat toys in there with you. Just make sure not to kick it." Jenny chuckled when she said, "I swear, those things get kicked more during a hunt than a soccer ball during a match."

Two of the guys passed the entrance to solitary confinement, one of them accepting the cat toy from Jenny's hand, then the blackness immediately consumed them. Hannah now thought they might be military, based on their high-and-tight haircuts and their tee-shirts, which all advertised an unfamiliar armed-forces logo. She giggled to herself when she thought none of them looked like they had missed arm day or chest day at the gym in quite some time. She squinted at the one who hadn't entered the blind cell to decipher the insignia on his shirt, but she couldn't place it.

"How is it in there, boys?" Jenny asked, not even leaning sideways to peer into the room.

"Creepy," said a male voice from somewhere in the darkness.

"Show us that you are here with us," Jenny said to the ghosts, now speaking louder than normal, "and touch the lights."

Nothing happened.

"Come on. We're friends. We just want to talk."

Nothing still.

"No need to be shy," she said in her raspy voice.

Nothing.

Christian cleared his throat, and Hannah glanced at him, hoping that hadn't been sarcastic.

Then the first green light blinked.

"Okay," Jenny said, her hoarse voice cracking from jubilation. "Thank you for trying. Could you do it again? This time try to make the orange light turn on."

Green light only.

"I know you can do it."

Green stayed illuminated.

"We just want to ask a few questions."

Orange light flickered.

"There ya go. I've brought some new friends with me, who would love to talk to you."

Orange illuminated steadily.

"See? I knew you could do it. Good job."

"*Why are you here?*"

Hannah almost screamed when the Casper-Capture app of the person next to her went off. And the blackness of solitary flashed in reds and blues from the nearby cat toy, making the men inside glow a flip-flop of colors and silhouettes.

"We are here to talk to you," Jenny said without missing a beat.

Hannah was impressed at how fluid this woman was with acting normal in this situation.

The cat toy ran through its cycle and stopped flashing.

"*Come inside.*"

That made the Rem Pod go off in the cell across the hallway. Green illuminated. Orange illuminated. Red barely flickered.

Now everyone stared at the woman who held the phone whose app was doing all the communicating.

"Who do you want to come inside?" Jenny asked.

"*Brother.*"

Jenny addressed everyone when she said, "Remember that this was a woman's cell. I'm thinking that whatever female had been in that cell wants a man to go in there. She probably went years without the company of a man." She narrowed her gaze at the lone military guy standing slightly removed from Hannah and Christian—an older bald man, with a whitening beard, also donning one of the tee-shirts with the unfamiliar military insignia. "You want to go in this other cell and see if anything happens?"

The LED lights on the Rem Pod darkened. Yet the cat toy inside the blind cell flashed resplendent colors, making the almost-dark hallway seem brighter than it was.

"I'll go in," the older man relented. "Can't ignore the cat toy. She obviously wants one of us in there," he finished with a nervous chuckle.

The green light flickered again.

"*Oooo,*" Jenny quipped. "She likes that. Why don't you tell her your name."

The man crossed the skinny hallway and submersed himself into the woman's cell. "My name is Heath."

"Did you hear that? You have Heath inside with you."

The man sat on the rusted metal cot devoid of a mattress.

"*I like him.*"

"All right, so we're doing well," Jenny said, commenting on whoever's Casper-Capture had spoken on their phone.

The green LED now remained steady. Hannah couldn't see any flicker. Someone coughed from the darkness of solitary confinement, and Hannah leaned around the doorway to see the two sets of eyes and two faces aglow from their phone screens, all with the app on.

"*Who is he?*" came from that darkness.

Jenny peered around the corner into solitary. "Whose app was that?"

"Mine, ma'am," a voice came from the darkness.

"Well, answer her. And don't call me *ma'am*."

A male voice wafted from inside solitary. "Dano."

Then silence.

Orange LED flickered from across from solitary.

"*Come inside,*" sounded from the darkness.

Dano mumbled, "Oh, shit."

"Well, Dano, sounds like she wants you to join Heath inside her cell."

Christian chuckled when Dano said, "Oh, shit," even louder this time.

"Go get her, bro," another voice from inside solitary said to him. "She's waiting for you."

"Shut up," Dano said as he emerged into the moonlight's ambient glow that splashed the only traces of light into the hallway—save the dimmed phone screens and the now-steady green and orange LEDs on the Rem Pod.

Dano sauntered across the hallway and paused at the entrance to the cell.

"*I want to talk.*"

"Yes," Jenny said, "we want to talk to you. You have Dano coming in now, and Heath is already waiting in the cell."

"This isn't right," Dano murmured as he entered and stood against the desecrated wall across from Heath, the two friends facing each other in the cell's darkness.

Red flickered now.

"I feel like this might be anticlimactic," Christian whispered to Hannah.

She shushed him and folded her arms.

"You've got your men in there," Jenny said. "What do you want to tell them?"

Silence.

No one spoke. No Casper-Captures went off. Everyone waited for something—anything—to happen.

Hannah's gaze danced between checking the end of the long hallway for any shadow figures or movement, to peeking into the darkness of solitary, to watching the two men inside the cell opposite from solitary.

Then all the LEDs darkened, as if someone had pulled a plug on the device.

"Well, that's not very nice," Jenny said. "We were obliging your requests. Why'd you leave?"

Silence.

The LEDs remained dark.

"Okay, well, if you won't hold up your end of the bargain, I guess Heath and Dano will just have to leave that cell so we can move on. They can't stay here forever."

"Or can they?" Christian whispered to Hannah, then made a spooky *wooo* noise.

She wanted to elbow him in the gut but refused to break the atmosphere that had descended upon the hallway.

Silence.

"So, do you guys know about the new feature that Casper-Capture added this week?" Jenny asked the group.

A collective of negatives emanated from the hallway, from the one guy in solitary, and from Heath and Dano behind the opened bars of the opposing cell.

"Oh, this is great." Jenny tucked her feet underneath her to stand, using the wall behind her as a crutch. "Everyone, go into the app, if you don't already have it loaded."

Hannah unfolded her arms and stared at the company's white logo of a beloved childhood ghost on her screen.

"See the three bars at the top left?" Jenny continued. "Hit those and—"

Green, orange, and red LEDs shot to full color and held steady.

"Oh, so *now* you want to talk. Why? Because we're not paying attention to you right now?"

All three lights flashed in unison. Then the cat toy activated.

"*You are annoying,*" someone's app chirped.

The guests laughed, and Hannah felt it was a necessary relief from the building tension.

"I know I am," Jenny said. "I've been told that my whole life. Now let me get back to talking to these fine folks, who are here to visit you."

Silence.

All three LEDs darkened. The cat toy finished its cycle.

"As I was saying, click those three lines, and you'll see two options: Casper-Vision and Casper-Conjuring. The Vision option allows you to detect EMF and to see if an entity is present. It detects anything living too, so make sure you don't have a person in the screen when using it, or you might get their energy instead. Go ahead. Try it."

Hannah hit the option for Casper-Vision and raised her cellphone at the group, as if she were taking a photo of them. Each person had an amber stick figure superimposed over their bodies, and it moved with the person, as if they held a marionette in front of them.

"So cool," Christian muttered next to her.

She panned her phone from person to person, and, sure enough, no matter what position the person was in, the amber stick figure mimicked that posture over their image.

"So, if you see what you are seeing now but no human is in your line of sight, then you know you are picking up something paranormal."

"Just when I thought this couldn't get more farfetched," Christian said louder this time.

"If you think this is a bunch of hooey," Jenny said, glaring at Christian, "wait until you see what the Conjuring function does."

Hannah giggled. "You know that was sarcastic, right?"

"I hate you," Christian whispered playfully but never lowered his phone. He pointed the camera down the hallway that grew darker the farther it was from them.

Hannah squinted at him, hoping he would catch her expression from the corner of his eye.

When he did, he asked, "What?"

"Farfetched, *huh*? Yet you have that thing pointed in the scariest spot that we can see."

"I'm just doing it to keep *you* safe. You know, *in case* something comes down the hallway, I can use my ninja reflexes to save you."

Hannah smiled inwardly. These interactions, these times with Christian, all truly made her wonder why she didn't give him an honest chance. Why did Dollard have such a hold on—

"*One more,*" demanded Hannah's Casper-Capture app, startling her with the voice being so close to her.

"Oh, so now you're talking," Jenny said. "We can't keep giving you more and more people. That's not how this works."

"*One more*," said Hannah's phone again.

Jenny spied Hannah with a quizzical expression that did not go unnoticed.

"What?" Hannah's heart rate increased, and small prickles covered her arms.

"They … They don't tend to ask or say the same thing twice in a row, especially not from the same person's app."

Jenny's stumble while trying to explain sent ice through Hannah's veins. Hannah didn't like that something out of the norm had just seemed to fluster this woman, who she would pick to be on her side in a bar fight. Hannah rubbed her bare arms for warmth, although the building's temperature wasn't what had caused the chill. Something else had descended upon the hallway.

"Christian?" she whispered. "Do me a favor."

"Anything, Banana."

"Can you keep pointing your phone down the hallway? Just … Just in case."

"Consider it done."

Hannah nodded in thanks, but she was sure he hadn't seen it.

"One more *what*?" Jenny asked. "You've asked for one more, twice, but we don't know—"

"*Him.*"

Hannah swallowed hard. Why was it her phone that suddenly was the only one communicating?

"Which *him*?" Jenny asked. "You must be more specific. There are a lot of—"

"*Christian.*"

Hannah almost screamed and dropped her phone. A shiver engulfed her that seemed to have come within her and spread outward. She side-eyed her friend to see his reaction.

Christian froze, his phone still pointing down the long hallway to catch any apparitions, but his widened eyes were glued to Hannah's phone.

"All right," Jenny said. "Is a Christian here?"

Christian's gaze quickly rose to meet Hannah's as he shook his head in quick movements, as if to say, *No no no no no, don't you tell her.*

"No? No one named Christian?" Jenny asked again.

Silence.

Hannah pursed her lips at Christian and tried to project a stern expression that said, *Tell her. Say it's you.*

Christian held his don't-you-dare glare at her, until …

"*The one next to you,*" came from Hannah's app.

Jenny craned her neck to see past Hannah. "Ah, Mr. NeverEnding Story himself. I think she's talking about you. Sometimes they get names mixed up."

Hannah kicked his sneaker to nudge him to confess.

"No, ma'am. My name is Christian."

The guests gasped under their breath, and a "No fucking way" wafted from inside the darkness of solitary.

"Okay, my man. She's asking for you specifically. By name. I don't think you have any choice."

Hannah placed a hand on Christian's forearm. She knew she could manipulate him into doing almost anything if she approached him with either a flirtatious or a soft manner. His tensed muscles relaxed under her grip. When he made eye contact with her, she pouted and batted her lashes. "For me?"

"That is so unfair, and you know it," he chided, then crammed his phone into his back pocket, let his backpack fall off his shoulder to the floor, and strode across the hallway and through the opened weatherworn bars of the cell.

Heath scooched over so Christian could sit next to him, facing Dano.

"I feel more comfortable sitting closest to the door," Christian murmured.

"I feel you," Heath said.

"You have Heath and Dano and your special request, Christian, in there with you. Will you talk to us now?" Jenny asked.

"I wish she didn't call me that," Christian mumbled, and the other two men inside the cell with him laughed. Nervously.

Silence.

"Come on. We just want to talk. Show us you're still here. Set off the lights again."

The LEDs stayed dark.

Hannah's gaze darted from her friend and the two strangers sitting inside a so-called haunted cell, to the lone set of eyes peering out from solitary. She slowly switched her Casper-Capture app from Speak to Vision and pointed her phone down the hallway.

"Okay, these fine folks have more to see and do tonight. I can't keep wasting their time," Jenny said. "If you won't let us know you're still here, we'll need to move on."

Hannah stepped backward. A flicker of one side of a stick figure dotted her screen—something deep in the shadows at the end of the hallway.

"What did you see?" Jenny asked.

Hannah didn't realize she had gasped and that her free hand covered her mouth. "Something down there." She pointed into the darkness. "Just a tiny bit of a stick person on Vision."

"They know we're here. They're trying to come out. It takes an enormous amount of energy for them to manifest, even for a split second."

Hannah drew her attention from her screen, still held upright and pointed down the hallway, and noticed every guest also had their phones trained on the darkness beyond.

"Guys, do you feel like we should maybe go out there too?" Christian asked Heath and Dano, still sitting in the darkness of a cell, by invitation of a female who had once been incarcerated here.

"No. I'm fine sitting right in here," Dano said, "where I can't see anything happening out—"

Christian screamed, leaped to his feet, and hurtled from the cell as the Rem Pod illuminated all three colors to their brightest capacity, with the nearby cat toy flashing its two-tone pattern. He practically flung himself into Hannah, and the collision knocked her phone from her hand.

All three LEDs blacked out.

Dano and Heath inside the cell were now on their feet, pale, their gazes darting around to figure out what had happened. The duo of women had stepped backward from where they stood, following Christian's outburst.

"Something grabbed my elbow," Christian said, panting.

Hannah furrowed her brows. "Are you sure?"

"Dude," Christian said, turning to face Heath. "Did you touch my elbow?"

Heath shook his head, his eyes wide.

Hannah noticed everyone stared at Christian, waiting for some follow up.

"Did you touch Christian?" Jenny asked the ghost.

Silence.

Hannah raised her phone and pointed into that cell. The amber stick men matched Heath's and Dano's bodies. She took a breath, held it a moment to embolden just a sliver of courage, and again pointed it down the long hallway. She checked the screen through squinted eyes, her eyelashes creating a natural barrier for her to fully see, in case anything unwanted appeared. She wanted to see something—yet she didn't want there to be anything.

"Don't go shy on us again," Jenny said, breaking Hannah from holding her breath.

The three LEDs illuminated simultaneously.

"*I want them to leave.*" This time the voice came from the phone inside the darkness of solitary.

"Who do you want to leave?" Jenny asked.

Silence.

"I'm not taking any chances," Dano said from inside the opposite cell and swiftly exited into the hallway, leaving Heath inside by his lonesome.

"It felt … It felt like," Christian stammered, regaining everyone's attention now that he seemed willing to describe what had happened.

Hannah had never seen him this shaken up. She pushed her glasses farther up her nose with the back of her hand and grabbed his hand.

Christian continued. "It felt like a hand on my elbow. I could feel the palm and the fingers. But it wasn't solid. It … It wasn't smoke either. It almost felt like …" He eyed Hannah.

She reassured him, flashing him the smile that he liked best.

Christian sighed. "As if water had taken shape, for only a split second. Then it was gone. Yet I could make out actual fingers and the palm of the hand."

"Like the water in the movie *The Abyss*," Heath said from inside the cell. "And what the hell am I still doing in here alone?"

The crowd laughed nervously, appreciative of the comic relief from the tension, as Heath stepped over the Rem Pod in the cell doorway and stood next to Dano.

"That's one of my favorite movies," Jenny said.

"Yeah, well, we're Coast Guard, so we have a weird fascination with movies that take place in the water," Dano said.

Hannah nodded to herself. That was why she couldn't recognize the insignia on their tee-shirts. It wasn't one of the four main branches.

"Are you okay?" Hannah asked Christian, watching him try to regain some composure. For all his joking and sarcasm, she knew him well enough to know he did not like to be embarrassed in front of strangers.

Christian ran his tongue across his teeth and exhaled loudly through his nose. His face brightened, and all fear left, replaced by his bravado. "You know how it is, rockin' and rollin' and whatnot."

Jenny shook her head. "You make a terrible Danny Zuko."

"Oh? You got the reference?"

"C'mon, I played Rizzo when I was in the drama club in high school. I ate and slept *Grease* for almost six months."

"Marry me?" Christian asked Jenny, making a puppy-dog face.

Hannah laughed and punched his arm as he gazed upon Jenny with star-swept eyes. Hannah knew Christian needed this dialogue exchange to shake off whatever he thought had happened to him inside that cell.

"I think that's the end of our hour," Jenny said. "Still, we got some good back-and-forth, some specific requests, and someone got touched." She smiled at Christian. "All in all, I would say this visit was a success."

The unnamed Coastie who had been sitting in the blind cell exited the room and huddled with Heath and Dano.

"*I want you to leave,*" spoke the voice again, now coming from the phone of one of the two women.

Christian's face paled for a split second.

"You sure you're okay?" Hannah asked. "You gonna make it, ninja?"

"Yeah, yeah. I'm sure that dude touched me. It ain't no thang," he said nonchalantly as he scooped his backpack from Hannah's feet and slung it over his shoulder.

"Right. I'm sure that's all it was," Hannah replied, giving him a narrow gaze.

Hanna focused on him as they followed Jenny from the women's unit. She noticed Christian's gaze darting left and right more than it had when they'd first climbed these steps. She removed her phone from her pocket and pointed the camera forward, with the Casper-Vision function activated.

"Please," Christian whispered, "just give it a break for a bit."

"Hey, man," Heath said from behind them. "Just so you know. I promise I didn't touch you. You scared me half to death when you jumped up."

"Yeah … I know you didn't."

CHAPTER 5:
THE GAS CHAMBER

Officer Duncan waited for them at the bottom of the stairs with another cluster of guests who he had escorted from a different location. Now he and Jenny would exchange groups, before Duncan took Hannah's group to the next location—the gas chamber—to meet up with Sara there.

Once Officer Duncan had completed the exchange, he raised his hand in the air. "Everyone who was just in the women's unit, follow me." He turned and headed across the yard.

Hannah listened to the footfalls on the pavement as her cluster of guests now walked not so much in three cliques but more as a single unit. It seemed the experiences in the women's unit had brought them closer together a bit. They had shared something unique, and she wondered what the gas chamber would bring.

They followed Duncan down a slope and through a gate, where the small square building, about the size of a bungalow, sat in front of them. Sara stood outside and gave

Officer Duncan the thumbs-up. He excused himself to sprint across the yard, his duty belt making a *schuck-schuck-schuck* noise against his police-issued tactical pants as he ran. Soon he would grab another group to escort them to their new location, then switch off again.

Hannah traversed the walkway toward the gas chamber and saw a white stone crucifix, about the size of a human, embedded into the walkway. Some people in front of her stepped on the cross, while others gave it wide berth, maybe not wanting to defile a holy symbol in a place rife with spirits. When she and Christian reached the crucifix, she found herself inadvertently sidestepping it. Christian's pace as he casually trampled over the cross confirmed that he hadn't even seen it. She wondered if it had been made from limestone as well.

The small boxlike building in front of them boasted two entrances. One side resembled the interior of a submarine. Strategically placed turrets adorned the edge of the roof, reminding Hannah of a row of sharp teeth ready to bite, chew, and tear any and all who dared to enter the belly of the chamber.

"Hey, guys," Sara said, standing between the two entrances to the gas chamber. "Where did you just come from?"

"Women's block," Dano answered from the back.

"Right on. Anything interesting happen there?"

Hannah eyed Christian to see if he would say anything, but she saw him studying his feet and refusing to look up. She had never seen him so shaken.

"That guy got touched," said one of the females from the duo at the front of the cluster, turning to point at Christian.

"Yeah, that's pretty common," Sara said without engaging Christian for any follow-up, as if such an event was just *so* common that it didn't even warrant further questioning.

Hannah allowed herself to relax with relief. She didn't think Christian could handle scrutiny about the experience, not until he'd had time to process it. And, knowing him, she was confident that she did; Christian would hide behind a curtain of sarcasm to mask how he truly felt.

Sara pointed at the building. "Welcome to the gas chamber. As you know, the prison executed a total of forty people here during the prison's 168 years of operation. Thirty-nine from hydrogen cyanide gas, and one in 1989 from lethal injection. The building is split into two sides. To your left is the viewing area, where both the victim's and the inmate's families could watch the process, integrated with each other. Tell me *that* wasn't a *Jerry Springer Show* episode waiting to happen."

Christian's eyebrows arched at Hannah in a *that's crazy* gesture.

Sara continued. "To your right is the chamber itself, and those two chairs are the original chairs where they executed the inmates."

Hannah raised herself onto her tiptoes to see over the heads in front of her to get a better view of the two entrances.

"Does anyone know what this is?" Sara raised a tablet-like device connected to headphones and a pair of orange-lensed goggles that mimicked something more from a cyberpunk movie than a paranormal device.

The group remained facing forward, waiting for Sara to give the answer.

"This is a spirit box. Does anyone know what it does?"

"Oh, I do," said one of the Coasties from behind Hannah. "It picks up voices within radio waves."

"Right. So, we're going to do the Estes Method here in the gas chamber—which requires noise-canceling headphones and blackout goggles. Two people can take turns sitting in one of the gas chamber chairs, while listening to the spirit box. The rest of us will be on the other side, watching and asking questions. The person inside the chamber will yell out anything and everything they hear in their headphones. Remember that the person in the chamber can't hear our questions."

"And how is this any different from our Casper-Capture app?" asked one of the women from up front.

"I was just thinking the same thing," Christian whispered to Hannah.

She shushed him but was glad that he seemed to have rebounded to his normal sardonic self.

"Good question," Sara replied. "The difference is that we are asking the questions and looking for a direct reply. And the person giving the reply didn't hear the question, nor can they see their surroundings, not with the goggles on. Casper-Capture says something, and we respond to *that* message. With the box, we are the interviewers and not just in constant reactionary follow-up mode."

Hannah nodded; it seemed to make sense.

"So, who wants to be the first in the chair?" Sara asked.

Hannah held her breath, feeling gazes from far away were on her, and she unconsciously slipped her hand into her pocket to rub the stolen piece of fabric—for comfort or to keep her awareness heightened, she didn't know.

"I will . . . ?" hesitantly said one the females, slowly raising her hand with much trepidation.

"You sure about that?" Sara asked. "Seems like you had to talk yourself into it."

A few guests chuckled, and the twentysomething woman, with dyed green hair and a Missouri State Penitentiary tee-shirt that read DON'T FEAR THE PEEKERS, stepped forward and stood beside Sara.

"Okay, great. The rest of you can find a seat on the benches here, and you follow me," Sara said to the green-haired woman. "What's your name?"

"Marie," she answered, then said, "And my friend in there is Alisha," as they disappeared into the chamber side.

Hannah followed Christian into the viewing side and waited for him to get his backpack situated before she slid onto the middle bench next to him. Hannah watched through two large rectangular windows. While Sara and Marie spoke, Hannah couldn't hear anything they said. Marie nodded, and Sara smiled and handed Marie the spirit box, the blackout goggles, and the noise-cancelling headphones.

Hannah glanced behind her to see the trio of Coasties had taken the back row, and Marie's friend sat on the first bench. Hannah watched Marie sit in one of the gas chamber chairs. The back of the chairs and the back of Marie's head faced the glass so Hannah and everyone else could only see her hair above the top of the white metal chair.

Sara left the chamber, veered around the front of the building, and entered the viewing area. "Okay, this is how it'll work. Marie's name may come into play at some point. It's important for us to know the translator's name. She can't hear us, so she'll give us a thumbs-up when she's situated."

Hannah inhaled deeply and held it. She glanced at Christian to see his deer-in-headlights look had now completely vanished, replaced with his signature cynical expression. She didn't realize how much she had missed this—his change in demeanor affecting her more than she had thought.

Marie raised a hand, all fingers lowered except her thumb.

"Looks like we can begin." Sara leaned against the window to the chamber closest to the exit.

Hannah studied the back of Marie's head, the two oval padded headphones secured on her ears like muffs, with the blackout goggles taut around her head.

"Does anyone have a question?" Sara asked.

The group remained silent.

Hannah scanned their faces. She wondered if this would be like a middle-school dance, where everyone *wanted* to dance, but no one wanted to be the fool who hit the dance floor first. It usually took just that first person to start the avalanche of courage and participation. She swallowed hard, steadfast that it would not be her.

"Sinner!" Marie screamed from inside the chamber.

Hannah's heart jumped a beat, startled.

"Remember," Sara explained, "Marie doesn't know if we are asking anything or not. The instructions are for her to yell—and she must scream or else we wouldn't hear her through the glass—"

"Run!" Marie yelled.

Hannah startled a bit. Something felt unsettling about the woman sitting in the gas chamber, just yelling random phrases that seemingly meant nothing right now.

"What did you pick for your last meal?" asked one of the Coasties from behind Hannah.

"Good one," Sara said and glanced through the window at Marie.

Marie remained silent.

After a beat, Heath began to ask, "Do you know what happened—"

"It's dark!"

"Keep asking," Sara urged, "even if she's not answering your question."

"Do you know what happened to you?" Heath asked again, finishing his question this time.

Hannah didn't realize her hands were balled into fists, until pain surged through her skin from her fingernails digging into her palm.

"It burns!"

Hannah gasped as their group whispered to each other. That felt a little too specific.

"Do you know we are here?" Christian asked, surprising Hannah that he would participate. Again based on that whole middle-school-dance theory.

Marie remained silent.

Hannah focused on the back of the woman's head.

"How many—" started Alisha, Marie's friend, but Sara raised a hand to stop her.

"Sometimes we need to let the question breathe and to be patient. It takes a lot of energy for the spirits to communicate. Let's give it a few moments."

Hannah pushed her glasses up her nose with the back of her hand and felt a thin layer of sweat on her skin. From the corner of her eye, she saw Christian cross his legs and bounce his foot. Nervous energy, she assumed. It certainly couldn't be boredom at this point. Not after something spectral had touched him.

"Yes! Go away!"

"See?" Sara said. "If we give them some time, you'll be surprised at how much they'll answer when they are in the mood."

"You're talking about them like they still have the ability to choose their behaviors," Dano said from behind Hannah.

"In a sense," Sara started, "I believe they—"

"Why is she here?" Marie yelled from the chamber.

Hannah's breath hitched in her throat. Was that directed at her? she wondered. Did the spirits suspect that Hannah was here because she had stolen something from one of their kind? Such a reason might be considered heinous to them. She heard her pulse in her ears as the silence drew on.

Thump. THUMP. *THWUMP!*

Hannah focused on the back of Marie's head and silently counted in her head to try to squash the onset of a panic attack—something she hadn't had to deal with in a very long time, not since before she had stopped drinking. The panic attacks always seemed to precede the appearance of the brimmed—

"I want her to go!" Marie screamed.

Hannah squealed just loud enough for the group to look at her. Her teeth clenched so tightly that she wouldn't be surprised if one of them snapped. Something was here—or was coming. She tried to breathe in steady breaths. She didn't want to know what might happen if she had a panic attack, here in the penitentiary, when the aftereffect was always a visit from her shadow-figure friend. *Please, not here.*

"You okay, Hannah Banana?" Christian gripped her left hand and unfurled her clenched fist. He slipped his fingers between hers and squeezed. "I got you. Concentrate on—"

"Return it!"

Hannah sucked in air, but nothing filled her lungs, like a fish out of water. It *was* talking about her. She was sure of it. And it knew. It knew she had stolen from it. Her heart accelerated, but she wasn't breathing. Christian squeezed harder, probably feeling her body go into full-blown panic mode—or now was under the same assumption as she was that whoever was talking through the spirit box directed it at her.

The brimmed-hat man was sure to be next.

"Missing!"

Hannah shot her gaze at Christian; she knew her eyes were wild. She needed help.

"What is missing? What do you need returned?" Heath asked the spirit.

Hannah spun her head to quickly glare at the Coastie. How could he ask that? How could he set her up like that? Didn't he know what was coming next? The shadow figure that she had kept at bay over this past year of sobriety …

"Run!"

Christian scooted closer to Hannah so his legs touched hers, and he leaned backward just enough to put his arm around her lower back.

Hannah knew he fully understood.

"Why do you want us to run? Are you going to hurt us?" Alisha asked the spirit.

Hannah tried to swallow. Tried to breathe. Tried to blink. Why were they egging on the spirit? Hannah needed to leave. She would take her chances crossing the yard by herself if it meant not hearing any more—

"It's dark!" Marie yelled.

Hannah bit her bottom lip, calculating the distance to the door that led outside, that stopped her from hearing Marie scream messages that seemed directed—

"Penance!"

Hannah made eye contact with Christian, pleading silently for him to get her to safety, for him to make good on all the times he had promised that he would keep her safe.

Christian's gaze softened, and he flashed her his signature smile.

She knew he was trying to bring her down from one hundred to zero without making a scene. She nodded and concentrated on his face.

"Are you apologizing, or do you want someone else to apologize?" asked one of the Coasties.

"I want to talk!"

"We are talking," Sara said before anyone could answer.

"What is it you want?" Heath asked.

"Nurse!" Marie yelled from the chamber.

"Is anyone a nurse here?" Sara asked.

The group collectively shook their heads.

"Do you need a nurse?" Dano asked.

"Stuck!"

Hannah felt her breathing and her pulse normalize. It appeared whatever—or whoever—was communicating with Marie had moved off the topic of Hannah's thievery and had graduated to a different subject. She relaxed her fingers intertwined with Christian's.

He released his hold and shook his hand. "Jeez, Banana, any longer and I would have to get my fingers amputated from blood loss."

Hannah smirked at him and pushed her glasses back up her nose.

"What was your favorite sport?" Dano asked the spirit.

"Ah, good one," Sara said, nodding in approval.

Marie remained silent while they waited.

Hannah noticed Sara check her watch and assumed it was getting close to the time to switch out participants. Hopefully whoever went in next didn't harp on Hannah's guilt of the stolen strip of fabric. She found her gaze flitting toward the opened door leading to the outside, hoping she didn't catch a glimpse of her brimmed-hat shadow figure. That panic attack had gotten too close for comfort before she could quell it and thankfully locked out the brimmed-hat man from appearing.

Marie stayed silent.

"Okay," Sara said and pushed herself off her leaning position against the glass window to the gas chamber. "If anyone wants to go next, and we'll only have time for one more, let me know when I come back in."

Sara exited to the outside and reappeared on the gas chamber side. Marie stood and removed the headphones and goggles, then handed Sara the spirit box. They exchanged some words, but Hannah couldn't hear them through the glass.

"You good?" Christian asked.

"Yeah, yeah. Thanks."

"For what?"

"Knowing what I needed, when I didn't even know myself. I was ready to get the fuck out of Dodge there for a few minutes."

A smile spread slowly across his face. "I know you were. And I know that wouldn't have solved anything nor fixed the problem of why we're here in the first place. I told you, Banana; I got you."

The worst part about it was, she knew he was the best thing for her. Yet old habits die hard—and familiarity kept winning over the road less taken. Still, she felt safer tonight, with Christian beside her, than she had in a long time. Even regardless of that unexpected onset of a panic attack.

Marie and Sara curved around the front of the tiny building to join the rest of the group on the spectator side, and Sara asked, "Well, has anyone decided whether they want to—"

"I will," Christian said, raising his hand.

Hannah leaned away from him, wide-eyed.

He caught her shock and winked at her, his hand still raised.

"Okay, young man. Come on down. You're the next contestant on Get Haunted's Gas Chamber Chat."

Christian stood, and Hannah slid her knees against the bench so he had room to shuffle past. When he scooted by her, he squeezed her shoulder, comforting her in so many more ways than mere words could have. That touch told her that he was doing this without menace, without using it as ammunition to belittle the exercise later. It told her that he was doing it because she needed to know he truly supported her now. Maybe he even did this a little bit because he couldn't shake the mystery of what had touched him in the women's unit cell.

Christian stepped away from the bench and into the pathway and stopped in front of Sara as Marie inched down the first row to sit next to her friend.

"Everyone, this is …" Sara pointed to him so he would finish the sentence.

"Christian," he answered.

"And the same rules and process will apply to Christian as it did to Marie. He will yell everything he hears, and we will be the ones asking the questions. We kind of let the spirits start to take the reins of Marie's session, so let's stay in control as the ones dictating the topics."

Sara escorted Christian out the door and through the entrance to the gas chamber. Hannah swallowed hard, unsettled to watch her—whatever Christian was—best friend talk to the Get Haunted co-owner through a window and not hear anything they said. Hannah smirked when Sara handed Christian the headphones, goggles, and spirit box. If someone had told her, just an hour ago, that this would be happening …

Christian sat in the same side chair that Marie had used, and now all Hannah saw of him was the back of his head. Sara's mouth formed a few more sentences, none of which the group could hear. Then she patted Christian's shoulder and exited the chamber side.

Hannah sighed, knowing Christian had volunteered for her sake, to help settle her mind, to take one for the team, to show he was here for her, among a sea of strangers. Then Hannah suddenly realized that her rock was now in a room—

a gas chamber—with a sound-deadening glass window separating them. What if the panic attack threatened to rise again? What if the brimmed-hat man flashed past her peripheral vision? She was in here, and Christian was in *there*.

Hannah sucked inside her lips as she pushed her glasses up her nose with the back of her hand and surveyed the people surrounding her. She felt comfortable around the group now—especially after what they had experienced in the women's unit together—but they were still strangers. And if shit went south, she would be alone.

"Come outside!" Christian yelled.

"Starting already," Sara said. "That's a good sign."

All Hannah's arm hairs stood on end when her friend's familiar voice yelled words that he was hearing, possibly from beyond the veil, through his headphones. It made her feel even more alone in the roomful of people. Marooned almost.

However, she was oddly proud of him, and if he could be brave enough to do this for her, she could be brave enough to endure sitting here by herself. Proverbially.

Alisha turned around to regard Hannah. "He's a keeper, that one. I can tell he's doing this for you."

Hannah politely smiled but didn't know how to respond—or maybe didn't want to deal with what that can of worms would open, regardless of what she replied. Instead, she shoved her glasses up her nose again and concentrated on the rear of Christian's head through the sound-deadening glass.

"Thief!"

Every time he yelled, Hannah flinched, like someone flicked an invisible finger at her nose.

"You guys don't have to wait for me to tell you to ask questions," Sara said. "Don't be shy."

"Did it hurt when they turned on the gas?" Heath asked from behind her.

Silence.

Hannah watched Christian place both palms on each side of the headphones, his hands now off the spirit box. She assumed he did that so he could hear more clearly. She didn't know what it sounded like, but she was sure the layers of static and noise proved difficult to decipher the words underneath.

"Smells!"

"Good, good," Sara said. "Keep the questions coming."

"What smells?" Heath asked again.

"Gin!"

A handful of guests chuckled, but Hannah gritted her teeth, not finding anything funny about this.

"For some reason, we get certain words frequently, without much rhyme or reason," Sara said.

"Run away!"

"Not!"

"Sinner!"

After his three machinegun-like outbursts, Christian added, "It's what I want!"

"What do you want?" Dano asked.

"What she stole!"

Hannah held her breath, watching Christian keep his hands pressed against the headphones. She wondered if he also sensed how his outbursts grew curiously specific to her situation and if he would cut his session short to spare her additional anxiety.

"Give it back!"

"Give what back?" Alisha asked, seemingly getting swooped up in the accelerated exchange between their questions and Christian's yelled responses.

"Keep her here!"

"Keep who here?"

"In her pocket!"

Hannah gasped, yet it resembled more of a squeal. She rose to her feet, her hand clasped over her mouth, as Christian leaped from the gas chamber chair, sending the spirit box clattering to the floor. The Coasties focused on the young woman who had practically screamed on the row in front of them, while the duo of women transfixed on the man in the gas chamber, who had torn the headphones from his head and pounded on the window, screaming.

Hannah's knees buckled, and she caught herself from completely collapsing on the bench by throwing out her arms. Sara had already bolted from this side of the tiny building, before Hannah registered that Christian needed help. Hannah spotted Sara run into the gas chamber and place a hand on Christian's shoulder.

He bent forward, visibly panting, while Sara kept her hand on him, her mouth producing words that Hannah could not hear.

"Are you okay?" Marie asked, leaning backward to see Hannah.

Hannah nodded in quick short jerks but did not trust her voice to speak without cracking—or her heart from exploding from her chest. A sound at the entrance to the spectator side made Hannah look there, and she saw Christian. His eyes were glassy and wide. She stood into a crouch to inch toward him.

She took his hands into hers. "That was too much for me too."

"No, no, no," he said, shaking his head. "That wasn't it."

The room fell silent as everyone waited with bated breath for what Christian might reveal.

"The bottoms of my feet started burning. I didn't think anything of it—thought it may have been my imagination. Then it rose over my feet and worked itself up to my ankles."

"Burning?" she asked.

"You know when after you get the worst sunburn you've ever had? And then the pain when you put on a shirt for the first time? It felt like that, all over both feet, and climbed higher. When it hit my ankles, the pain became almost unbearable."

"How do you feel now?" Sara asked.

Christian panned his gaze from Hannah to the woman. "It dissipated immediately as soon as the headphones fell off me, like it had never happened. I'm sure it was just some self-suggested hallucination or something. You know, hyperaware of every little thing because we are looking for it."

"When they pumped the gas into the chamber," Dano asked from the back row of benches, "where did it come from?"

Hannah watched Sara grimace and take a few breaths, as if stalling. She finally said, "From the floor at their feet so it could rise and fill the chamber."

CHAPTER 6:
A-HALL
(HOUSING UNIT 4)

Hannah noticed Officer Duncan bound toward them, a cluster of guests in tow, down the walkway toward the gas chamber. She sighed in relief that this excursion was over, and they could move on, hopefully to a location where she wouldn't experience so much targeted attention. Then she realized Christian had been affected both times. He had come as a skeptic and had twice put himself in the direct line of fire, and both times he had experienced a personalized encounter with a ghost.

But what if all the targeted attention that she assumed this place had directed at her was really paranoia? What if she was *looking* for it to be about her—her guilt manipulating the events as a punishment for her past behaviors? She slipped her hand into her pocket to fondle the keepsake.

"Thank God," Christian mumbled when he also noticed Officer Duncan leading the next group forward. Christian leaned into the second row of benches to snatch his backpack, then returned alongside Hannah.

"All done?" Officer Duncan asked Sara.

Hannah squinted to see if the woman would give any indication that something bizarre had just occurred in here.

"Oh yeah, I think they got their money's worth." But her expression remained stoic, not revealing anything. "Especially that one." She pointed to Christian.

There it is, Hannah thought. They either just can't leave well enough alone or they thrive on calling out people who had just suffered a traumatic experience—or was it just something about Christian? Maybe because he was a vocal critic? Because the fingers kept pointing to him when the subject was raised.

"Good job, troops," Officer Duncan said to Hannah's crew. "We gotta skedaddle to A-Hall so I can take *that* group to Reese and Rob in Death Row."

When Officer Duncan turned his head, Hannah saw the beads of sweat glistening on the man's forehead. It subliminally caused her to push her glasses farther up her nose, sliding over the compounding slime of humidity on her face too.

The group of Coast Guards shouldered through the door to the outside, with Dano stopping to ask Christian, "You okay, bro?"

Christian nodded and mumbled a, "Yeah, thank you."

Dano sympathetically clapped Christian's forearm, as if Christian had just attempted the game-winning field goal and missed.

Hannah slipped her arm around her friend's back as they filed down the pebbled pathway, some sidestepping the white stone crucifix in the ground, some unconsciously trampling it. "You sure you're good, Halifax?"

"Right as rain, Banana." He flashed her his best poker-face smile.

They snaked up the incline, around the bend, with Officer Duncan leading the parade, until they reached A-Hall again, where Get Haunted had kicked off tonight's event—where the peekers lived—and where the dungeon breathed with a life of its own below ground.

The hall was in complete darkness except for a green floor-to-ceiling LED matrix grid that covered the back second half of the four-story building. Some *oohs* and *aahs* came from the guests, as what had once been a looming macabre building now resembled something from inside a ride at EPCOT Center at Disney World.

"Those splashes of green dots on the walls and ceiling are like those projectors used in kids' bedrooms to replicate stars," Christian mused.

"It's oddly beautiful," Hannah added, marveling at the crisp green pinholes that had turned the hall into a wonderland.

Lisa stood behind a wooden table that held the projector spraying the LEDs across the hall. In front of her were the rows of metal folding chairs they had sat in during the original introduction. "Come in. Come in. I know you guys already sat in here for what felt like a while when you first got here, but this time we'll have some real fun."

"I'd like to be front row for this," Christian said.

Hannah eyed him sharply. "You sure? Are you a glutton for punishment?"

"*Nah*, just feel like I need one of these locations to *not* taunt me. You know, to prove it was a coincidence and that this place didn't single me out."

"If you say so, hotshot." Hannah followed Christian to the front row and raised an eyebrow when he plopped into the dead-center chair. "Brazen."

"It's how I roll, Banana." He winked at her as he lowered his backpack to his feet.

Lisa waited for their small group to settle into their seats. "The space looks different from before, huh? And keep your eyes peeled for those peekers that Reese mentioned earlier. They've been *very* curious during the last two groups."

Heath, who sat directly behind Hannah, said, "Looks like something from *Tron*."

Lisa pointed at Heath with a finger-gun. "Can anyone guess what we use the LED grid spray to detect?"

"Ghosts?" Marie answered, but it sounded more like a question.

"Not just ghosts but shadow figures. Entities that consume light as they pass it."

"But wouldn't someone walking in front block it out too?" Dano asked.

Christian pivoted to face Dano. "No. See, the LED would then reflect onto the person's body, so we'd still see the light on *them* now and not against the wall. If a shadow passed in front of it, the light would disappear." Christian turned, front-facing now, and glanced at Hannah.

She nodded and flashed him an approving smile, glad to see him participating—and glad that he had known the reason so fast.

"That's correct," Lisa said. "So occasionally check the back wall for any LEDs that disappear, then reappear, as a shadow figure moves across the hall."

"*Remorse,*" said someone's Casper-Capture app.

Lisa continued without missing a beat. "And I have placed two cat balls on either side of the projector."

Hannah leaned forward so she could see the two toys on the table.

"We'll try to coax them to light up the balls. Does anyone know what was one of the most important items in prison? Their currency?"

"Cigarettes?" Marie asked.

"Exactly. People would get shanked in the yard over a single smoke, so we'll use those as—"

"*Bribed.*"

"No, no one's bribing you," Lisa said to the ghost. "This isn't a bribe. If you can make the cat balls light up, you can have the cigarettes."

"*I don't believe you.*"

"We're telling you the truth. We wouldn't lie to you." Lisa placed two fresh cigarettes on either side of the LED projector. "Just touch the cat balls, and you can have the cigarettes."

Heath, Dano, and the other guy who comprised the Coast Guards in attendance all rose, approached the table, and stood next to it. Hannah watched Dano activate the Casper-Vision function on his phone. "Look. Something's trying to form."

Hannah and Christian leaned to the side to see Dano's screen better. The amber stick figures flashed and danced, pieces of the limbs appearing and disappearing, in front of the table.

"It's trying to collect enough energy to manipulate the balls," Lisa said.

"If you make one of the toys light up, you can have the cigarettes," Dano coaxed the spirits, the stick figure on his screen not disappearing as often, the limbs staying solid longer.

"It's trying."

Christian leaned forward more, craning his neck to see better.

"You're really getting into this, aren't you, Danny Zuko?"

"*Pffftt* … no way. Not me, babe," he said in his best John Travolta impression, pretending to flip up an invisible collar on an invisible leather jacket.

"Look, look. There's two of them," Marie said, now standing with the trio of Coasties.

Hannah and Christian rose so they could have a better vantage too. The screen showed the first stick figure, about 80 percent formed, with now a second one trying to manifest.

"Think they're gonna fight over them?" Christian asked.

"That's why we have two cigarettes," Lisa answered.

"You're almost there," Dano coaxed the nearest spirit. "Just a little bit more. Make those cat toys light up, and the cigarettes are yours."

"I even have a lighter to light them for you," Heath added, and a few people chuckled.

Hannah watched the first stick figure flash even less and seemingly had pulled itself into a solid form on the app. Her gaze darted from Dano's screen of the two stick figures that represented the two wraiths standing in front of the table, to the space between the table and the front row of seats. Back and forth, the app confirmed that two entities stood right there in front of them but were invisible to the naked eye.

The second stick figure gained solidity, its limbs flashing less and staying on the screen longer.

"*I want one*," said one of the Coastie's app.

"You have to light up the cat ball first," Lisa said, "then you can have one."

Both cat balls ignited in a red and blue dance of colors. Hannah forgot herself for a moment and almost clapped in celebration.

"Very good," Lisa commended. "Each one of you can have your smokes now."

From behind Lisa, in the entranceway to a cell, the same device that Jenny had used in the women's unit—a Rem Pod—illuminated all its colors. Lisa faced the rear of the hall. "Well, I think our friend in cell 10 is jealous that someone got cigarettes." She glimpsed at the group. "The entity in cell 10 is known to be a bit cranky. Sometimes a sore loser. That's why I put the Rem Pod in his doorway."

The green, orange, and red LEDs on the device remained fully lit.

"Okay, anyone want to investigate what he wants with me?"

Hannah eyed Christian, literally curious if he would keep the streak going. It did not surprise her when he raised his hand and shifted his weight from one leg to another. He was either really stupid or doing this for her sake. Knowing Christian, it was probably a mixture of both.

"All right, we have a *tribute*," Lisa said, smiling, her eyes glinting.

"The hand touching you in the women's unit and your feet burning in the gas chamber wasn't enough for you, Halifax?" Hannah asked. "You don't have to keep trying to impress me."

As Christian circled to the other side of the wooden table where green LEDs peppered Lisa's body, he said loudly so their whole group could hear, "Oh, Banana, at this point, I'm waiting for Slimer to come shooting from a cell."

The Coasties behind her laughed as the younger-looking one—the one whom she had not learned his name yet—said, "I'm outta here if it's the Stay-Puff Marshmallow Man."

Hannah chuckled and turned to smile at the Coastie.

Dano punched the young man in the arm, chuckling in a teasing manner. "Dude, Stay-*Puff*? You're an idiot."

"What?" the young man asked, his hands out in question, and glimpsed Hannah.

"It's Stay-*Puft*," she said. "Your friend is just being a jerk."

"Hey!" Dano retorted. "What have I ever done to you? Besides protect your boyfriend when a horny ghost touched him and freaked him out." Then Dano smirked at her in a way to show he was just playing around with her too.

"Yeah, like hell you did," Christian said from the other side of the table, now next to Lisa.

Hannah noticed that Christian didn't correct Dano about him not being her boyfriend.

"You were ready to take me out at the knees to get out of that cell if it touched you too," Christian quipped, then winked at Hannah as the Coasties laughed, sending an encapsulating warmth through her—a warmth, for the first time in a year, that didn't involve alcohol hitting her stomach and spreading like tendrils through her body, numbing her.

Hannah shook her head to clear her reverie; she was *not* that Hannah anymore. She had spent the last year working the steps. Making amends. Apologizing. Knowing it could never reverse the past, but it might just be enough for a brighter future. No, that old Hannah would finally die. Here. And tonight.

She slipped her fingers into her pocket to feel the fabric, to remind herself that she was both on a quest to move forward and on a mission to right a wrong.

Hannah glanced at the Rem Pod at the entrance to the cell down the left side of the hall. All three LEDs remained illuminated, and the two cat balls on the table blinked to life simultaneously, sending their red and blue flashes across the faces of the group.

"Ready?" Lisa asked Christian.

He turned to give Hannah a thumbs-up and the goofiest, most cartoonlike ear-to-ear smile he could muster.

The cat balls finished their cycle and went dormant.

"You guys are more than welcome to come watch. I'll be using that Casper-Conjuring feature on the app, which is still in beta testing." Lisa homed in on Christian's face. "You ready to be the guinea pig?"

"Story of my life, babe." Christian pointed the finger-gun at her.

"Oh, for Christ's sake. Could this night get any weirder?" Heath said behind Hannah, making her chuckle to relieve some tension.

Lisa turned and headed for cell 10, Christian keeping pace beside her, as the rest of the group filed in behind them.

As they crossed the hall floor, passing cells on their left and right, Alisha exclaimed, pointing to the second floor, "I saw one! I just saw one of those peepers."

Hannah followed the woman's finger to the cell above them, the weatherworn entranceway holding the possibility of seeing something straight on.

"Peekers," Lisa corrected, also gazing upward at the second deck, as she lumbered toward cell ten.

Christian turned and walked backward to face Hannah. "You would think she could get their name right. I mean, her friend *is* wearing a DON'T FEAR THE PEEKERS tee-shirt and all. Maybe I should buy one, if we ever come back."

Hannah shushed him, then asked Alisha, her voice lowered, "What did it look like?"

"It was so fast. Just like they said. Saw it out of the corner of my eye. And, when I looked, it disappeared into the cell."

Hannah scanned the openings to the cells above, filled with darkness, as they walked, until they reached the Rem Pod.

Then the device went from fully illuminated to dark, as if someone had unplugged it.

"Weird," Lisa mumbled.

Hannah didn't know if she liked Lisa's tone. It felt … cautious.

Lisa faced the group when they reached the entranceway. "You guys watch from out here. See how tiny these cells are?"

Hannah peeked above Christian's shoulder to observe the thin rectangular cell, no more than six feet wide, with the darkened Rem Pod in the entryway.

"Lower your voice," said someone's Casper-Capture app.

"We're not even talking," Lisa answered, then turned and stepped over the Rem Pod and into the cell, as if replying to the app was the most normal thing in the world, and motioned for Christian to enter with her.

He lifted his leg to clear the ghost-hunting apparatus, and all three lights shone like mini-flashlights, illuminating his body. Christian yelled something that sounded like a *whoa* and danced on his tiptoes to avoid the glow of the lights, as if they could be tangible and touch him. He stumbled, hopping on one foot into the cell, then regained his balance.

"Jesus, that scared me," Christian whispered. He composed himself and put his hands on his hips, his face blushing.

"You okay?" Lisa asked, touching his arm.

"My boy there has been the center of all the spirits' attention tonight," Heath said, laughing.

Hannah watched Christian shoot him a look, as if to say, *Shut up. This isn't funny anymore.* Then Christian flashed Hannah a reaffirming smile. He was putting on a brave face for her, she knew now. She could see his signature Danny Zuko façade cracking—the close encounters finally toying with his mind.

When Hannah flashed her playful smile at him, Christian answered Lisa, "Yeah. Yeah. I'm good."

"Well, whoever is in here seems to like you, with the Rem Pod going off like that."

"That seems par for the course tonight," Christian said.

Hannah moved to the edge of the doorjamb so she had a better angle on seeing the entirety of the cell and to give Marie, who was shorter and standing behind Hannah, more of a view.

"So, this function is called Casper-Conjuring." Lisa launched the app on her phone. "We will ask whoever is in here to show us, on the screen, what they are seeing."

A few of the group mumbled in disbelief.

"Sometimes the images don't make any sense, like taking a handful of different pictures and scrambling them together. So don't hold your breath for anything specific. But we still like to try."

"I don't like it," said Alisha's app.

Marie leaned into Hannah. "Maybe they shouldn't do this."

Hannah regarded her with furrowed brows. "What do you mean?"

"Your boyfriend has already had something happen to him at each station. And it just told us that it didn't like what we are doing."

Lisa interjected, "Sometimes the things the app says don't always pertain to what's actually happening in the moment." She cleared her throat and raised her phone screen to eye level. "Okay, if you can hear me"—she espied the illuminated Rem Pod—"because I know you're still here, can you show us what you see right now?"

Christian leaned closer to Lisa and somewhat blocked Hannah's view of the phone. The room fell silent as everyone waited for something, for anything to happen on the screen. Or visibly inside the room.

Hannah thought Christian could *not* handle a full-blown apparition at this point.

"Look. Something's happening," Lisa said.

"We can't see out here," Marie said.

Christian glanced behind him, noticed he was the obstruction, and apologized as he put some space between him and Lisa.

Hannah squinted at Lisa's phone, now raised a bit higher so everyone outside the cell could see. Red patterns of waves and swirls covered her screen. Splotches and dots of something solid formed for just a moment, then returned to what resembled moving sand art.

"Why is he here?" asked Hannah's phone in her hand. She jumped, almost as if someone had shocked her. She had forgotten that she had launched the Casper-Capture app and had it running on her phone.

"Why is *who* here?" Lisa asked from inside the cell. "Show us who you mean by *he*. Show us what you are looking at."

Marie screamed, her voice ricocheting through all the empty cells on all four floors, as Christian backpedaled so fast that he tripped over the Rem Pod. He collided with some of the guests as he stumbled, and threw his hands forward just in time to break his fall to the cement floor. The Rem Pod skidded across the hall and came to rest in front of the descending staircase to the dungeon.

Lisa spun around, strode to Christian, and crouched to ask if he was okay.

Hannah pressed her hand against her chest in concern and confusion. *What the heck just happened?* She took a few steps toward Christian, who was already halfway to getting to his feet, and put her hand under his forearm to help guide him the rest of the way.

"You okay, bro?" asked the young male who was afraid of the Stay-Puft Marshmallow Man.

"Yeah, yeah. I'm good." Christian wiped penitentiary dust from his jeans and tee-shirt.

Lisa looked sternly into his eyes. "You sure you're good? If you're hurt, we'll need to report it."

"Nah. No reason to. Tip-top shape." He flashed her a haphazard smile.

Lisa narrowed her gaze at him, unconvinced.

Hannah pushed her shoulder into Christian's arm to get closer and asked Marie, "What happened? Why did you scream?"

"Show her," Marie said to Lisa.

"Show me *what*?" Hannah asked.

"Do you want to see it again?" Lisa asked Christian.

He shook his head.

"Something spooked good ole boy here," Dano said.

"You didn't see it?" Marie asked him.

Anxiety and impatience rose and bubbled inside Hannah. "Will you guys just shut up and let Lisa answer?" Hannah took a deep breath and held it. She felt ashamed of her outburst; she hadn't let her emotions get the better of her since … well—and it hurt every fiber of her being to admit—since before she had gotten sober. "I'm sorry, everyone."

Lisa smacked her lips and offered her phone to Hannah.

Hannah gasped and covered her mouth when she saw a perfect image of the backs of Lisa's and Christian's heads. The ghost in cell 10 had been watching them from behind.

"Stay with me …" added the spirit.

Lisa collected the Rem Pod from the other side of the hall. "If you're really feeling fine, I think we should move to the next location."

"You sure you're good, Halifax?" Hannah asked.

Christian nodded in quick jerks. "Yeah, Banana. Two enthusiastic thumbs-up, Roger Ebert style."

Marie wove through the small group, now dispersing from the front of cell 10, toward Hannah and Christian. "I'm sorry if I scared you and made it worse."

"I would've screamed too," Hannah said. "I'm almost glad I had some warning that *something* had happened before Lisa showed me. At least I was a bit more prepared than you two were, seeing it in real time."

Lisa placed the Rem Pod, its LEDs still unlit, on the wooden table next to the laser projector and faced the group.

Hannah slipped her hand into Christian's and intertwined their fingers. She didn't fully realize she had done it, until he gave her hand a quick squeeze. She glanced at him, and he stared at her, his gaze full of thanks and something else—hope? She didn't want him to jump to conclusions about what her holding his hand signified—because she was unsure herself about what it signified.

Lisa clapped once to get everyone's attention. "Okay, we're gonna head down those stairs behind you into the medieval-style dungeon nicknamed *The Hole*. It was where they literally threw the troublemakers. Or if they even *thought* you were a troublemaker. If you know what cave darkness is like, that's what they experienced down there. Dark enough where you can't see your hand in front of your face. The only light they would see in a twenty-four-hour period would be for the few seconds when a guard would open a small slit in the door to slide some bread and water through. And each cell could have five or six guys in it. Sometimes the number of slices of bread didn't match the number of men in that cell. How do you think that went down?"

"Oh, God," Marie whispered beside Hannah.

Hannah cleared the lump in her throat.

Lisa traipsed toward the staircase that was just a hole in the floor from this perspective. "Most of them were forgotten about once they went down there. One of the most extreme cases involved an inmate staying down there for up to seventeen years, without ever seeing light."

"What happened when they came back up?" Marie asked.

Lisa reached the top of the downward staircase and stopped to face the group behind her. "He came out blind." Lisa descended the steps, the group following her. "They had a whipping post down here, and the guards would whip the inmates with a cat-o'-nine-tails. They were only allowed to whip them up to ninety-nine times. The inmates came out bat-shit crazy. Some committed suicide by ramming their heads into the walls. Over and over and over. They even killed each other. Some starved to death. Disease ran rampant. They were literally buried alive down here."

The bottom of the stairs gave birth to a larger square room with an open shower stall at the back. An entranceway sat to Hannah's left, which staved off the darkest nothingness Hannah had ever seen. Unlike the solitary confinement room in the women's unit, she was sure the blackness down here in the dungeon would devour any light shone into it.

"Behind me, through that doorway," Lisa continued, "is a single hallway. All the cells will be on your left-hand side. The unique thing about these cells is that each one is known for a different trait. I'll explain each one as we walk." Lisa slithered into the dark hallway, the nothingness consuming her.

Hannah wouldn't have been surprised if the tour guide had actually vaporized from existence. Hannah, still holding Christian's hand, sliced through the entryway and joined Lisa in the blackness. The rest of the group filled the space in the dank hallway behind the tour guide, Hannah, and Christian.

"Is everyone in?" Lisa asked.

"Is everyone *innnn*?" Christian intoned in a whisper to Hannah, mimicking Jim Morrison's voice when he sang that lyric in The Doors' song "The End."

"Nice to see you've bounced back quickly from your scare." And Hannah slipped her hand from his with a little too much zest than she had intended. From the corner of her eye, she saw him casually tuck his hands into his jeans pockets, as if her sudden break of connection hadn't meant something to him—typical Danny Zuko reaction. Typical Christian Halifax reaction.

They reached the first cell on the left. None of the cells had bars or doors, and the entranceways were only large enough for one person to pass through at a time.

"This first one is the Growly cell. People hear growling noises inside that cell."

The group shone their handheld flashlights or the torchlights from their phones into the cell.

Hannah realized the ceilings were still arched, like in the cells upstairs, but were much higher, almost cavernous.

They continued to the next cell on the left.

"This is the Touchy-Feely cell."

"So is that cell in the women's unit," Christian quipped, and the trio of Coasties behind them chuckled.

"Next is the Tuggy cell. Different from the Touchy-Feely cell, here people's hair and clothes get pulled."

They reached the first corner, turned to the right, and shambled into the blackness, only marred by the concentrated beams of light hitting the walls.

"Can you feel me?" asked someone's Casper-Capture app.

"That doesn't sound ominous at all," Dano teased from the rear of the group.

They turned right at the next corner and followed the dungeon's horseshoe pattern.

"Here is the Sparkly cell."

"Ooh, that sounds fun," Marie said.

"That cell has the most orb sightings," Lisa clarified.

They marched forward, and Hannah now discerned the end of the hallway ahead, a limestone wall facing them. They passed the next cell.

"Cold spots." Lisa pointed into the blackness of the cell, until the group's searching light beams chased away the darkness.

"It's what we want," said Marie's app, right behind Hannah.

"And this last cell is the In-Your-Face cell. Its name is pretty much the description of the aggressive behaviors of the ghosts in there." Lisa stopped on the opposite side of the entranceway so the group had room to peek into the cell. "We have countless stories of people taking selfies in there, and then a face is directly behind them in the photo. Or people feel someone's breath on their neck or face. Or hair gets pulled. Or people get pinched."

Hannah peeked over Lisa's shoulder at a door flush with the wall. "What's that for?"

Lisa glanced over her shoulder. "We have no idea."

Now she had piqued the group's interest away from the In-Your-Face mystique of the cell they stood in front of. Lisa moved to the end of the hallway and stopped in front of the medieval-looking door. No knob.

"It's coming."

"What's coming?" Lisa asked the Casper-Capture app. She waited only a few ticks for a response, then continued. "That door has been sealed since before any of us started working here."

Hannah stepped closer to inspect the door. She ran her hand across where the wall met the change of color and texture, signifying where the door started. The door didn't have a handle or a locking mechanism nor did it have hinges.

A rusty hole that seemed to have been blown out by a small explosion scarred the door on the right-hand side.

"Whoever put up this door wanted to ensure nothing ever got in there," Marie said.

"Or to make sure whatever was on the other side never got out," Heath said from behind them.

Hannah crouched at eye level with the hole and shone her flashlight through. She could see iron bars, like the cell doors upstairs. On the other side of the bars was another limestone wall, sealing the room off even further. Hannah stood and replied, "Whichever way it was—to keep us out or to keep them in—whoever was in charge of doing this went the extra mile to make sure we'd never know." Hannah faced Christian. "Take a look."

When he bent to peer through the hole, Hannah explained to the rest of the group, unprompted, "Cell bars are on the other side of the door, then another wall against the bars."

"Great. You found the Fort Knox of haunted houses," Dano said and chuckled.

"I don't think I *want* to know what they were trying to hide away," Christian said, straightening his posture. He shone his flashlight at the group of faces in the hallway. "That shit is sealed up tighter than the Velociraptor cages in *Jurassic Park*."

"Do you just live your life on movie quotes?" Marie asked, giggling.

"Oh, you have no idea," Hannah said, rolling her eyes.

"I want to leave."

"Me too, ghost voice, me too," said the scared-of-the Stay-Puft-Marshmallow-Man Coastie.

A few chuckled, then Lisa announced, "I only brought you down here to acclimate you with the different rooms so you can explore them on your own during the free-roam hour."

"Definitely sitting in the In-Your-Face cell," Dano mumbled to Heath, and they fist-bumped.

"That concludes my part of the tour," Lisa said. "We should get you guys topside so Officer Duncan can bring you to your final location, before free roam." Lisa shoulder-sliced her way through the group in the skinny hallway so that she led the pack again. "Where haven't you guys gone yet?"

"Death row," Christian said.

Hannah shot him an inquisitive look about his newfound level of enthusiasm and knowledge of the itinerary. This was the man who, just a few hours ago, had known nothing about the place—and had seemed proud of it—and now he had integrated himself fully into the experience.

She didn't realize she was smiling at him, while they followed Lisa out of the dungeon, until Christian asked, "What . . .?"

Hannah shook her head and slipped her gaze to the floor as they walked, refusing to give him the satisfaction of admitting anything that he might construe. Then she suddenly noticed the weight of the stolen piece of fabric felt heavier in her pocket now, as if it had just gained five pounds.

They turned left, then turned left again, completing the horseshoe-shaped corridor, then climbed the stairs to the main floor of Housing Unit 4 above. With each step on the staircase, the fabric seemed to grow larger and heavier inside her pocket—bulging even. Hannah was sure it was just her imagination playing tricks on her, but she also felt it harder to raise her right leg—the side that held the item—than her left. She reached into her pocket to ensure she hadn't gone crazy, that the fabric was, indeed, the same size and weight.

Her fingertips corroborated what her mind was telling her; the stolen keepsake remained in its original state. When she removed her hand from her pocket, just as she crested the top stair from the dungeon, all imaginary sensations dissipated. The piece of cloth felt normal again. Well, as normal as a stolen item could, from the cell of the penitentiary known as *the bloodiest forty-seven acres in America*. For all she knew, the item had belonged to a possible serial killer.

The group congregated atop the stairs, the projector on the table down the other end of the hall dotting their faces and bodies with green LEDs.

Hannah beheld the massive expanse before them, prison cell upon prison cell, on either side, climbing four stories high. The catwalks on each floor that connected the two sides hung in the darkness in midair, like doomed silhouettes of planks.

And then she saw a peeker—in a cell on the second floor to the right of the farthest catwalk. Yet just how everyone had described, the shadow disappeared too fast back inside the cell for her to discern anything tangible.

Hannah heard Lisa talking about something to do with waiting at the front of the hall for Officer Duncan, but the tour guide's voice faded, until a ringing in Hannah's ears replaced it. Tears welled in her eyes, and pressure squeezed the inside of her skull. Goose bumps and a shiver enveloped her body.

The brimmed-hat shadow man had stepped from that same cell and now glared at Hannah below. And he wasn't disappearing this time.

Hannah's body reacted before her mind could catch up with what it was doing. She dug her heels into the floor and bolted for the front of the building, not completely convinced she was fleeing to leave. When she reached the staircase that would bring her to the second deck, her feet unceremoniously changed direction and plunged her into the stairwell's darkness.

Christian's voice echoed through the hall behind her. "Hannah!"

He had sprinted after her, and, with their mismatched speeds, he would probably reach her before she reached the top of the stairs. But she pressed onward, needing to know if the cell that the brimmed-hat man had stepped out of was his actual cell. It only made sense. As her sneakers hit every cement step, she convinced herself that he had shown himself to her so she could return the stolen item to the correct location.

Her breathing came out in short bursts as the muggy air became heavier in the stairwell. Almost palpable. Like every inhale tried to lift a fifty-pound weight.

She hit the first landing, where the stairwell veered to the left, and fumbled with her phone. Christian's footfalls reached the bottom of the staircase. Her shuffling up one stair at a time was no match for what sounded like him bounding two or three at a time. She raised her phone to eye level and swiped up on the app to activate the Casper-Vision feature. If the brimmed-hat man was no longer visible to the naked eye when she reached the second deck, she still wanted to know if his essence had remained there.

"Hannah!" Christian yelled from below, closer now.

"He might be showing me his cell," she yelled back.

She hit the top of the stairs, turned left, and the extremely narrow open walkway, with a railing overlooking the massive hall below, spread far in front of her, almost into an endless abyss of a green LED grid pattern. And the brimmed-hat man was no longer in the spot where she had seen him from below. The catwalk across and the walkway in front of her were clear of shadow men.

She stopped just long enough for the app to acclimate and for her to steel herself. She would have to pass the entrances to all the cells, all on the left side, mere inches from their openings. If anything wanted to pop out in front of her—or even tried to grab her—she would have zero space to maneuver away from it. She knew that once she started down the walkway, she must keep moving until she reached the first catwalk, where her brimmed-hat man had been standing in front of that cell.

Christian was halfway up the second set of stairs, directly behind her. "Wait, Hannah. Let me go with you."

She didn't know why that felt like a bad idea, but it seemed his words were what brought her from her pregnant pause and propelled her forward down the walkway. The railing to her right was so close that it almost grazed her arm, with dark cell openings to her left so close that a hand could grab her without the rest of its body emerging. She calculated that the cell where the brimmed-hat man had exited from was about eight or so cells down. That would be eight opportunities for someone—or something—to touch her.

Hannah powerwalked past the first cell, the walls and arched ceiling exposing their sordid history within the layers of different-colored chipped paint. She forced herself not to glance into any of the cells. Just kept her gaze and her phone trained on the spot where the brimmed-hat man had just stood moments earlier.

The second cell went past her peripheral vision. Outlines of shapes took form. She didn't know if it was cots or sinks or shadow people. The edge of her phone screen picked up a piece of each cell as she now passed the third cell, and the telling amber figures that represent a possible entity blipped on the screen. Something more than just furniture was in that cell.

Just keep moving, she told herself as claustrophobia set in the farther from the event horizon she traveled. With each step toward the center of the walkway, Hannah had to commit even more to keep going.

Christian had started after her down the walkway, moving a tad brisker than she was.

The cells passed more in a blur now. Almost there. Yet the amber outlines on her phone screen seemed to grow in intensity. And the silhouettes of whatever else was in the cells grew more insidious. Cell, shape. Cell, shape. Cell, shape.

She knew that if something startled her—or if something pushed her just two inches to the right—she would fall to the concrete floor below.

She skidded to a halt when she reached where the catwalk that connected to the opposite side met the walkway, where the brimmed-hat man had been standing.

Christian was now directly behind her, panting.

Hannah stood still but panned her phone very slowly across the spot. The screen was now blank of any amber outlines. "He was standing right here, Christian. And he didn't disappear. It looked like he was staring *at* me."

"You guys okay up there?" Lisa called out from below.

Hannah's gaze darted to the right and downward to see the tour guide and the rest of her group all looking up at her and Christian. "I–I think so."

"We're good up here!" Christian replied with more confidence and assurance. Then whispering quietly to Hannah, he asked, "Are you positively sure it was your same shadow figure?"

Hannah pocketed her phone and wrapped her arms around him, burying her face into his chest. Her muffled voice said, "I'm absolutely sure. I haven't seen him since the night I checked myself into rehab last year. Now he's back."

"You said yourself that maybe he was showing you which cell was his so you could give him his shit back."

Hannah pulled away from Christian's chest and inclined her chin to look him in the eyes. "Do you think I should just leave it in"—she glanced at the doorframe adorned with white numbers—"forty-three?"

"We gotta go, peeps!" Lisa called out from below, now escorting the rest of the group to the front entrance of the hall, their bodies pimpled with green LED lights the closer they got to the projector. "Officer Duncan is here with my next group."

"What do I do, Christian? Hurry." Hannah could not formulate cohesive thoughts right now, never mind make a decision that determined her mission on the fly.

"Let's go!" Lisa now yelled. "You'll have more time to explore the peekers up there during free roam."

Christian focused intently on Hannah's eyes. "She has a point. That feels … right. We'll come back during free roam. We could be making a huge mistake if we are rash about this decision. Especially since you just saw him again for the first time since …" He let his voice trail off.

"So, it's *we* now?"

"Is that okay?"

She nodded.

"C'mon, Banana. Let's go downstairs." Christian let her go first toward the direction where they had come, toward the staircase, and put his hand on the small of her back.

Hannah assumed it was his way of showing he was all-in with her now. She wished the walkway was wide enough for two people to walk side by side so maybe he could wrap his arm around her shoulders. They felt unusually heavy and downtrodden right now.

They forged past the cells slower now, her phone tucked away so she had no way to know if anything was inhabiting the cells other than the cots and desks that she could see with her own eyes. Maybe that was for the best anyway. Hannah slipped around the corner to descend the stairs.

Halfway down the first set of steps before the landing, Christian stopped her from continuing by saying, "Hannah? Have you considered that maybe he appeared just now to scare you *away*? And not to help you?"

"Why …" Hannah swallowed hard, afraid of his reasoning, and faced him. "Why would you think that?"

The blackness behind Christian seemed to approach him, darkening and thickening, as if trying to engulf him from behind. "If you were an inmate in this godforsaken place, and someone had broken you out, and you were free, would *you* want them to bring you back to prison and just hand you over?"

Hannah's eyes widened in realization. "So, he might be trying to stop me from leaving it here."

"Just a theory. But c'mon, I don't want that lady to have a stroke if we don't rejoin the group."

Hannah plopped her feet on each step leading to the ground floor, unable to stop her swirling thoughts that maybe she was doing the wrong thing by returning the piece of fabric. Maybe she was doing the exact opposite of what her brimmed-hat man wanted. And what if he became violent to ensure she returned home with it still in her pocket? With him still a freed soul?

CHAPTER 7:
DEATH ROW
(HOUSING UNIT 3)

Hannah and Christian reached the bottom of the staircase and stopped behind their group, who stood in a semicircle around Lisa and Officer Duncan.

"Oh, shit. My backpack," Christian whispered and darted inside A-Hall alone.

Hannah watched him leave from the corner of her eye and had forgotten he had even brought in his backpack. And then remembering what he had smuggled into the penitentiary inside his backpack made her anger flare. Heat rose to her cheeks with the image of the vodka bottle stashed inside his belongings. For all his attentiveness toward her, he certainly could be just as clueless with his decisions sometimes.

"Okay, fine folks," Officer Duncan addressed Hannah's group, "huddle together and stay close. It's gotten pretty dark outside. Gonna take you over to Death Row."

Christian appeared at Hannah's side, as if he had manifested from nowhere, his backpack slung over his shoulder.

Hannah glared at it, almost feeling betrayed. A constant reminder of her past that he inadvertently kept shining a light on tonight—a night supposed to represent her sliding the last brick into that wall to seal away the old Hannah forever. Kind of like that door without a handle or without hinges below in the dungeon.

Hannah caught Christian's gaze, and he asked, "What? What's that look for?"

Hannah tsked and shook her head to dispel the fog of aggravation. If he couldn't get it on his own, with how much he claimed to *get* her, how could she possibly explain it to him in a way that wouldn't cause him to just make light of it?

They filed behind Officer Duncan, his duty belt creaking with every step he took, as they crossed the yard toward Death Row. Hannah walked in silence, mulling over both what Christian had said about her brimmed-hat man not wanting to return to prison, as well as talking herself down from the ire she harbored about the alcohol in his backpack.

The group shuffled up the limestone steps and through the double doors leading into Death Row. Reese greeted them atop the stairs that descended behind her.

"Welcome, welcome." She paced as she spoke, almost like a caged lion with too much energy trapped in a small space. "My name is Reese, if you didn't remember from the introductions. I will bring you down one floor to the cells of Death Row. Then you'll go down another floor into 3D, where Rob and Trevor are resetting all their ghost-detecting gear. After that, you'll be released for free roam."

"Thank God," said the Stay-Puft-Marshmallow-Man Coastie.

"What?" Reese asked in a tone of sarcasm and teasing. "You don't think I'm good enough for you to stay with for the rest of the night?"

Hannah chuckled and beheld the young man's face.

He shot his gaze to the floor and shifted on his feet. "I–I didn't mean anything—"

"I'm just playin' with ya," Reese said, a huge rascally smile decorating her face. "We're here to have fun, right?"

Silence.

"Oh jeez, people. If you can't do better than that, I'm not taking you guys anywhere. We're here to have fun. *Right?*"

Now most of the group gave a halfhearted *hooray*.

"That's more like it. Okay, follow me down the stairs, and we're gonna stop in the guards' room."

"Ten-four, Reece's Pieces," Christian said.

Hannah punched him in the gut and furrowed her brows as the group followed the guide. "What is it with you and using food nicknames?"

"Clearly that one slice of pizza in the lobby wasn't enough."

"Clearly," Hannah parroted with a sarcastic tone.

At the bottom of the steps, they filed into a large rectangular room.

"This is where the guards would stay. Who knows anything about the riot of 1954?" Reese asked.

Everyone eyed each other, lips pursed and frowns drawn, as if to say, *Not me.*

Alisha raised her hand.

"Whatch'ya got?" Reese said to prompt Alisha to speak.

"I know a bunch of inmates broke out of their cells, then got the keys to other cells, and unlocked those cells. And some inmates were killed. And half the place was on fire."

Reese flashed Alisha her signature smile. "Well, that's the blurb version of it. You can't imagine the chaos both sides must have felt—guards and inmates alike. Especially since inmates turned on inmates."

"What is happening?" asked someone's Casper-Capture app.

Hannah rubbed her bare elbows, her arms crossed. A chill she hadn't felt in any of the other buildings shot through her. She made eye contact with Christian and favored him with a smile, hoping he would return the smile to set her nerves at ease. She had calmed herself, but the air itself felt different here.

If she focused on steady breaths, she might stifle any panic attack that threatened to rear its head right now. But obviously a panic attack was no longer synonymous with her brimmed-hat man. He proved he could exist independently now, regardless of Hannah's state of mind. Or body.

"Around 6:00 p.m. on September 22, 1954, in a different housing unit than this one, a nineteen-year-old inmate named William DeLapp complained to a guard that his sheets were wet from a recently repaired broken pipe and that he felt sick. When the guard opened the cell door, DeLapp and his cellmate overpowered the guard and stole his keys. They opened cell doors, releasing inmates. Those freed inmates then helped to empty additional cells. And those who were freed helped open even more doors. They raced around the compound, unlocking whole buildings of inmates. I think you can get an image of how fast they overran the entire property."

"For fuck's sake," Alisha murmured.

"They estimate that nearly half of the entire prison participated," Reese added.

"And how many is that?" Marie asked.

"About seventeen hundred."

"*Sooooo* … seventeen hundred divided by two?" Christian asked.

Reese laughed. "Oh no. Seventeen hundred *is* the divided number. So, can you imagine, seventeen hundred angry inmates, from five different housing units, let loose across the whole compound? And a dozen or so guards trapped inside with them?"

"Goddamn," Christian muttered. "Were the guards armed?"

Reese confirmed, "Yes."

The air didn't get any lighter for Hannah. While she was thankful that the air didn't get any heavier either, each breath was still labored.

"When the inmates reached the dining hall, they smashed out the windows and broke apart the chairs to use as weapons against the guards. They stormed the prison shops and set anything flammable on fire. A total of five buildings were ablaze during the night: the prison's recreation building, vocational building, tobacco shop, license plate factory, and the dining hall—which housed a chapel and a school. They got three-in-one with that building. When it was all said and done, four inmates were dead, sixty were injured, and one had attempted suicide." Reese approached a discolored part of the wall that appeared to be comprised of a different material. "See this area that doesn't match the rest of the wall?"

The group nodded and mumbled their acknowledgment.

"On the other side of that gate, outside this room, was where they kept a prisoner in protective custody, after he had testified against a gang who had carried out a string of armed robberies in St. Louis."

"Snitches get stitches," Dano said.

"Or, in this case, a sledgehammer," Reese countered.

Hannah's face flinched from the thought of a sledgehammer pummeling her face.

"And, yes," Reese added, "the inmates here viewed Walter Lee Donnell as exactly that—a snitch—so they wanted to take street justice into their own hands. When the rolling wave of inmates reached Death Row, they were gunning for Donnell. A guard posted inside Death Row, thinking he was making a good decision, tossed the ring of keys through the gate and out of reach of the inmates, probably assuming the guards would figure out a way to retrieve the keys after the riot was done."

"Sounds like both a smart and a stupid move," Dano said.

"Damned if he did, damned if he didn't, right?" Reese said. "Well, the inmates had already pilfered the compounds, so they were already armed with broken pieces of chairs, makeshift weapons, and that sledgehammer that they would eventually use to kill Donnell."

"Let me guess," Heath said. "They stormed the guards' room here and smashed through that wall with the sledgehammer."

"Right-a-mundo! Right here." Reese slapped the center of the discolored section of the wall.

"See? I'll be a detective yet," Heath said.

"*Detective Heath Bar* will look good on his nametape," Christian whispered to Hannah, and she jabbed the side of his stomach to tell him to knock it off.

"You got something to say to my face, wise ass?" Heath's glare shot invisible daggers.

Christian raised both hands in an *I surrender* gesture. "Calm down, Ponyboy. Can no one take a cool nickname anymore? *Sheesh*."

Hannah placed a hand on Christian's forearm and squeezed to indicate for him to quit it.

"Are you two children done?" Reese asked, her face scrunched, both hands on her hips, one foot tapping.

"What should I do?"

"How do I use it?"

Two different Casper-Capture apps on two different people's phones spoke simultaneously.

"What is it that you want to know how to use?" Reese asked.

"Do you think those two messages are referencing what you're talking about?" Marie asked.

Hannah swallowed a collection of saliva that had collected underneath her tongue and forced herself to exhale. She had forgotten to breathe, which wasn't good for warding off threatening panic attacks. She captured Christian in her stare, who seemed so engrossed in the story that he didn't notice her rising anxiety.

"C'mon, now the fun part. I'll show you cell 18, where the murder happened. And keep your eyes peeled for a unique resident. He doesn't always make an appearance on a hunt, but he likes to come out and play sometimes."

Christian eyed Hannah. "You okay, Banana Peel?"

"*Uh-uh.* Nope. Knock that one right out of your vocabulary. I'll tolerate *Banana*, under very specific circumstances, but I'm putting my foot down with *Banana Peel.*"

"*Eh …*" He shrugged. "Just trying out something new."

"But, to answer your question, I'm struggling a bit. Just let me know you're here, until I can get control again."

Christian took both her hands in his and faced her. "Panic attack?"

She gave a sharp, curt nod.

He bit his bottom lip and softened his gaze. "Let's go see a cell where a man was brutally murdered during a violent riot. That always makes everyone feel a bit better."

Hannah chuckled and put her arm around his lower back. "Thanks for making me laugh."

Reese bee-bopped through the group to get to the exit of the guards' room and to stand next to the gate to Death Row.

"Watching you," said Hannah's phone app, muffled, in her back pocket.

"Wonderful," she breathed.

"The police didn't even start to get the riot under control until 7:00 a.m. the next morning," Resse continued as she walked to the right, and a long expanse of cells on the left side stretched almost as far as the eye could see. A floor-to-ceiling fence split the hallway. "So the violence and beatings and fear happened throughout all hours of the night. You can walk on either side of the fence. The right-hand side was where the guards patrolled, and obviously the left-hand side contains access to the cells."

"Are the ghosts more active during the night because of how bloody the riot was?" Hannah asked, choosing to traverse the guard side. She felt like she already had experienced her fill of walking shoulder to shoulder past the entrance to dark cells earlier.

Reese side-eyed her with a smirk. "Honey, there's a reason why we don't have afternoon ghost hunts."

The group chuckled nervously.

Then Hannah noticed Reese glancing over her shoulder, eyeing the length of the fence behind them, her expression a tad concerned and laser-focused. For a split second, Hannah saw something break through the guide's carefree persona.

Reese continued. "When we compare the differences of residual hauntings and intelligent hauntings, who's to say the riot isn't happening right now? All around us? But we just can't see it with our own eyes," Reese suggested.

"You mean, like they are trapped here, repeating that night, over and over?" Alisha mused.

"Could be." Reese winked at Alisha. "They could be rushing in here right now, all around us, to smash through that wall with the sledgehammer to get to the snitch on the other side. To kill him. Again. Every night. Like replaying the scene of a movie." Reese glanced over her shoulder again.

This made Hannah glance behind her also. The guide was certainly checking for something behind them.

"She keeps looking behind us, like she's *expecting* something to appear," Hannah whispered to Christian.

"Like how you keep darting your attention into the cells we pass, *expecting* to see your shadow man?"

"That's not fair, and you know it," she retorted. "Look. She's doing it again."

This time Hannah knew Christian had seen the guide check the length of the fence from where they had come.

Christian opened his mouth to say something, but Marie screamed, and Dano yelled, "What the fuck?"

The whole group, regardless of what side of the fence they were walking on, squeezed far from the center of the hallway, while the shadow form of a small man slithered past the group on his belly, in an army crawl, but traveled along the middle of the fence. Stuck to it, like he was a spider and like the fence was his web.

The trio of Coasties who had taken the inmate side of the hallway shuffled backward into random cells to get away from the man—creature?—while Hannah, Christian, and the two women who had picked the guard side pressed themselves against the walls.

Reese remained steadfast and unfazed in the center of the aisle, watching this shadow form that *could* be a human, if it had discernible limbs or a head.

Hannah gasped when the silhouette scurried now along the top of the fence and leaped onto the ceiling above their heads, defying gravity. Wide-eyed, Hannah watched the spider figure disappear around the corner. It reminded her more of the way Samara, from *The Ring* movies, moved than anything human.

"What. The. Actual. Fuck. Was. That?" Dano asked from the darkness of one of the cells.

Hannah put her palm to her hammering heart. They were all okay. Nobody was hurt. They had just watched a shadow creature scamper along the top of a fence right past all of them, then not jump down but jumped *up*, to turn the corner at the end of the hallway.

"Wait for it." Reese held up her index finger to stop anyone else from talking.

"What else could we be possibly waiting for?" Christian asked, a tremor in his tone.

The sound of a cluster of bells jingling filled the hallway from around the corner where the shadow creature had gone.

"There it is. The Creeper is friendly, playful mostly, but aways announces his exit by ringing those bells hanging around the corner. I just wish he would announce his *arrival* too sometimes."

"You call that thing *the Creeper*?" Marie asked, her face blotched with red patches.

"Gotta call him something. He hangs out enough with us."

"*Jeebus*, they got peekers and creepers in this place. Sounds like a bunch of pedophiles, if you ask me," Christian said to Hannah.

Hannah grabbed the front of Christian's shirt and balled it into her fist. He took a step sideways to free himself from her grip, but she pointed at the empty cell that Heath was exiting.

The brimmed-hat man stood motionless, his head lowered a bit. His eyeless gaze was pointed at her.

"He's standing right … there," she said through gritted teeth in a forced whisper.

"Who?" Christian asked.

"My shadow figure, you idiot." Coldness spread through her capillaries.

"What does she see?" Marie asked, backing up farther.

"Someone see something else?" Reese asked.

Hannah locked gazes with the almost figureless shape donning a very distinct brimmed hat. She clenched her back teeth so tight that she thought they would snap in half. Her head vibrated from how tense her neck muscles were. Yet she refused to break eye contact.

The brimmed-hat man didn't move.

"I am *not* coming out this cell until someone tells me what the *fuck* is going on!" Dano yelled from inside the cell where he hid.

Hannah's eyes started to dry out from not blinking, but if her shadow man wasn't moving, then she wouldn't blink, for fear of missing it if he left.

"I don't see anyone," Christian whispered.

"Because he is attached to *me*."

"Girl, if you don't start telling us what you—" Reese began.

"Will you just be quiet and give her a moment?" Christian said in almost a yell. Then to Hannah, he asked, "Is he still there?"

All she could do was force herself to nod once. She slipped her hand into her pocket and fiddled with the piece of fabric that belonged to the faceless shadow across from her.

The brimmed-hat man raised a blurry, shimmery black arm and pointed at her.

Startled at his movement, Hannah removed her hand from her pocket, breaking contact with the piece of fabric.

Hannah's shadow figure turned and moved so fast down the hallway, in the same direction of the Creeper, that she could only think of it as a *whoosh* of blackness.

Hannah grabbed the links in the fence and ran as fast as she could, past Christian, past Marie, past Alisha, past Reese, and hit the corner where both shadow figures had eventually disappeared to. She stopped and was met with a smaller hallway, a cluster of five small bells swinging from atop a cell and dangling from green yarn, no longer colliding with each other enough to ring.

The hallway was devoid of the Creeper or her brimmed-hat shadow figure.

"Boy, you're lucky I like you, to talk to me like that," Reese said to Christian, then took a few steps to stand alongside Hannah. "What did you see? No one else saw anything."

The adrenaline spiking in Hannah now tried to find a way to metabolize it all out. She became racked with tremors and covered both eyes to force herself not to burst into tears.

Christian approached from behind and put his hand on her shoulder. "Is he gone?"

Hannah removed her hands from her eyes and nodded, still facing down the hallway with the swinging bells.

Reese reached up and cupped the bells with her palm to stop them from swinging. She let them go, and they remained motionless.

Until the Creeper makes another pass, Hannah thought.

Reese regarded Hannah. "If you don't want to tell us what you saw, that's fine, but I have never had a sighting where only one guest sees it. I don't mean nothin' by this, but usually, when that happens, the person who saw something was either mistaken or was making it up."

Hannah turned slowly to address the woman. "He is my demon and mine alone."

Reese's eyes turned into slits. "We don't like to use those words in here. It's misleading and can open unwanted energy."

"I–I meant my personal demon. Figuratively."

Reese tilted her head at Hannah. "Do you want a hug? You look like you could use a hug. You're paler than the limestone in the walls."

Hannah didn't know she was on the brink of crying until the tour guide drew her in for an embrace. The trio of Coasties who had darted into the cells to hide from the Creeper finally emerged, Dano especially glancing around wildly, as if the next unnatural-looking entity was about to run past.

"Is your shadow dude gone?" Christian asked in a whisper behind her.

"Yeah." Hannah pulled herself from the guide's embrace. "He was already gone when I turned the corner." She faced Christian. "He's never remained fully formed like that, not even on my … worst days. And he's obviously not afraid to show himself anymore." She regarded Reese. "Is that Creeper thing what you kept looking back for? I noticed you kept checking behind us."

"Oh, no, sweetie. The Creeper is far from anything that worries me down here."

"Then, what were you checking for?" A part of Hannah wondered if maybe the guide had also been looking out for the brimmed-hat man.

"Something much more sinister—the apparition that we believe is the warden of all the ghosts here. Big Boy. He primarily patrols Death Row, both up here on this level and below in 3D."

"Do you call him *Big Boy* because he is the warden?"

Reese chortled. "I wish that were all. We call him that because he is a seven-foot-tall shadow man who will rise from the floor, usually behind someone. He is known to wrap guests in his shadow, making them disappear for a few seconds, until he moves on down the hallway."

Reese stepped backward to put some distance between her and Hannah and Christian to address the whole group.

"Who is she?" asked the Stay-Puft-Marshmallow-Man Coastie's app.

Hannah swallowed hard. Were they asking about her specifically? Asking maybe why *she* was so important to *him* tonight? Did they want to know so they could team up and *help* the brimmed-hat man with whatever message he was trying to convey?

"Who is *who*?" Reese responded to the Casper-Capture app.

All apps remained silent.

Reese waited for a response but not for too long. "Rob and Trevor should be finished resetting the gear downstairs from the previous group, so let's head down there."

"What happened in 3D?" Marie asked.

"That's where they kept the criminally insane," Reese said. "And where Big Boy hangs out the most."

Christian moved Hannah from the group a bit and whispered, "Tell me what exactly happened."

"He pointed at me when I touched the fabric. And he took off when I removed my finger from it."

"I'm telling you that he doesn't want you to return it. He doesn't want to be stuck here again."

"I just need some time to think through this. For the first time in my life—and I can't believe I am saying this—I'm not afraid of him anymore. Never in my life have I wanted to run *after* him before."

"In a weird way, I think that's good," Christian said. "You're turning a corner."

The rest of the group reached a descending staircase, only wide enough for a single-file line. Christian urged Hannah to move to catch up with them.

"Rob, you ready for them?" Reese called down the stairs.

"All set!"

"All right, I'm all done with you guys. Hopefully I'll run into you during free roam." Reese homed in on Hannah. "And I'll be watching the rest of your night with much curiosity."

"Come down, guys," Rob called from the bottom of the stairs, focusing on Hannah and Christian at the top.

As they descended into 3D—the "insane asylum" of the penitentiary—Hannah felt the darkness grow darker, thicker.

Rob waited for the group to reach the bottom of the staircase before he spoke. "We're going to the end of the unit. This is the space where even the tour guides won't go."

They passed wider cells than above, and, when they turned the corner, Hannah saw the youngest Get Haunted crewmember, Trevor, standing behind a skinny tripod, with a camera affixed atop.

Rob waved them onward through a gate and into the last section before the corridor ended, all cells on their right-hand side. "Gather around," he said, removing his Get Haunted baseball hat, and wiped sweat from his brow with the back of his sleeve. He sat on a wide and deep windowsill on the left-hand side to face the rows of cells, about thirty feet from where the hallway met a dead end.

Hannah surveyed the section of hallway and noticed a shower in the back corner and a single metal folding chair against the wall that ended the hallway.

"Welcome to 3D." Rob searched their faces from where he sat on the sill, manhandling a black device that had a small screen in the center. "Down here is where they locked away the criminally insane to rot and die on their own. Behind me in that shower"—he inclined his chin toward the corner shower that Hannah had noticed a few moments ago—"was the scene of a gruesome murder."

"Still okay, Banana?" Christian asked into her ear.

She nodded.

"See him again?"

She shook her head.

"Do me favor. Since I'm in the thick of it now with you, could you let me know as soon as you see him, if you do see him again? I don't like surprises."

She smiled at him. "Of course."

"We're going to do two quick experiments," Rob said, "then I'll release you to free roam."

"That's what I'm talking about," said the Stay-Puft-Marshmallow-Man Coastie, now chuckling.

"Well, we just got our first volunteer," Rob said.

"Oh, shit," the young man said.

Hannah giggled.

"Stop fangirling," Christian whispered and winked at her.

"He's angry," said Trevor's Casper-Capture app.

"What's your name, Coastie?" Rob asked the young man.

"Glad someone recognized the logo," Dano said.

"Go Army," Rob said, laughing. "I'm a veteran. So, your name?"

The young man, only known to Hannah up to this point as a *Ghostbusters* reference, wrung his hands and bounced from foot to foot. "Parker, sir."

"You nervous, Parker?" Rob asked.

"I wouldn't say *nervous*, but I did count how many churches we passed on the drive here from Fort Leonard Wood—that's where we're training this month. You know, just in case I need some holy water in the morning."

"Oh, I know Leonard Wood very well. And you have nothing to worry about," Rob said with a chortle, as if Parker was being ridiculous. "The haunts can't leave here. That's not how it works."

Hannah absentmindedly slipped her hand into Christian's and intertwined their fingers. He gave a soft and comforting look. Hannah knew by Christian's expression that he didn't need her to verbalize what storms brewed inside her. She felt helpless that even Rob, from Get Haunted—one of her heroes—had the process oh-so-wrong. Hannah slipped her free hand into her pocket and grazed the strip of cloth with her fingertips. *Oh-so-wrong.*

"All right, Parker." Rob wagged the small item that looked like a vintage FM/AM radio at the young man. "Do you know what this nifty device is?"

"No, sir." Parker ran a hand through his bushy black hair.

Hannah thought the young man looked more nervous than she felt.

"We can record voices on it. Voices that we can't hear with our own ears." Rob scanned the faces of his audience. "To get the voices, we have to ask questions. Sometimes we need to coax them into having an actual back-and-forth conversation, so we ease them into it by starting off with simple yes/no questions. Get them comfortable talking to us."

A cat ball to their right toward the shower blinked red and blue.

"That's good," Rob said. "We didn't even need to persuade them to make an appearance. Makes our life a tad easier. Now, Parker, I want you to think of a simple question, with a yes or no answer."

Hannah became cognizant of how sweaty her palms were, but it didn't seem that Christian minded. His grip on her hand remained steadfast. Her eyes seemed to adopt a life of their own as she couldn't help darting her gaze down what remained of the hallway, to where the wall came to a dead end.

"Give it back," said someone's Casper-Capture app, which echoed through the empty cells.

Hannah broke her hold on Christian's hand so she could cross her arms and pull herself tighter, as if a winter chill had just shaken her bones.

"Have you thought of a question, Parker?" Rob asked.

"I believe so, sir."

Rob stuck the radio-looking device closer to the middle of the semicircle that they had created around him and nodded for Parker to ask his question.

The cat ball on the floor in front of the shower fell dark. The only illumination now came from the ambient glows off their group's cellphones.

"Do you regret what you did?" Parker asked.

Hannah's eyes widened, while the rest of the group murmured among each other.

Rob raised a finger to hush them. After a few ticks of the clock, Rob broke the silence. "Wow, okay. That's pretty gutsy for the first question. And, guys, we need complete silence after the question so we don't get cross-voice contamination from one of us. Let's rewind and see if we got an answer."

The cat toy tossed shadows against the dead-end wall and into the shower as it burst to life.

Hannah narrowed her eyes at Parker. If someone poked him from behind right now, he would be like one of those *Tom & Jerry* cartoons where, when startled, their bones ran away first, then their skin caught up to them a moment later.

Rob pressed Play, and Hannah strained her ears to hear, even though she wasn't quite sure *what* she was searching to decipher.

Parker's voice replayed through the small speaker on the device, filling every nook and cranny of the end of the corridor where they stood.

Hannah heard the few murmurs, then … something else.

Rob must have heard it too, because he rewound the soundbite and pressed Play again. Parker's question came through the speakers, and Hannah found herself squinting to try to hear better.

"Definitely a voice," Marie said.

Rob looked up to make eye contact with her. "For sure. I think I'm hearing a *no.*" Rob rewound the sample and pressed some buttons. "There's a theory that the spirits exist on an energy plane that operates on a slightly different frequency than ours. Therefore, their voices, when we hear them on our plane, sound sped up. I'll slow it down to see if we can get a clearer word."

Rob pressed Play, and Parker's question wrapped around them again from the speaker. Then silence between his last word and when Hannah knew the answer would come felt like a two-ton weight.

"No!"

Rob looked up at Parker. "Well, I don't know if that makes you feel any better."

Parker shook his head.

"Do you want one more question before we get to the good stuff?"

Parker drove his hands into his back pockets. "Sure," he replied meekly.

Rob pressed a few buttons and held the device closer to Parker, then nodded for him to continue.

"Does God exist?"

Rob tilted his head inquisitively at Parker. Hannah thought everyone had stopped breathing in anticipation. After what felt like a much longer time than Rob had let the silence continue for the prior question, he hit the Stop button and rewound the sample. "All right, let's see if we got anything." He pressed Play, and Parker's voice came from the speaker. Then a sound came, like from layers of voices, all on top of each other.

"That sounded like a … growl," Dano murmured.

"Let me slow it down," Rob said.

Rob replayed it, Parker's voice elongating and sounding like a record playing on the wrong speed.

The layers of voices were more distinct this time but still not clear enough to pinpoint actual words.

"Still sounds like a growl," Rob whispered. "What the heck?"

"Great." Heath slapped Parker's forearm. "You pissed it off."

"Wait, wait." Rob pressed the button to slow down the words. "I've … I've never heard a voice like this before."

The group stepped forward, tightening the semicircle in front of Rob, all ears tuned in. Hannah thought that if she tried to strain her hearing any more, she might pop a blood vessel in her brain.

Rob leaned his face closer to the device and pressed Play.

Parker's voice became so slow that if Hannah hadn't known his question, she never could have picked out the words. Now the space of silence before the growl was even lengthier in this slowed-down playback.

A roar came from the speaker, not a growl, so sharp that Hannah flinched and covered her ears. Marie gasped and grabbed Alisha's arms in reflex. The device flipped from Rob's hands and hit the cement floor. The back casing of the device broke off, leaving the machine shattered in two pieces.

Now on high alert in the almost-blackness of the criminally insane hallway, Hannah slowly scanned the group's expressions, then checked the gate that segregated this section of 3D from the cells behind them—so dark that she couldn't see past the entryway. Then she focused on the dead-end wall in front of the shower.

"Well, that's a first," Rob said as he bent to collect the broken device.

Yet his voice sounded a million miles away to Hannah when her gaze landed on the bodiless silhouette of a brimmed hat levitating in the shadows.

"Did you get that on video?" Rob asked Trevor, behind the camera on the tripod.

Trevor nodded and gave a thumbs-up.

"Did it jump out of your hands by itself?" someone asked.

Hannah's focus remained laser-locked on her shadow figure's brimmed hat, floating in front of the shower. "Christian?" she whispered in more of an exhale than truly speaking.

Christian must have seen her expression, because he wrapped his arm around her shoulders to follow her gaze into the shadows at the end of the corridor. "He's there?"

"*Uh-huh.*" It took every ounce of Hannah to nod once.

"Is he moving?" Christian whispered.

"Not yet."

The voices stayed muffled behind her as she stepped more into the center of the corridor and away from the semicircle. She thought she heard Rob ask if she saw anything, but whatever was happening behind her with the group might as well be happening on a different planet.

"I don't want to scare him off," Hannah whispered to Christian.

"Scare who off?" Parker asked, now behind her.

Rob rose from the windowsill in Hannah's peripheral vision. "Does anyone else see anything? I don't know what she's looking at."

"Why is he talking about me like I'm not here?" Hannah whispered to Christian.

"I dunno. I'll go with you … if you want to get closer. Is he still there?"

Hannah nodded and shuffled two steps closer toward the dead end. "Yeah, but it's only his hat."

Christian sharply turned his head to look at her. "You only see his hat?"

"Whose hat?" Rob asked. "We're all in this together. You need to share what you're seeing, because I don't think any of us—"

"Look. Back off, pal." Christian used his free hand to point aggressively at Rob across the corridor. "Just give her some fucking space. Jeez, what is wrong with all you people?"

Rob raised both hands in a surrender gesture.

"Sorry," Christian whispered the Hannah.

"You'll need to apologize to Rob later, but right now I want to keep moving forward." Hannah narrowed her gaze for clarity. *Yep, that is his brimmed hat, all right. But where is the rest of him? And why hasn't he moved yet?* Then she remembered what had happened last time.

"I'm going to touch the cloth. Last time, that's what set him off."

"But he ran away last time," Christian countered, both of them shuffling, inch by inch, toward the dead end of the corridor.

"Man, this is bullshit," Dano said. "Nothing's there. She's messing with us."

Hannah saw the Coastie stride past her and into the dead end. "No!" she screamed to get him to stop.

But Dano charged forward, as if storming the shadows on purpose to ruin Hannah's standoff.

Christian tried to grab Dano's arm as he passed, but Christian was too slow.

Hannah's gaze darted in front of the shower, and she caught just the edge of the hat's brim *whoosh* deeper into the shadows. But where was *deeper* when a wall was there?

"Dammit!" she yelled and shook her head.

"See? Nothing here," Dano said when he reached the dead end, vacant except for one folding chair. He turned and extended both arms, as if to say, *Told you that no monsters were under the bed, silly child.*

"Asshole!" Hannah yelled at Dano, her voice ricocheting off the dead-end wall, then disappearing behind her.

"What did you see exactly?" Rob asked, circling so he now stood in front of Hannah and Christian. Then he glared at Christian, demanding he don't answer for Hannah.

Hannah pursed her lips and scrutinized the faces eagerly awaiting to hear what the *crazy lady* was about to say.

"Give it to me." Dano's Casper-Capture app went off in his pocket at the end of the corridor.

Rob tilted his head to peer at Hannah from just below his eyebrows and studied her through slits. He nodded and straightened his posture as he clapped one time. "Okay, some of these sightings can be very personal," he addressed the group. "And that's what makes ghost hunting so much fun. Everyone is searching for something different and will have different experiences."

"I think she's full of shit," Heath said behind her.

Hannah immediately intervened to stop Christian's reaction by grabbing his arm and squeezing it. "Don't," she warned through gritted teeth.

Christian relaxed under her grasp.

Sometimes it amazed her that she knew him so well, only after one year of friendship. "I only wanted time to get him to react. On my terms. Just for once," she answered Christian.

He nodded without looking at her. His glare was still trained on Dano at the end of the corridor, Christian's nostrils flaring with every breath.

"Please calm down. For me," she whispered.

"Since you are already at the end of the corridor and next to that chair, I have volunteered you to be the subject of our next experiment," Rob called down the fifteen yards or so to where Dano stood in front of the shower.

"Fantastic," Christian mumbled, dripping with molasses-thick sarcasm.

"Bro, you just got fucked." Parker pointed and laughed at Dano.

Hannah could hear the young man trying to sound brave through the vines of terror in his tone.

"Calm down," Rob said, standing in the middle of the corridor, facing Dano, his back to the rest of the group. He turned to glance at Hannah. "You sure you're okay? Speak up now if you want to leave, or we're gonna continue with the experiment."

Hannah blinked fast a few times. A flash of consideration of maybe just calling it a night and trying another time fired through her synapses. Or maybe she should just keep the cloth—and the brimmed-hat man who came with it—as a reminder of a past that she promised to never repeat.

"He belongs here," said Marie's Casper-Capture app.

"See? Even the haunts of 3D want you to do this experiment," Rob said to Dano.

Hannah's heart pattered, and she swallowed hard, knowing Rob had wrongly assumed who that message had been meant for. She felt a bit more comfortable knowing the voice on the app had just decided for her; she would stay to return the inmate's belongings to its rightful cell.

"Have a seat in that chair," Rob ordered Dano. He rummaged through his duffel bag and removed a black blindfold.

Heath and Parker chuckled. "He won't like this," Heath said.

Rob traversed the distance between the group and where Dano now sat on the metal chair, the back of the chair a few inches from the dead-end wall and directly to the right of the shower opening.

"Oh, hell no!" Dano exclaimed when he saw the blindfold in Rob's hands.

Rob stopped, the blindfold dangling from his fingers. "I can't make you do this, but think of it as retribution for cockblocking this young woman's experience."

Hannah smirked and had to suck her lips into her mouth to not show a full-blown smile. *Fangirl* was right.

"*Pffftt*. I got this," Dano said. "C'mon. Give me your best shot."

Rob strode the rest of the way to Dano and handed him the blindfold.

"You're not gonna do the honors?" Dano asked.

Rob dropped the blindfold into Dano's lap and eyed Trevor standing behind the tripod of the camera, recording it all. Trevor gave Rob an unprompted thumbs-up.

Dano slipped the blindfold over his eyes and adjusted the strap behind his ears.

Rob walked back to the group, all facing Dano sitting on the chair.

Parker said, "Hold up a sec." He trotted the distance between the group and where Dano sat and stopped beside his friend. Parker reached into the collar of his shirt and retrieved a small rabbit's foot hanging on a silver chain. He hung it from the chairback where Dano sat. Parker trotted back to the group, mumbling, "Sorry. It's for good luck."

"Wow, you weren't kidding," Rob said to him.

"Not taking any chances," Parker said, chuckling.

"Okay, Dano," Rob said. "This is what I need you to do. Your job will be really easy, but if we get the results we're looking for, you'll have a story for the rest of your life."

Dano crossed his ankles and adjusted his posture to sit ramrod straight in the chair.

"He's scared," Parker said to Heath.

"The way spirits manifest is they usually need to draw power from somewhere and use it to manipulate," Rob said to the group. "That's why people's phones will sometimes run out of battery very quickly. But one of the best charging stations, if you will, for them is us. They can pull some of our energy, without hurting us, and use it to manipulate things or to manifest just a tad longer."

"So, you're using me as a ghost battery?" Dano asked.

"Something like that," Rob answered.

"It's not yours," said a Casper-Capture app.

"See that?" Rob said just above a whisper. "Look at his shadow behind him on the wall."

Hannah bit the inside of her cheek as she focused on the dead-end wall behind Dano. His shadow moved when he tilted his head slightly. She got irritated when she couldn't quite find what Rob saw.

Now Rob pointed.

"Holy. Fuck," Christian murmured and stepped backward.

Dano's shadow behind him stretched and climbed the wall, then distorted so much that the definition of his shoulders and his head blended.

"Guys?" Dano asked. "Should I take off the blindfold? What do you see?"

"Trevor, are you recording?" Rob yelled.

Trevor nodded, and the gate behind them that separated this section from the rest of 3D swung closed so hard that it shook the whole fence. The sound startled Hannah to make her look at the gate, but she knew the shadow figure still climbed the wall behind Dano.

Marie turned to run for the now-closed gate, but an invisible force yanked her across the corridor and sucked her into the cell she was passing. Alisha arched through the air, as if something had plucked her from the fence, and flicked her into the cell with Marie. The large metal bars moved, groaning in protest from years of being idle, and slid shut with a resounding *clang*—defying Jenny's number one rule of not closing doors.

Dano jumped to his feet and ripped off his blindfold as the group huddled against the wall farther away from the few open cells. Away from where Marie and Alisha were now trapped.

Marie grabbed the cell bars with both hands and shook them, as if she could rock herself free. "Get us the fuck out of here!"

Dano sprinted the length of the hallway toward the closed gate, which had locked all of them into a small section of the corridor, like rats in a cage.

Rob ran across the corridor to the cell where Marie and Alisha were stuck inside and yanked. The door didn't budge. "Just stay calm. We'll figure this out." Rob turned to run to Dano to help him open the gate that had also closed. They slipped their fingers into the small crisscross pattern of the metal and pulled. The gate didn't budge.

It took a few moments for Hannah to register that Rob had switched to full-blown panic mode when she saw him and Dano tugging on the gate.

"Fuck it," Christian said and charged toward the locked fence, which made this whole dead-end section of the corridor now a cell—or a tomb.

Hannah fixated on the shadow figure still growing behind the empty chair where Dano had been sitting. From the corner of her eye, she saw the rest of the group bolt to the locked gate and yank. To no avail.

"Guys!" Marie screeched from inside the locked cell. "Get us the fuck out of here!"

"What do we do?" Christian asked Rob.

But Hannah couldn't focus on Christian and the rest of the group tugging frantically at the locked gate. She couldn't concentrate on Marie's and Alisha's screams to be freed from inside the locked cell. All Hannah could focus on was the shadow at the back of the wall, growing taller and wider behind the lone chair. Her gaze followed where his face should be as it climbed higher.

Hannah remained frozen to her spot in the middle of the corridor. Screams and gate clanging came from behind her. Marie's and Alisha's cries for help pierced the air from Hannah's right. But all sounds and chaos slipped from her senses as the hallway seemed to shorten—without her moving.

Hannah slipped her hand into her pocket and pinched the fabric for comfort. She was surprised that Christian had not checked on her yet, but she assumed he was hyper-focused on getting them freed from the locked gate. Hannah wasn't sure how she knew it, but, somewhere deep in her core, she knew this shadow figure was here because of what she had in her pocket.

The figure rose to its full seven-foot-tall height, then extended both its shadow arms left and right, but the arms didn't stop stretching until its hands reached either side of the corridor.

Then it took its first slow and deliberate step.

Hannah clapped her hand over her mouth to keep herself from screaming and to keep the panic from spilling out. *So, this is Big Boy, the warden. This is definitely not my brimmed-hat shadow man. Great, now I'm seeing even more ghosts.* She glanced behind her again. No one was paying attention to her.

"Why aren't you guys using your cellphones to call one of the other guides?" Alisha yelled from behind the cell bars. "Mine's in my bag."

Rob spun to face the cell where the two women were trapped. "We tried. None of us have a signal." He raised his phone and waggled it at them, as if they could see the tiny NO SERVICE bar from all the way in their cell.

Just as Rob returned his phone to his pocket, his body hit the floor, and something dragged him across the concrete toward an empty cell. His arms flailed as his fingers tried to gain purchase on the cement. Marie screamed and backed away from her cell bars. Rob's shirt had bunched to his chin from the friction.

For a split second, he had gotten some leverage, but then whatever invisible force dragging him had one more heave-ho, and it flung Rob into the empty cell next to Marie and Alisha. Before he could scramble to his feet, the door slid closed. He reached the bars just as the lock clicked securely. Rob grabbed the bars and pressed his cheek against them so he had a better view of the corridor.

Hannah stood transfixed on the seven-foot-tall shadow at the end of the hallway, his arms outstretched, gliding toward her. She knew it was looking at *her,* was homed in on *her.*

The three Coasties had resorted to banging on the fence gate with their fists and screaming for help. But all that ruckus was so far in the background for Hannah that it might as well be happening in another building.

The shadow figure at the end of the hallway drooped one side of its head to meet its shoulder in a Jesus Christ pose, his arms outstretched like a crucifixion.

Next, an invisible force dragged Dano, Heath, and Parker on their bellies from the fence and past Hannah, one of their flailing arms striking her ankle as they zoomed by. The three disappeared into the open cell next to Rob, and the bars slid shut so violently that some metal flakes from the door fell to the floor.

"I never should have taken off that rabbit's foot," Parker said, almost sobbing, from somewhere inside the darkness of the cell.

Trevor yelled something that sounded like a cross between a gulp and a yelp as he flew backward through the air, folded at the waist, his hands reaching for nothing, and landed into the last cell before the shower. He grunted when he collided with the back wall, and the metal bars slid closed in a reverberating *boom.*

The seven-foot-tall shadow, maintaining the Jesus Christ pose, quickened its approach toward Hannah, who now stood alone in the middle of the hallway. Only Christian remained free with her in the corridor. And she realized he had stopped banging and screaming from behind her.

She chanced to steal a glance over her shoulder to see Christian standing with his back pressed against the fence, his eyes wide as he pointed down the corridor at the approaching shadow that had swallowed the folding chair.

Hannah noticed she could no longer see the folding chair sitting somewhere at the end of the corridor. The seven-foot-tall black figure had moved in front of it, and she could not see anything through the phantom mass.

"Is that Big Boy?" Christian breathed from behind her.

Hannah nodded. "I think so." She scanned the four locked cells that contained the rest of her group, plus Rob and Trevor. They were either banging on the bars or screaming, but it seemed fear had consumed any and all external noises. Or maybe the warden was altering her senses. Yet she didn't think he was *that* powerful.

Hannah balled her exposed hand into a fist and clenched the piece of fabric secreted in her pocket with the other.

"*Psst.* Why the fuck aren't you moving?" Christian asked from a million miles away.

She swallowed hard. "Where the hell would you like me to go?"

Hannah's pulse remained steady, even if she drew quick and sharp breaths. Somewhere deep inside, she knew Big Boy's appearance had everything to do with the stolen item in her pocket. And if he really was the warden, this item was rightfully his, as was the inmate who the stolen item belonged to as well.

Hannah chose bravery to see how this would play out. A tiny piece of her thought that maybe if the warden really did want his escapee back, then he was revealing himself right now to *help* her with whatever cell she needed to return her contraband to.

The warden glided past Rob's and Trevor's cell, his shadow slowly devouring everything it passed from Hannah's vision. Not only did Rob and Trevor disappear from her sight, but their voices and all the sounds they made also vanished. Gone. Consumed. Swallowed by the darkness of the shadow figure.

"*Hannnaaaahhh!*" Christian yelled, elongating her name to get her attention. "Did he kill them? Are they fucking gone?"

The warden, his arms still outstretched, his right ear still touching his right shoulder, glided past the cell of the three Coasties, which severed their yells and banging, as if they were just a movie and someone had clicked off a TV.

"Oh my god. Are they dead too?" Christian yelled.

Marie and Alisha screeched so loudly that their voices cracked in a discord of terror, then resorted to a whisper-scream when their vocal cords gave out.

"I don't think so," Hannah answered calmly.

Christian bolted between where he was pressed against the fence to where Hannah stood. He grabbed her hand and tried to tug her backward. "C'mon. Move backward. Get against the fence with me."

Hannah panned her gaze from Christian's frantic expression to the seven-foot-tall shadow figure, now just a handful of yards from her.

The moving darkness absorbed Marie's and Alisha's cries for help, like a black hole sucking in light.

Christian squeezed Hannah's hand. "Please, Hannah. Move backward. I can't lose you."

She yanked her hand from his hold. "I can't explain it, but I'll be fine. I need you to get back … just in case."

Hannah heard his heavy breathing while he wrestled with obliging her request or doing what seemed to come natural to him—wanting to keep her safe.

His fingers slipped from hers, and he walked backward toward the locked gate. Hannah smiled internally at how he continuously proved that she could count on him—even if it went against all his instincts. When Christian's back pressed against the fence, it made a clatter.

Hannah realized how deathly silent the corridor was now. She couldn't see or hear any of the rest of their group. The sound of Christian's panting and the clanging of the gate reverberating sounded like it came from concert-hall speakers in contrast to the silence that had been borne from chaos a few moments ago.

The shadow warden now loomed over her, its black form towering. Hannah could not see anything past him down the corridor from where he had come. She now had to look up to see the space where a face should be. And, even without the shadow having distinct facial features, she knew he was looking down atop her head.

Hannah snatched her phone from her back pocket, surmising she had just seconds before he reached her, and quickly launched the Casper-Vision mode of the app to see if the superimposed amber stick figure would ascertain where the warden's shadow actually started and stopped as he elongated.

The seven-foot-tall phantom exploded in a burst of speed that Hannah had not been prepared for, and she dropped her phone as she backpedaled.

"Hannah?" was the last thing she heard from Christian behind her, before the warden's long outstretched arms wrapped themselves around her like a swaddle.

Even though Hannah's eyes remained open, darkness cocooned her in all directions. And the silence was deafening.

Hands grabbed her from underneath her armpits to assist her to her feet.

"Banana, you okay?" Christian asked, his voice hoarse.

Hannah blinked and shook her head to clear the mental cobwebs and to orient herself. She was sitting on the floor, leaning forward but propping herself up with both palms. She nodded, stretched herself to collect her fallen phone from the floor, and let Christian help her to her feet.

The three cells made a loud *clank* sound as they unlocked and slid open. The rest of her group scrambled and poured from the cells, clamoring as fast as they could to get as far from where they had been imprisoned as possible.

Marie ran straight to the gate and yanked on it. It swung open effortlessly, as if it had no lock on it at all. She grabbed her duffel bag and said, "We'll see you guys outside. I can't be down here. C'mon, Alisha."

Rob and Trevor stepped from their cell with a deliberate and measured gait toward Hannah. Calm—as if what had just transpired was something as common as brushing their teeth.

"Can you find your way out?" Rob asked Marie.

"It's just straight, then up the stairs and out the front doors," she answered.

Rob nodded at both women. They turned to leave the building, and he made eye contact with Hannah as he strode toward her. He placed both hands on her shoulders and leveled his gaze at her. "What did you see when you were in *there*?"

Hannah removed her glasses and wiped both eyes with the back of her hand. "First, I want to know what *you* saw from out here."

"You were j–j–j–just … gone," Trevor said.

Hannah darted her gaze at him. "That's what happened to the entire hallway for me. All of you just disappeared into the abyss. Even sound. Everything. But everyone saw him, right?"

"Yeah, we fucking saw him," Heath said, standing in front of the wide windowsill, alongside the other two Coasties.

"You guys good?" Rob asked them.

Dano nodded.

Rob refocused on Hannah. "Big Boy doesn't target specific people. He usually just shows up and treks down the hallway. He was focused on you."

Hannah rubbed the back of her neck and stepped backward from Rob's intense gaze.

"Do you have any affiliation with the penitentiary?"

"What?" She glanced at Christian. "No."

"No relatives who either were incarcerated here or worked here as a guard?"

"We're from the Northeast," Christian answered for her. "She doesn't have any ties to Missouri, other than a friend who went to college here."

Rob stood ramrod straight and lifted his shirt to reveal floor-rash burns, pimpled with pieces of dirt and cement flakes from when the invisible force had dragged him across 3D. "*This* is also completely off Big Boy's usual MO." Rob lowered his shirt and placed his hands on his hips. "There's gotta be some reason why he separated all of us from you, minus your friend here, and then set his sights only on you. You can't think of anything as to why he picked you, out of all of us?"

The piece of fabric in Hannah's pocket weighed her down—the prize she knew the shadow warden had been after. Hannah stole a glance at Christian, hoping he wouldn't rat her out. *Snitches get stitches*, after all.

"No. There's nothing," she reiterated. Hannah could feel the accusatory glare radiating from Christian's expression.

"You s–s–seem oddly c–calm," Trevor said to her.

Hannah scratched her eyebrow, then adjusted her glasses. "I never felt threatened. It felt"—she glimpsed at Christian to signal that she was about to convey so much more than what her word said—"inquisitive."

Christian grabbed his backpack from where he had left it leaning against the wall and hefted it over one shoulder.

"What time is it?" Hannah asked Christian, panning between her smartwatch and her cellphone.

Christian pulled his phone from his back pocket, and the voice from his Casper-Capture app filled the small corridor. *"Why are you here?"*

"Is it asking *me* that?" Christian regarded Rob.

"I dunno. Sometimes to get clarity with them, we must follow up a question with another question."

"Right." Christian nodded.

"Hey, Halifax. Please tell me what time it is," Hannah interrupted before Christian went down the rabbit hole of talking to disembodied voices.

Christian checked his screen. "Just past midnight."

Hannah tilted her smartwatch toward her face and held her cellphone in her palm. "No. The *exact* time."

"It's 11:03 p.m."

Rob narrowed his gaze at her. "What are you seeing?"

"How long would you say that you couldn't see me?"

"Maybe five minutes?" Christian answered.

She raised her wrist so Rob could see her watch. "It's four minutes behind my phone, which shows the real time."

Rob gently grabbed her wrist to tilt the smartwatch face toward him. "So, you're saying you think time *stopped* while you were … *in there*?"

Hannah thought that *in there* was an interesting way to put it. But it wasn't incorrect. "I dropped my phone, so it wasn't on me when Big Boy surrounded me."

"Let me see." Christian snatched her phone from her hand without permission. He found her Settings app and scrolled down to Connected Devices.

"It's still synced, if that's what you're looking for," she said.

"Just humor me for a moment." Christian unpaired her watch from the phone on the app.

Hannah saw the face of her smartwatch go dark.

Christian pressed two buttons on the side of the phone to cycle it through a hard reboot. He tapped his foot rapidly as he waited for the company's logo to reappear on her phone screen. When it illuminated and announced that it had restarted, he launched the Settings app and paired her watch again.

Hannah's watch vibrated on her wrist, signaling it had connected. She nodded at Christian and checked the time. She raised her wrist so he could see the clock face.

"Motherfucker," he whispered, then showed her the phone. "Still four minutes off."

"Have you ever seen anything like this before?" Hannah asked Rob.

"A time shift?" He shook his head.

From the end of the corridor, where Dano had been sitting, Parker yelled to the group, "My rabbit's foot is gone!"

CHAPTER 8:
OUTSIDE OF MISSOURI STATE PENITENTIARY

"I think Rob might be able to help me—or at least give me some advice," Hannah said to Christian as they stood in the lobby, looking through the glass doors at Rob, Sara, and Jenny having a smoke break on the front steps of the penitentiary.

"But then he would know you lied to him down in 3D," Christian countered.

"And I can justify it by saying that I didn't feel comfortable admitting to the theft in front of a group of strangers."

Christian chortled. "Oh, Banana. After what we've gone through with these people tonight, I would hardly describe them as *strangers*."

"Fine." Hannah pushed her glasses farther up her nose with the back of her hand and flipped her black-haired French braid to the front of one shoulder. "You can either stay in here, with all your new *friends*, or you can come outside and join me." Hannah pushed through the closed glass doors without hesitation.

She smirked, knowing Christian would be behind her regardless of the ultimatum, and strolled the few feet toward the Get Haunted co-owners and the tour guides, including Officer Duncan, all taking their first break of the evening, now that free roam had begun on the property.

"There's the coveted one," Rob said with an ear-to-ear smile.

Jenny took a long, deep drag of her cigarette. "We heard about you. Got your money's worth in 3D, *huh*?"

"Does *nobody* find any of this odd or scary?" Christian asked, his gaze darting between the Get Haunted owners and the guides, then to Hannah. "Like, you're talking to her as if she just ate an award-winning cupcake for free. This is *not* normal."

"You're right. That's why it's called *para*normal," Sara said. "When this is what you do for living—and as a passion—you find wonderment in these moments and not fear."

"Really well said," Hannah mumbled.

"People don't come to these events to get scared," Rob added. "If they wanted that, they would watch a jump-scare horror movie or go to a cheap haunted house at a fairground. The people who attend these events try to discover the undiscoverable. Or try to discover something about themselves. Fear tends to be left at the door. Apprehension? Yes. But not fear as you're thinking."

Hannah gulped. "Can … Can I talk to you?"

Rob tossed his half-smoked cigarette on the ground and mashed it with his shoe. "Sure." He turned and walked a few yards from the front steps and from the rest of the crew and guides, and Christian followed suit.

"I–I wasn't completely honest down in 3D," Hannah started.

"I'm not a psychic, far from it, but I saw a look in your eyes that said you were hiding something."

Christian placed a hand on Hannah's shoulder for support.

"For my twenty-first birthday, I was out here visiting a friend at one of the colleges. We got shitfaced and came for the overnight ghost hunt."

Rob shifted his weight. "This already isn't starting off to have a happy ending."

"I don't remember anything about that night, but I must have taken this from one of the cells." She pulled the piece of fabric from her pocket—the first time it had been exposed to air since she had left the hotel room to come to the penitentiary tonight. "So, I wasn't completely lying when you asked if I had any relatives who had connections here. I don't. Except *I* am the one who now has a connection to this place."

Rob scratched his salt-and-pepper goatee, then removed his Get Haunted baseball hat to wipe the sweat from his brow. "Okay. Wow. So, I feel like the story doesn't end there. Why would you return, after . . .?"

"Seven years," she added.

"Seven years later, you came back to return it? Sounds like an awful lot of trouble for something you could have just thrown out."

When Rob made that suggestion—to discard an artifact belonging to someone who was part of these walls' legacy—her stomach roiled and churned. Just the consideration to drop this item, steeped in so much history, into a trash bin along with household waste, only reaffirmed the steadfastness of her mission. She didn't expect to be so appalled by the idea, but here she was. And it reignited the fire to get it back to its rightful owner.

"I'm an alcoholic. I've been in recovery for a year tonight. This is part of step nine."

Rob nodded and adjusted the brim of his baseball cap. "I'm all too familiar. You don't have to explain further. No one ever regrets *not* drinking the night before, right?"

Hannah sucked in her lips to form a thin line and exhaled the humidity.

"One of the hardest personal stories I can share is how Sara and I even became partners," Rob continued. "In February of 2022, I was in a bad place, the lowest place I'd ever been. I'd lost a very well-paying job after twenty-four years. My marriage was already rocky, and it wasn't getting any better. My kid was struggling. My dog was getting kicked around the house by a ghost. My now ex-wife—yes, I got a divorce—hated the paranormal. But here it was, in my own house."

"I take it your ex didn't see what you saw?" Hannah asked.

Rob shook his head.

"What about your child?" Christian's tone implied that he was invested in the story, to Hannah's secret delight.

"My kid saw things at school, and I just didn't know what to do. I tried to find help. I tried to cleanse the house. Nothing seemed to work. The morning of February 2, 2022—"

"That's a whole bunch of twos, mister," Christian said in a faux Goofy voice.

"Don't think that's not lost on me. Five twos and one zero. That morning, I woke up, took a shower, and grabbed a pair of socks from my sock drawer, which is where I keep one of my guns, exposing the handle of the firearm. And then came a real voice. My dog, still a puppy, was in his crate next to the bed. And I heard this voice that told me to grab that gun. And, for a brief moment, it seemed like a really good option."

Hannah tried to stifle the short gasp that had escaped her lips. The idea of Rob from Get Haunted being so low, so depleted of options, resonated with her—well, resonated with the ghost of Hannah past. Deep down, she prayed this story would reveal a healthier Rob—one that resonated with the ghost of Hannah present.

"I shook it off. It's not who I am. I looked down at my dog and was like, dude, we're going to burn down this fucking house. We'll go live in the woods. Instead, I sat with this for most of the afternoon, until another voice said I should reach out to Sara. At the time, my only interactions with Sara had been when I was a guest on her show, Paranormally Blonde, aside from few comments back and forth on social media. I reached out and was like, hey, have I ever told you my story? When she said no, I spent quite a while just dumping all this on her—story after story, feeling after feeling."

Hannah smirked at Christian and rubbed his forearm with her free hand.

Rob tilted his head and squinted at them. "That meant something to you guys, didn't it?"

"I met her right after she had gotten out of rehab. It was kind of a"—Christian glanced at Hannah—"not-so-chance meeting? At least I don't think it was, even though it might sound accidental or coincidental—God, I hate that word when it comes to our situation—to people who didn't know us."

"I know that exact feeling. Serendipitous. That's how I feel about me and Sara meeting and about the events that transpired for us to get so close."

"It was more than a right-place/right-time encounter," Hannah added, absentmindedly fondling the piece of fabric between two fingers. "He's been my rock from day one of sobriety. The weird thing is, I didn't know him prior to that. But he has had the most positive impact on my new life, even if getting sober in the first place was 100 percent all me."

Rob snapped his finger and pointed at Hannah. "Exactly. That's the same with me and Sara. It wasn't until I decided to pull myself from the doldrums that I could be receptive to having such a positive force surrounding me. I wasn't supposed to get divorced, but I did. I wasn't supposed to lose that job, making two hundred grand a year. As great as it was to have that money, I was unhappy. I hated it. But the universe took that all away from me—it just exposed me—and that lady literally saved my life that day."

Hannah nodded. "It's like when we choose to heal, we then open ourselves to the people who can truly make the largest difference in our lives going forward. Please, continue. This is fascinating how mirrored it feels to the story of me and Christian."

"Well, Sara asked me some of the most bizarre questions anybody has ever asked me. She doesn't remember them, and she'll tell you that she's not psychic, but she just knows things. By the end, I had spilled all this stuff. Before Sara hung up, she said, 'Rob, did you ever think that those demons you're fighting belong to you?'"

Hannah saw Christian raise an eyebrow at her—a sympathetic eyebrow—when Rob had mentioned the idea of fighting personal demons.

"So, I get the *why* of you feeling the need to return what you stole. But now I need to know the *who*."

"I'm not following."

"You are returning it as part of your personal healing. But *who* made this item so special? Like how Sara made my proverbial items special."

"It started the morning after I got home from the trip—"

"And home is where?" Rob asked.

"Salem, Massachusetts."

"The Witch City. Love it there. Continue."

"I started seeing a shadow figure. He's short and wears a brimmed hat."

"Where would you see him?"

"Everywhere. Didn't matter. Home. My bedroom. Rearview mirror of my car."

"Only at night?"

Hannah shook her head. "The sunniest of mornings to the most overcast of nights."

"That's a little purple-prosy there, Banana," Christian said and smirked at her.

She liked that he always gave her shit, even in high-tension moments like this. It always brought her down two to three notches. She realized she hadn't boiled over in a year. She had attributed that to her sobriety, but now she wasn't so sure that it was the *only* thing contributing to her newfound wellbeing.

"And you haven't seen him since you got sober," Rob added.

Hannah nodded and pushed her glasses up her nose with the back of the hand that held the piece of fabric, its stiff construction grazing her cheek with each side-to-side sway.

Rob continued. "I started a journal of all the big experiences I'd had at this location, and then it all made sense. Almost every experience was tied to a question that Sara had asked me—some things relating as far back as when I was eight years old. Those experiences were clues to traumas I'd had in my life. Her statement about those demons belonging to me was the most accurate thing I had ever heard. It all made sense. There wasn't evil in those visitations. The ghost wasn't trying to destroy my life. It was trying to fix it."

Hannah's eyes widened as she hyper-focused on Rob's face. "You think my brimmed-hat shadow figure wasn't haunting me to be a negative force in my life?"

"Sometimes a paranormal entity will present itself to you in a way that will wake you up. And I believe mine said, *Hey, Rob, your life is a fucking disaster, and it's time to fix it. Here's all the shit you've got to work on. Go do it, or I'll do it for you.*"

"See?" Christian interjected. "Maybe we shouldn't be killing ourselves trying to return the stolen item. Your shadow man might be your personal guardian angel. And you're just ready to toss him back into general population."

"Can I hold it?" Rob jutted his chin toward the item in Hannah's hand.

Hannah gave Rob the long rectangular piece of fabric, and he turned it over in his hand, inspecting it. "And you've seen him tonight … for the first time since you stopped drinking?"

Hannah nodded. "I need help returning it. I was hoping maybe you had some advice."

Rob stopped studying the article and met Hannah's gaze. "What kind of advice?"

"I have no way to remember what cell I took it from. Heck, I don't even remember anything specific about being here at all."

"Thankfully some incriminating photos prove she was here," Christian added.

Hannah frowned at his tone, which made her think Christian might nudge Rob with his elbow and say something in a frat-boy voice, like, *You know what I'm talkin' about.*

"First, let's see what this thing even is," Rob said and called Jenny over to their palaver.

Jenny pushed herself off the outside wall next to the entrance and sauntered toward them.

"Can you tell us what this is?" Rob held up the fabric for the tour guide.

Hannah's heart jumped. She had never considered the fact that she might get in trouble with *humans* during this whole journey of returning the item. She had been so hyper-focused on the *nonhumans*. What if Jenny, who Hannah wouldn't want to cross on a good day, kicked out Hannah and Christian?

Or worse, what if Jenny informed Officer Duncan that Hannah had stolen something from the state, and Hannah's mission ended in a pair of handcuffs and a ride in the back seat of a Jefferson City Police patrol car? And surely they would arrest Christian for being an accomplice. And then they would search his backpack. And find the contraband vodka. This was turning into an avalanche that could snowball into a soup sandwich—total fuckery.

She had never pondered those implications. Never for a second. But here she was, on the precipice of being arrested for just wanting to do the right thing, to right a wrong.

Jenny eyed the strip in Rob's hand and didn't even need to touch the fabric. "Easy. That's what the inmates nicknamed their *closet strip*. It was bolted to each cell wall, and that's how they hung their clothes. That strip was literally their entire closet. How did you get one?"

Hannah swallowed hard and interjected before Rob could explain for her. "I took it. Last time I was here." Hannah consciously chose to use the word *took* and not *stole*. She thought that might make the difference between Jenny throwing the Officer Duncan bat-symbol into the sky for him to come take her away.

Jenny's cigarette dangled from her bottom lip, seemingly stuck there, probably from the humidity. "Yep, pretty cool souvenir. Every cell had one. About half of them still do."

"Well, Banana, that narrows your search down to *half* of a few hundred cells," Christian whispered. "I like these odds." He playfully winked at her, then refocused on Rob and Jenny.

The front door opened, and Rob snapped his fingers over his head. "Trevor! Come here, bud."

The young ghosthunter plodded down the steps and toward Rob.

"Have you reviewed that footage in 3D yet? With …" Rob paused, then chortled. "I've only heard him call you *Banana* so far."

"Hannah," she answered.

"Hannah." He eyed Christian with a look that said, *What are you? Three years old and on* Sesame Street*?* "We usually don't review any footage until we get home after an investigation, but this one proved to be … special."

Trevor exhaled so long and so heavily that Hannah couldn't believe a human could have that much air in their lungs. "It's j–j–just s-static."

Rob furrowed his brows. "The whole thing?"

"Yeah. Like wh-wh–when the TV channel in *Poltergeist* signs off for the n–n–night in the beginning of the m–m–m–" Trevor had to pause to collect himself. "Movie."

"Please tell me that you got some sound," Rob said.

Trever shook his head. "Nothing. S-Static."

Rob nodded, and Hannah saw the disappointment in his eyes. "I'll see if I can extract anything at the house. Maybe something is hidden underneath the static. Like the roar from Parker's question."

"What made you want to bring the closet strip tonight?" Jenny asked Hannah. "Are you using it as a method to draw them out more?"

"Oh God, no," Hannah said, sounding almost offended that anyone would suggest such a thing. "I want to return it to the cell I got it from."

Christian adjusted the backpack on his shoulder.

The fear of the staff finding the vodka bottle inside pulsated in Hannah's ears like the telltale heart.

Jenny took a drag of her cigarette and glared at Hannah with wise and knowing eyes. "I have a feeling I know why, but I want to hear you say it."

"Something—or someone—came with it."

"*Uh-huh.* A shadow figure? Doesn't surprise me. Rob was telling us about what happened in 3D. You know Big Boy is their warden."

Hannah nodded.

"If you ask me, your inmate attached to that closet strip doesn't want to come back. And the warden's job is to account for all the inmates. So he will do whatever it takes to get an escapee back and to keep them here. That's probably what that little show of intimidation was in 3D. Big Boy probably exhausted all the energy he had collected to manifest long enough to manipulate our bodies and the cell doors."

"What about him surrounding me for those missing four minutes?" Hannah asked. "How did Big Boy have enough energy to stay there?"

Rob reached over and tapped Hannah's smartwatch. "Like a trickle charger on a car battery. That's why it stopped recording time."

Hannah unconsciously rubbed her free hand on her wrist wearing the watch, as if to soothe it.

Jenny lit another cigarette. "And I'll just add that it seems the quote/unquote lower-level spirits, no matter how much energy they siphon, can't manifest for longer than a second. Maybe two if we're lucky."

"The peekers," Hannah whispered to herself, wondering if her brimmed-hat man was just a lower-level spirit—a peeker—but maybe her mental state when she had been inebriated expelled a more potent charge for him?

Christian scoffed. "I love how you said if *we're* lucky when speaking of ghosts having more time. I still can't wrap my head around how much drive you all have, the guests included, to contact these ghosts."

"Most people would say if they ever saw a ghost in person, they would run screaming out of there," Jenny said. "We're that small band of fools who welcomes it with open arms, who run *toward* it."

"That's confirmed by the fact that, after what just happened to us in 3D, no one in our group has left yet."

"That's the allure," Rob said. "We're here to experience that. And now that they've had a taste, they'll want more. Fact is, Hannah, you need to return the closet strip." He regarded Jenny. "Was that right? They're called closet strips?"

Jenny nodded. "A sergeant who worked here for twenty years, all the way up to the day it closed, told me that because it didn't have a technical name, the inmates referred to it as their closet. The guards then called it that also, just so they were all speaking the same lingo."

"Even in the spirit world, your shadow figure doesn't belong beyond these walls," Christian added. "You've just been keeping him like a pet."

Hannah grimaced in disgust. "You think I was keeping him as a *pet*? You think I liked never knowing when he would appear in the corner of my eye? You think I *wanted* to wake up some mornings with him standing at the foot of my bed, watching me sleep?"

"I suggested that Hannah just leaves it anywhere on the property," Christian added, ignoring her retort. "The ghosts seem to have full roam of the place. Or try to sell it as prison memorabilia at that mall we saw coming in—Awesome but Unnecessary Antiques—and make some moolah on it."

"It doesn't work that way," Rob said, disregarding Christian's lame attempt to add dark humor.

Christian faced Hannah and took her hands in his. "Hannah, it doesn't matter what happens to your stupid shadow figure anymore. The most important thing is that *you* will be rid of him. Then your personal plight will end here, even if it doesn't for scary brimmed-hat shadow dude."

Her gaze shot daggers at him. "I am done being selfish, Christian. Being selfish was all I did for years. It defined me. Not anymore."

Christian argued, "It's unfair to use the memory of a dead convict as your vehicle to cleanse your own soul."

Silence hung heavy, uncomfortable.

She turned her head slightly to regard him from the corner of her eyes. "Really? You're going to say something like *that* to me? Now? For fuck's sake. Maybe *you* should be the one who leaves." Hannah spun on her heels and headed toward the front doors.

"Where are you going?" Christian yelled after her.

Without stopping or slowing, she hollered over her shoulder, "I gotta pee. Is that okay with you?"

Hannah grabbed the handle of the front door and yanked toward her with such force that she thought she might have broken the glass if it had struck the building. She stormed through the lobby, weaving through other guests from the other groups who were mingling and sharing stories from their guided part of the hunt. Hannah sucked in her lips and felt her breath coming out hot and fast. *The nerve of him!*

She reached the backside of the lobby where the Porta Potties were located and scanned each door. The three bathrooms all showed red next to the handles—occupied. She stood, waiting, tapping one foot like a jackrabbit, her arms crossed.

Sometimes Christian found a way to get so close to breaking through her armor and to make her consider exploring her feelings deeper. Then other times, he could say that one thing that would force her to push him away with all her might.

The left-side Porta Potty clicked to green, and the door swung open. An unfamiliar woman gave Hannah a quick smile and scooted into the lobby, and Hannah entered the potty. She closed and locked the door and sat on the toilet.

After tempering her anger toward Christian, she now heard more distinct sounds coming from outside the bathroom door. She recognized Parker's voice, speaking with his two Coastie friends. She assumed they had gathered to wait for an available toilet.

It wasn't just his voice that she tuned in to. It was some of his words. She strained to listen closer.

"It would be so funny," Heath said in response to whatever Parker had suggested.

"She might just pee herself," Parker said. "So, you guys wanna do it? She's been so jumpy that I think we could get her good."

Hannah felt her blood boil. They were talking about scaring her. On purpose. She wanted to get out of the Porta Potty as fast as possible to face them. To berate them for even contemplating something so juvenile at her expense.

She finished hastily, rose, pulled up her pants, and swung open the door—fists clenched, ready for battle.

To nothing.

She scanned the darkened yard, then the path that led to A-Hall and the path that led to Death Row. She spotted the backs of the Coasties' heads climbing the steps into Death Row, then they disappeared into the darkness of the building.

She cursed under her breath.

Hannah knew she would have to tell Christian, even if talking to him was the last thing she wanted to do right now. Not until her temper cooled a bit. It always did, but it took time.

Hannah padded through the lobby, now a bit more thinned out than when she had just come through. The guests had obviously finished with their break and left to take advantage of the free-roam time—the permission to go anywhere unaccompanied on the property to hunt. She pushed through the front door and made it a point to stand between Sara and Trevor. Hannah glared at Christian across their mini-circle so he would know that she had consciously decided not to stand next to him.

"Another thing," Rob added, "that young man's missing rabbit's foot from the chair in 3D isn't sitting well with me either. The ghosts don't usually take something. Now, move it? Yeah, all the time," he said with a guffaw. "But keep it?"

Sara's face illuminated when she noticed Hannah had returned. "And your shadow figure, Hannah, doesn't have any identifying features other than his hat?"

"No. He's shorter than me though. I'm five-foot-five, so I think he's about five-foot-even. He's a good five or six inches shorter than me."

"That narrows it down a bit more," Sara said. "But I don't think you realize that your closet strip could have belonged to any inmate ever incarcerated here, from 1836 to 2004. The number of inmates throughout the history of this place, when all combined, is probably a few hundred thousand or more."

"And we certainly don't have records for every inmate," Jenny chimed in. "Your hat man might be an inmate from 1850 or 1950."

Hannah sighed. "I get your point."

"Told you. Fruitless," Christian said.

"That's enough. You need to stop," Hannah scolded him. "You've always been on my side. What happened in the last half hour?"

"Oh, I don't know. Maybe I watched everyone in our group except me and you get sucked into cells by an invisible hand. Then they got fucking locked inside the cells. Behind doors that *she*"—he pointed to Jenny—"forbade us to close, because they would not open if we did. Guess what?" He laughed like someone ready to crack. "They fucking opened. On their own. Not to mention Hannah gets swallowed by some ogre ghost—"

"I said, *enough*!" Hannah stomped her foot once. "I get that you're scared. And I think it scares you even more that no one else is scared, even after they were the ones who were molested. It's abnormal behavior to you but not to them. Not to …" Hannah looked at her sneakers. "Not to me." She raised her eyes to meet his gaze. "So, like I've already told you just recently, get on board or go back to the hotel."

Hannah let the silence punctuate her last statement.

"Every minute I'm out here arguing is another minute that I'm not looking for the cell." And Hannah turned on her heels and stormed through the lobby, not caring if Christian followed her or not.

CHAPTER 9:
A-HALL (HOUSING UNIT 4)

Hannah bit the inside of her cheek as she powered past the Porta Potties and charged toward A-Hall. A hand grabbed her elbow from behind, and, while she didn't shrug it off, she didn't slow her pace either.

"Hannah, come on. Slow down," Christian said. "Let's talk about this. Where are you going?"

Without turning her head to regard him, she answered, "I'm going to start where I saw him in A-Hall."

Christian finally matched her pace alongside her. "On the second floor? When we came out of the dungeon?"

"*Uh-huh.*"

They reached the entrance, and the darkness inside consumed them. Hannah considered letting her eyes adjust first, but her rising anxiety—both from running out of time for the task at hand and from Christian's sudden brattiness—made her soldier toward the staircase in the corner, the one she had fled up just a few hours ago. Her heart hammered when it dawned on her that when she reached the top of the stairs, she would again be faced with that skinny walkway to cell 43.

Murmurs and shuffling feet of other humans enjoying their own personal hunts wafted from below. Hannah realized she had not *seen* anyone when she had entered, now that the building was in lights-out mode for the rest of the event.

Hannah hit the top of the stairs and froze. She heard Christian mutter a curse word behind her when he almost slammed into her back.

"You okay, Banana?"

She tightened her lips into a taut line, partly angry because she knew Christian hoped that using his term of endearment for her might soften her a bit and partly because she knew she would have to pass all those even-darker cells, her left shoulder only inches from each opening.

"Follow me if you want," she grunted and strode forward, like navigating a minefield in the dark—but the explosions wouldn't come from underfoot here. No, they would come from shadow figures directly to her left and without warning.

Christian's hurried footsteps behind her synced in time with her racing heartbeat as she focused on the spot on the walkway floor directly in front of cell 43. She refused to even entertain sneaking a peripheral peek into the soulless abysses of nothingness she passed. Hannah reached the cell where she had seen her brimmed-hat man, blinked for a beat longer than normal to prepare herself for coming nose-to-nose with her shadow figure, and spun into the cell.

Silence and darkness seemed to drip from the deteriorating arched ceiling, until Christian turned on his flashlight with the red LED bulb, splashing the cavernous space with a blood-colored hue.

"Fuck," Hannah whispered, crossing the distance from the cell's entryway to the back wall in three strides.

Christian stayed quiet, not inquiring what she had seen.

Hannah saw the red beam from his flashlight focus on the wall above the cot, where she looked too.

"I'm sorry, Banana," Christian said behind her, and she heard the genuineness in his tone.

Hannah exhaled a long breath that she hadn't realized she was holding, and her fingernails dug into her palms. She felt a juxtaposition of emotions, feeling relief about not having an apparition greet her and yet feeling disappointment at what hung on the wall.

"It's not his cell," Hannah said, cupping the piece of fabric bolted to the wall—one that mirrored the one in her pocket. She drew it away from the wall ever-so-slightly, acknowledging how strange and yet familiar the strip of fabric felt in her palm.

"It was a brilliant guess though," Christian said.

"Why did I think it would have been that easy?" She turned to face him, the red light from his flashlight refracting off the tears dotting her eyes.

"Because it made sense to start at the place where you saw him first."

"But I didn't see him here first. I saw him in the women's unit. I think he was just following me around in there. Of course his cell wouldn't have been in that building, so I defaulted to maybe it being here. It would have been counterproductive to start in the women's unit." Hannah trembled, a tear escaping the bottom edge of her eyelid.

Christian closed the distance before she even knew he had moved, his flashlight now tucked into his back pocket, his arms engulfing her, holding her tight, wrapping her head and pressing it ever-so-lightly to his chest.

Hannah snorted some snot back into her nostril and stepped backward from his embrace. She wiped her nose with the back of her arm and let her gaze dart around the now pitch-black room.

Christian adjusted his backpack on his shoulder, grabbed both of her forearms, and lowered his face so he was eye level with her. "Where do you want to go next?"

Hannah used the back of her hand to push her glasses up her nose by the bottom of the frames. "Death Row. That's where I saw him next."

"Him and that spider-walker," Christian mused.

Hannah giggled. "That thing was pretty freaky."

Christian's face lit up in a grin. "The creepiest, but not as creepy as those abhorrent Teletubbies."

Hannah held his gaze for a beat and felt her cheeks blush, trying to stifle giving him the satisfaction of bursting into laughter. "Come on, goofball. Let's head to Death Row."

"Still such an odd thing to say out of context," he murmured as she passed him and headed for the exit.

The ball of anxiety that had been rolling around in her stomach was now gone. Even though she hadn't yet found the brimmed-hat man's cell, she felt less weight bearing down upon her—even if the darkness in the cell as she exited was palpable.

Hannah turned right out of the cell and onto the shoulder-width walkway toward the stairs.

A black figure launched from the next cell in line, facing her, its darkened feet landing square on the walkway. Two hands reached for Hannah's face, its fingers splayed wide like skeletal branches, and she screeched. Her ear-piercing tone clawed the walls of the housing unit and zigzagged like a ping pong. She jumped backward, colliding into Christian.

Christian stumbled backward and grabbed the thin railing to stop himself from tumbling and falling to the cement floor below. The momentum still landed him on his backside, with an audible *oof.*

The figure doubled over in a fit of laughter, and Hannah heard the giggles from two other male voices in the cell. The figure pulled a black hoodie off its head, revealing Parker, the whites of his teeth and his eyes shone in the darkness, accentuating his scare tactic.

Hannah still heard the residual sound of her scream echoing through the rafters long after she had stopped making noise. She brought her trembling hands to her face, and she couldn't decide whether to cover her eyes or her mouth. She glanced behind her to see Christian clutch the thin railing to hoist himself to his feet, his rage burning in his eyes, his face flushed.

Heath and Dano stepped from the cell that Parker had jumped from, holding their sides from laughter. "I wish I could have seen the look on her face," Heath said.

Parker, almost unable to answer for laughing still, said, "It was exactly what we thought it would look—"

Christian lunged past Hannah, using every inch of free space available between her shaking body and the railing on that skinny walkway. He collided with her shoulder on the way by, knocking her sideways into the wall between cells. He balled a fist, cocked it back, and before Hannah could register the unfolding events, Christian swung at Parker with all his might, his backpack sliding off his shoulder and landing on the walkway from the inertia.

The young man shuffled backward to avoid the punch, but his feet caught on themselves, and he stumbled to gain balance.

Hannah knew she had screamed, "No!" but the sound still startled her as Parker's two friends grabbed Christian from behind and spun him to face them.

Parker's momentum finally got the best of him, and he fell diagonally, his upper body dangling off the walkway ten feet above the cement floor.

"What the fuck, man?" Heath yelled, the collar of Christian's shirt balled in his fists.

Hannah regained clarity and heard Lisa screaming from below for them to stop as the tour guide sprinted toward the back corner for the staircase. Then Hannah heard Officer Duncan's duty belt *schuck-schuck-schuck*-ing as he ran behind Lisa.

"Get the *fuck* off me!" Christian grabbed Heath's wrists to twist them free from his shirt.

Parker rose behind Christian, trapping Christian between the Coasties on the narrow walkway.

Hannah's thrumming pulse in her ears muffled the sound of Lisa and Officer Duncan reaching the top of the stairs and plodding toward them. Hannah unconsciously stepped backward, now standing in front of the entranceway to cell 43.

Christian turned to face Parker. "What the fuck is wrong with you?"

"Break it up!" Officer Duncan yelled as he and Lisa stormed down the walkway toward the group, his command ricocheting through the vastness of the hall.

"Oh, shit," Parker murmured loud enough for Hannah to hear and turned to face Lisa and Officer Duncan.

Heath and Dano stepped backward to distance themselves from Christian, whose shoulders heaved with every breath.

Now that the situation seemed to be calming down, Hannah felt an eruption inside her stomach that she couldn't suppress, which plumed up her throat and burst through as a sob—a single sound that encapsulated not just the frustration of the evening but the struggle of the entire previous year, every second of struggle throughout the previous year.

"You, downstairs." Officer Duncan pointed at Parker. "Sit in the chairs and wait for me." He stepped closer, now Christian being the next person in his line of sight. But instead of giving Christian an order, he glanced over Heath's and Dano's shoulders—who still separated Hannah from Christian—and asked, "You okay, miss?"

Hannah grabbed both her elbows as a barrier and nodded.

"This one with you?" Officer Duncan asked her, thumbing toward Christian.

"Yes, sir."

"The two of you"—Officer Duncan waggled his finger over Christian's shoulder at Heath and Dano—"go sit with your buddy down there."

Lisa pushed past Officer Duncan and Christan and delicately laid her hands on Hannah's shoulders. "Are you sure you're okay? You scared the bejesus out of me when you screamed."

Hannah nodded again.

"What happened?" Lisa asked.

Hannah swallowed hard and eyed Officer Duncan speaking with Christian, who was using exaggerated hand movements while he talked. She knew Christian only did that when he was either super angry or super excited. She would joke and say his inner-Italian from his mom's side was coming out. That thought tugged the corners of her lips, even among the cloud of anxiety swallowing her head.

Hannah answered in a mousey, meek tone, "When I was going to the bathroom, I–I overheard them planning to scare me because they thought it was funny how freaked out I got when I saw the shadow figure."

Lisa's expression hardened as the guide spun to face Officer Duncan.

Officer Duncan put a hand on Christian's shoulder to lead him toward the staircase at the end of the walkway.

"What's going on?" Lisa asked the police officer as she strode to catch with him and Christian, Hannah now following behind.

"I'm gonna escort all of them out," Officer Duncan replied, a handful of Christian's shirt now in his fist, as he guided Christian from behind, down the skinny hallway and toward the staircase.

"Wait, wait!" Lisa said, quickening her pace.

Officer Duncan stopped and turned, Christian also turning slightly. Hannah saw Christian's expression mixed with deep apology and festering anger.

"Do you want to tell him what you told me, or do you want me to?" Lisa asked Hannah sympathetically.

Hannah pushed her glasses up her nose and shifted her weight from foot to foot. "Christian was acting in self-defense. I overheard those guys joking that they wanted to scare me." She saw the police officer's face go from a stoic command presence to a softer understanding.

"I would like to request, Officer Duncan"—Lisa glanced at Hannah—"that you remove those three below from the property."

Hannah chanced a look over the railing at the three men sitting on the metal folding chairs below, all six eyes seeming to shoot daggers at her. She was sure they had heard the tour guide's recommendation.

Christian raised both hands in an *I surrender* gesture. "Sir, I understand if you want to throw me out. I did push him, and that breaks the rules. I'm well aware that he could've fallen."

"Our rule of not intentionally scaring people trumps someone reacting in self-defense *because* they were *scared*, by that person," Lisa added.

Hannah thought she saw Lisa shoot Christian a look that said, *Shut up and let me handle this.*

Officer Duncan sighed. "Okay, but I have to ask the young man if he wants to report it as an assault. If he does, I'll have to write it up and escort this one from the property too."

"But look how terrified—" Lisa began.

"He *did* shove another guest." Officer Duncan locked his gaze on Lisa's.

"I understand." Lisa turned to Hannah. "C'mon. Let's go downstairs."

Hannah followed behind Officer Duncan, his hand still on Christian's shoulder to lead him forward, with Lisa bringing up the rear. Hannah bent slightly to scoop up Christian's backpack and slung it around one shoulder. It felt particularly heavy to her, knowing what contents hid inside, her stomach churning at the thought. They descended the staircase, the red beams from their flashlights like individual portals bouncing against the walls.

"Stay here," Officer Duncan instructed Christian and Hannah, then he and Lisa approached the three men on the chairs.

Hannah strained to listen to what they said, and, even in the quiet hush of the hall, she only discerned a few words here and there. But the Coasties' expressions said it all. Parker's chin dropped to his chest in defeat. Without resistance, the three rose from their seats, gazes downward, and none of them acknowledged Hannah or Christian as Officer Duncan escorted them through the metal bars of A-Hall and into the darkness outside.

Parker added just as he exited, "I'd still like my lucky rabbit's foot back."

With a solemn look, Lisa traipsed toward Hannah and Christian. "I'm really sorry they did that you. Are you absolutely sure you're okay?"

Hannah nodded, then murmured, "Yeah. Thanks."

With that, Lisa headed back to her post.

Christian placed a soft hand on Hannah's shoulder and whispered, "I overreacted. Sorry."

Hannah met his gaze, her eyes welling up again, and wanted to wrap her arms around him. She felt that her ability to keep holding her proverbial breath while trying to locate this improbable cell was running thin. As was her time.

"I'm fine. I think now I'm angrier that he robbed me of precious time to finish this than I am mad at being scared." Hannah reached into her pocket and fiddled with the closet strip to remind herself of her target.

"I'll take my backpack," he said.

Hannah shrugged it off her shoulder and handed it to him, thankful to be freed of its contents.

"Come on. Let's go to Death Row and see if that cell where you saw your guy is the winner." Christian put his arm around her shoulders and headed out of A-Hall with her. "Let's not let Parker Brothers back there set us off course."

Hannah stopped and glared at him with one eye half closed. "Seriously? Parker Brothers?"

"*What?*" Christian shrugged, with a rascally puppy-dog smirk. "I couldn't think of a food item that went with his name."

"You're ridiculous." With a chuckle, Hannah laced her arm through Christian's and led him across the threshold of A-Hall.

When they stepped into the humid night, and Hannah saw the backs of the three Coasties disappear into the lobby area, Officer Duncan keeping a tight distance behind them, she chortled.

"Penny for your thoughts, Banana," Christian said.

Playfully she quipped, "The irony that you were the one who had made the joke about why this place needed a cop here for a ghost hunt—and tonight it was because of *you*."

CHAPTER 10:
DEATH ROW
(HOUSING UNIT 3)

Christian yanked open the entryway doors of Housing Unit 3 and turned left into the Death Row side. "I think it was this way," he said, turning left again.

"*Uh-uh*, that's the way to the stairs to go down into 3D," Hannah replied, slipping right to travel along the inside fence that separated where the guards walked and where the cells were. "We saw the Creeper first right up there, then my shadow man came from that cell toward the end."

Hannah quickened her steps, conscious of the silent ticking of each second that passed. She heard music from down the hallway and saw the hue from flashing lights spill on to the floor from ahead, near the cell where Hannah had thought she had seen her brimmed-hat man.

"Is that …?" Christian began.

"Johnny Cash? Yep. Sometimes music can help coax them to make contact," Hannah said, striding toward the cell bustling with sights and sounds.

Christian hefted behind her, and when she reached the cell aglow in an LED light dance party, she turned quickly into it and stopped.

Four amateur ghosthunters sat on the two metal cots, sans mattresses, and looked up at her when she appeared in the entryway. "You can join us, if you want," one said.

Hannah scanned the multitude of Rem Pods, K2 EMF meters, and other ghost-hunting devices that contained blinking lights.

When she didn't say anything for a moment, one ghosthunter said, "They are dancing to the beat."

Hannah's gaze flitted quickly to each device. All the lights on all the apparatuses blinked in sync with the signature Johnny Cash boom-chicka strumming.

Christian pressed his chest into Hannah's back to get a better view over her shoulder. He muttered some kind of astonishment. Then he whispered, "You sure this is the cell? It seems too large to be a normal one. Too … wide."

The song stopped playing from the ghosthunter's phone, and all the LEDs simultaneously died, shrouding the cell and the adjacent hallway into darkness.

Hannah leaned outward to peer up and down the row of cells. "I'm, like, 99 percent sure. Gosh, we all were still reeling from seeing the Creeper that I don't know if I can trust my memory right now."

Chubby Checker's "The Twist" started, with a more upbeat tempo than the Johnny Cash song. The LEDs from all the devices illuminated so fast and so brightly that Hannah put a hand to her eyes and almost shuffled backward a step.

If the circumstances were different, if she didn't have a stolen item to return, with a countdown nearing double zeros, what was happening in this cell would have entranced her and made her join the people on the cots to watch the ghost-detecting version of Dance Party USA.

But the urgency of free roam neared its end, and the weight of the closet strip in her front right pocket made her turn to the right and take a step. She had just enough reflexive time to close her eyes, turn her head, and raise her hands halfway before her cheek slammed into a shirt—and a body. Hannah recoiled, cold adrenaline coursing through her veins, as she brought her hand up the rest of the way in defense.

"Oh my god, girl!" Reese said. "I think you scared me more than I scared you."

Hannah put a hand over her heart, trying to slow the pneumatic drill in her chest. Then she laughed in a release of tension, while a disco seemed in to be in full swing behind her. "I have had more scares during free roam from humans than I have had with apparitions."

"Story of my life." Reese chuckled.

"Excuse me," Christian asked Reese, "do you know why this cell seems so much bigger than the others on this row?"

"This was hardly ever used as a cell. It was a shower area for years, and then I heard after they removed the showerheads, they used it as a dry cell."

"So, no one would have ever stayed in this cell as their assigned place?" Hannah asked.

"Not in that one. And, even if someone did, could you imagine how the other inmates would take out their jealousy on the person who *was* in there, getting a cell double the size?"

Hannah sighed louder than she had expected and pushed her glasses up her nose with the back of her hand. "Okay, Halifax. Let's go to 3D. My faith in finding anything down there is about as good as finding a pot of gold at the end of a rainbow."

Hannah didn't wait for him to respond before she headed toward the descending staircase to the criminally insane level below. Time was not on their side, and she couldn't chance Christian wasting more time by also not being on her side.

Hannah reached the bottom of the stairs, descending into a darkness that felt palpable, heavy, like wet towels draped on her shoulders.

"Hannah, listen." Christian stopped a few steps from the bottom. "Think rationally for a minute. Do you really think they let the criminally insane have those in their cells? If you just leave your strip somewhere, your ghostly attachment might not be returned to his actual cell, but at least he'll be *here* and not with *you* back home."

Hannah stopped walking, crossed her arms, and put her back against the windowsill so she could see both Christian to her right and the cells to her left. They were now on the level where the warden had consumed her at the end of the horseshoe. She refused to be blindsided if he was about to have round two.

Christian adjusted the backpack on his shoulder and stared at her.

"No," Hannah answered and removed the closet strip from her pocket. "If I can't find the exact person who I took this from, then I am leaving with it, and we'll try again on the next hunt."

"It took you seven years to do this one. When do you think we'll actually be back here? Be realistic, Hannah. This was the equivalent of a legit vacation, with the miles we traveled and the money we spent to get here. Just leave that strip wherever."

As she pushed her glasses up her nose, and the lenses readjusted over her line of sight, she caught a glimpse of her brimmed-hat man standing behind an opened cell door a few cells down the row, his fingers clutching the bars. She pushed herself off the wall and sprinted diagonally across the hallway toward the entryway to the cell.

She reached where he had been standing and slowed her trajectory by grabbing onto the bars and swung herself inside the cell. She had been prepared to confront him—to maybe get some semblance of a clue of where she needed to go, with just the few minutes they had left before the hunt ended.

Huffing and catching her breath from the quick burst, along with the disappointment of the cell being empty of any shadow figure, she didn't turn to face Christian when she retorted, "I won't just leave it. I'll take him back with me, until I can make plans to get back here and do it properly. I–I don't think he's dangerous anymore." She crammed the fabric into her pocket for punctuation. "And that's my final answer. I'd rather take it back home than leave it for the wrong … inmate."

"But that inmate doesn't *want* to be returned. And what do you mean exactly when you say to come back here again to *do it properly*?"

"Don't use that tone with me, Halifax."

"Can you hear him?" Someone's Casper-Capture sounded from the blind corner of the horseshoe, and Hannah heard a few whispers from guests.

Hannah took a deep breath, held it, and pinched her lips into a taut line as she glared at her friend.

"Okay, sorry," Christian conceded as he retrieved his phone from his pocket. "Have you consider just asking what number his cell is? You are so convinced that these apps are worth a shit, why don't you put your money where your mouth is and ask? Put faith in what you believe."

"Because, idiot, if what Rob says is right, my shadow man doesn't *want* to be returned. It's also what you've been preaching to me for the last hour. So why would he answer?"

Christian slapped his forehead in frustration. "You can be so dense, Hannah. You think your shadow man is the only one who can answer? What if the warden answers? Because, you know, the whole *warden wanted his escapee back* thing. If he really wants his guy back, he'll give you the cell number. Too easy. Why wouldn't *he* help you?"

A cluster of guests came from around the corner and approached Hannah and Christian, on their way toward the stairs leading out of 3D.

Hannah checked her watch and mumbled rhetorically, "How has it been an hour of free roam already?"

The group of guests politely smiled and nodded at Hannah and Christian as they passed and ascended the staircase, disappearing out of sight at the top. Hannah heard the front door close with a clatter, and she realized they were probably the only ones still in this building.

"C'mon. We gotta go. Time's running out anyway. They need us out of here, and I don't want to be accidentally locked in here." Hannah pushed her glasses up her nose with the back of her hand. "So, thanks for wasting valuable time arguing with me, when I could have been figuring out this shit. We're not done talking about this."

Christian snatched her arm a little more forcefully than she felt was comfortable. "Don't tell me that you blame me for failing."

"I didn't before." She yanked her arm back and away from his grip. "But I'm starting to think that asking you to be my wingman on this was a terrible idea. I can't believe I'm going home without returning this thing"—she took the fabric from her pocket and wiggled it in Christian's face—"and that somehow *you* got the one thing I had been fighting against all night." She stuffed the closet strip into her pocket and passed him to head up the stairs, then stopped, one foot on the bottom step, when Christian spoke.

"It would behoove you to stop being so fucking irrational and to think with the smart part of your brain—not the one so hellbent on fixing your past. This is one part of AA's steps that you might just need to be okay not working right now. You don't have a monopoly on failure."

"I hate you," she growled in a measured hiss, then steeled herself and spun to face him, with every intention of telling him to go to hell.

Except all the air expelled from her lungs before she could scream. Her mouth was silently frozen open as she grabbed Christian's hand to tug him away from the shadow mass that had filled the corridor, its head lolled onto its shoulder in a Jesus Christ pose, growing taller and wider.

Christian must have seen the shock and fear in Hannah's eyes because he jumped aside and looked backward at the warden.

Hannah had only turned halfway toward the ascending stairs when a solid yet somehow ethereal arm wrapped around her waist and dragged her backward. Her vocal cords felt like someone had injected vials of Novocain into them. She reached for Christian with both hands, her fingers splayed so taut that she thought her skin would crack, as the shadow arm pulled her backward.

Christian opened his mouth to scream, but Hannah didn't hear any sound escape from his mouth. The warden's other arm wrapped around Christan's waist and yanked him backward as well.

The world went silent, as if someone had hit the Mute button, even though she was sure their kicking feet produced *some* noise in the corridor of the criminally insane. She tried to scream again, but her voice seemed to be trapped underneath a heavy blanket in her diaphragm.

Hannah caught sight of bars in her peripheral vision, understanding now that the warden was pulling them backward into one of the cells. She glanced at Christian as her heels tried to find purchase on the concrete floor.

He flailed, trying to reach for her, his mouth silently opening and closing, like a fish left to die out of water.

The spectral arms backpedaled Hannah and Christian into a cell and released them, the force causing them to stumble backward a few more steps, before gaining balance. Hannah screamed at Christian, asking if he could hear her, and he shook his head and shrugged, not understanding.

Blackness consumed the entryway into the cell, as if someone had hung a curtain outside the opening that encompassed every inch of empty space. Not a blip of ambient light from the corridor on the other side penetrated it.

Hannah, panting and trying to will the rising panic in her heart to stay at bay, reached to touch the cloak of darkness covering their exit.

Christian grabbed her wrist, shaking his head frantically, his eyes darting back and forth, wild with fear.

Hannah cleared her throat—and the sound filled the cell. "Thank fucking god! I can talk again."

Christian replied with his own resurrected voice, but she didn't pay attention to what he had said. Her ears became attuned to how odd her voice had sounded when she spoke. She raised a finger for Christian to stop talking.

"Help!" she screamed. "We're stuck in here!"

Christian must have gotten the gist because he not only matched her in volume but seemed to be screaming loud enough to rip his vocal cords.

Yet Hannah sensed something was not right. She dug deep again and belted the longest, loudest scream she could muster—hoping, praying someone outside heard them. And then she realized what felt amiss.

Hannah put her hand on Christian's arm to get him to stop screaming for a moment. "Listen. I'm going to scream, and you tell me what you think sounds weird."

Christian adjusted the backpack on his shoulder and nodded.

Hannah belted as loud as she could, for as long as her lungs had air, until a coughing fit overcame her.

"It … It doesn't sound like our voices are leaving the cell."

Hannah felt her face flush from the racking coughs and put her hand on her chest to help center her breathing. "It's like our voices are bouncing back at us."

Christian opened his mouth and screamed a war cry. Then he said, "No, the problem is they're *not* bouncing back at us, Hannah. The black shadow is absorbing them, so the sound is just stopping."

"I'm gonna touch it." Hannah raised her hand to chest level and stepped forward. "I don't think it's the warden himself."

"It might be some kind of seal," Christian mused, with his hands in a steeple formation, his lips pressing against the sides of his index fingers and his thumbs under his chin.

"But maybe it's *just* a shadow, and we can run through it." Hannah pressed her palm against the draped cloak of blackness. "I can't push through it, but it's not solid."

"Fucking wonderful," Christian spat. He slapped the sides of his thighs as he turned, placed both palms on the far wall, and hung his head between his outstretched arms. With his chin against his chest, he said, "What if we never get out of here, Hannah?"

Hannah pushed on the black shadow covering the entryway of the cell, but it was futile—she could have been pushing on one of the limestone walls.

Christian spun to face the black shadow curtain when they heard the front door of Death Row open, and Jenny's voice carried down the stairwell into 3D. "Anyone still in here? We're closing up for the night!"

Christian crossed the short distance from the back wall to stand alongside Hannah in front of the shadow curtain.

Screaming over each other, their voices sounded like a cacophony of chaos filling the small cell—

"Hey!"

"In here!"

"Help!"

"We're still here!"

"Don't lock up!"

"Hey!"

"Can you hear us?"

"Help!"

—yet Hannah knew deep down that their voices weren't penetrating the shadow barrier in front of them. She took a breath and considered giving up, but she eyed Christian and saw the determination commingled with desperation on his face. She recognized that he was here solely because of her. And it was *not* her right anymore to give up before he did. She owed him that, at least.

So, Hannah opened her mouth and released the most blood-curdling scream for help that she had inside her. When she had to stop to take a breath, she heard Jenny from the vestibule area of the building call out again, "Last chance! Anyone in here? Gonna be locking up for the night!"

Christian now resorted to pounding on the shadow curtain with both fists, his face so red that Hannah thought he might suffer an aneurysm right here in the cell.

When Hannah screamed again, the tendons in her neck tightened to the point of almost snapping. As the scream left her mouth, and as the shadow curtain absorbed her cry for help, she knew Jenny had already left the building.

And had left Hannah and Christian alone, to fend for themselves.

CHAPTER 11:
THE LOBBY (HOUSING UNIT 1)

Hannah slipped her hand into Christian's. Her stomach roiled, signaling that if she screamed one more time at that same level of intensity, she might just vomit all over the place.

Christian's fingers intertwined with hers and gave a reassuring squeeze.

She eyed him, her breaths coming at the speed of her thrumming heart, and she saw him swallow hard.

He forced a feigned smile and raised both eyebrows. "Well, Banana, this is uncharted territory."

Hannah checked her smartwatch. Pixels and colors danced across the screen as it glitched. She raised her wrist to Christian's eye level. "Same as last time when I was engulfed in the warden's shadow."

Christian dug his phone from his pocket and sighed. "Still no service."

"And my smartwatch is not worth a shit too, thinking it's four minutes earlier."

Then, without warning or any sound, the shadow curtain dropped from top to bottom, as if someone had been holding it by its top corners and just let go.

Hannah and Christian exchanged a nanosecond of a glance before bolting from the cell and into the corridor of 3D. Hannah quickly checked their right-hand side to ensure no embodied apparitions would be flanking them on the way out, then followed Christian up the stairs to the main level of Death Row, leaping three stairs at a time.

As soon as they hit the top step, they resumed their barrage of screams for help.

"Wait!"

"We're still in here!"

"Can you hear us?"

"We're coming out now!"

Christian reached the front doors of Death Row first and exploded through it like a wrecking ball.

Hannah used her palm to push through the door as it closed behind Christian, and they bounded down the outside limestone steps, then raced along the pathway toward Housing Unit 1. Hannah fixated on the closed door ahead that would lead to the lobby, and hopefully to a straggling employee, all before the staff closed the metal bars that secured the only way in or out of the penitentiary.

Hannah thought her upper body would topple her forward, as her feet were not keeping pace with her flight. The closed door that hopefully would gift her a way to freedom jiggled in her sight as she ran, her breaths exhaling more like uncontrolled puffs of air than steady breathing. Her lungs stung. And her thighs and calves burned from the sudden burst of speed.

Christian stayed a step or so ahead of her. The speed of the wind entering her lungs matched the breeze whooshing past her ears. With each knee raise of her right leg, the weight of the closet strip in her pocket seemed to grow heavier, almost as if the newfound weight was intentional.

"Hey!" Christian yelled at the door they approached. "If you're still in there, don't leave!" He reached the door, skidded to a stop—inertia propelling his body into the wall next to the doorjamb—and yanked the heavy metal door toward him.

Hannah watched him disappear into the lobby and followed a tick behind. He had stopped in the center of the lobby, frantically scanning the room—a room that just less than an hour ago was teeming with tour guides, ghosthunters, and guests. Now it was vacant. The chatter and excitement of earlier was quiet enough now to hear a pin drop, like the emptiness had stolen the ecstatic vibrations of humans.

And left Hannah and Christian to its devices.

"Hello?" Christian yelled, his feet spread shoulder-width apart, as if preparing to run or to fight. He pivoted at the waist and looked toward the three steps that led to the gift shop area. "Anyone still here?"

The blood drained from Hannah's face as she noticed the front doors. She padded forward, inch by inch, her lips parting slightly in an almost defeated response. She shuffled toward the only exit on the property—the same door they had so freely been able to go in and out of earlier to chat with Jenny and Rob and Sara and Trevor on the front steps—and gripped the closed metal bars with both hands.

Hannah leaned forward and rested her forehead on the cool steel, the rusted chips embedding themselves into her sweaty skin. But she didn't care. "Christian," she whispered.

"Oh, fuck," he breathed behind her. His footfalls shambled toward her and stopped when he appeared alongside her. "We're … locked in here."

"*Uh-huh.*" She nodded as she agreed, the skin on her forehead scraping loose some more rusty chips from the bars.

Keeping her gaze trained on the floor, she glimpsed Christian gripping the bars next to her, mirroring her stance. "How in the world did the staff not notice that we weren't all accounted for?"

"It's not like we signed a log or anything. Heck, I think I even saw a few groups of people leave after the guided tours ended, when we were on the front steps. So how are they supposed to keep track of all that? The front steps"—Christian's voice rose in volume and anger as he shook the bars so hard that Hannah thought he might dislocate his shoulder—"that are right *fucking there.*"

Hannah pursed her lips and surveyed the empty stairs just beyond the metal bars and the glass doors, not ten yards away. "I think that may have been the warden."

"Big Boy? Oh, ya think? But why didn't he just keep us trapped in there, if he wants his escapee back so much?"

"I feel like he had only built up enough energy to keep us trapped in there long enough for the staff to leave."

"Well, hopefully he's depleted enough where he can't affect us again, before we find a way out."

She stood upright with a start, her heart beating faster with hope. She stripped her phone from her back pocket so quickly that she thought she might fumble it and have it crash to the floor, but she regained some dexterity and held it firmly. "I think I had service when we were out front earlier. We're close enough now …" She waited with bated breath for her phone to search for a signal. She held it high above her head and slipped it between the bars to press it against the glass.

"Be careful. If you drop it, we'll never get it back, until they open in the morning. Wait." His brows knitted together at her. "*Do* they open in the morning?"

Hannah pushed her glasses up her nose with the back of her hand. "*Yeesss* ..." she muttered on an elongated breath, catching on to what he was implying. "They have history tours in the mornings."

"See, Banana? We just gotta hang out for a few hours. We'll explain the misunderstanding, and I'm sure we'll all have a good laugh about it on the way home."

"I'm coming for you."

"Ah, shit. That was my phone," Christian said, retrieving it from his pocket. "Is it irony that the apps still work without a signal so we can't communicate with living people, but the ghosts of dead people can speak to us?"

Hannah sucked her lips slightly into her mouth and shoved her phone back into her pocket. "I don't like this. Something doesn't feel right. Like ... like the air has changed. It's thicker."

"Well, I'm all ears if you have a different plan." Christian ran his hand through his hair and blew out an exhale that puffed both cheeks.

"Scale one of the fences."

"Scale ... one of the"—he nodded as he finished—"fences."

"Fences, yes."

"The fences are out of the question. Look at all that barbed wire. They are at least twenty feet high. We are in a level-five maximum-security *prison*, with a Death Row, and you think we could just ... climb a fence?"

"Can't leave until it's returned."

Hannah snatched her phone from her pocket and glanced at the screen.

Christian cocked his head at her.

Hannah snorted. "So much for your theory of Big Boy needing some time to recoup after his magic trick in 3D." She stepped into the center of the lobby and projected her voice. "If you want him back so badly, tell me what cell number was his. I will march his closet strip over there right now and gladly return it to you. Then you can have your escapee back."

"He is mi—"

"Don't want to stay."

"Oh, for fuck's sake. Are they arguing through the app?" Christian's eyes widened with disbelief.

"My brimmed-hat shadow man isn't strong enough to manipulate physical items." Hannah pinched the bridge of her nose as she paced in a circle, her thoughts and theory pirouetting in her head faster and faster. "But he is strong enough to communicate through the app. The warden—"

"Big Boy," Christian clarified.

"Right. Maybe he hasn't built enough energy to speak over my shadow man."

Christian pointed at Hannah to accentuate his point. "And, of course, your brimmed-hat dude doesn't want to come back, so he'll probably try to interrupt the warden giving you that information."

"God, this all sounds so hokey," Hannah whispered to no one but herself.

"Done with games," came from her phone.

"Games are done?" Christian regarded Hannah with a grimace. "Which one is saying that? Your shadow dude or the warden? And what do they mean by that?"

"You are mine too. Punishment. No escape."

"I guess that answers that," Christian said. "Let's go test your fence idea. Maybe there is a break we can squeeze through."

They headed for the back door of the lobby that led to the yard.

"What made you change your mind?" Hannah tried to match his determined stride.

Christian regarded her with a desperate expression but flashed a forced smile. "I don't think Big Boy plans to let us make it until morning."

CHAPTER 12:
DEATH ROW (HOUSING UNIT 3)

Hannah and Christian quickened their pace when they got through the metal door at the rear of the lobby. The night was deathly quiet. Hannah only heard her and Christan's labored breaths as she frantically scanned the fence lines between the buildings.

"See anything?" Christian asked.

Hannah squinted at the small section of fencing in front of A-Hall. "I think I see it pulled up from the ground a bit."

Christian didn't give her any semblance of a reply—verbal or visual—before kicking into a powerwalk toward where she had pointed.

Hannah followed behind on the paved pathway between the two buildings and cocked her head to hear better. She wasn't quite ready to alert Christian or to take him off his trajectory toward the fence line, but she strained her ears to decipher what she heard—or even in which direction it came from.

As they neared A-Hall, Hannah realized the sound grew louder. Her gaze darted from the compromised spot of the fence—at least she hoped it was compromised and not just a trick of the moonlight—to the closed front door of A-Hall. Back and forth, as they approached. Fence. Door. Fence. Door.

They reached the line of sight of the front door and were close enough to inspect the fence. Hannah sighed and bit her bottom lip in disappointment.

"It's bowed outward, but it's still secured into the ground," Christian said softly.

Hannah grabbed Christian's arm, now no longer concerned with the state of the fence's integrity. She squeezed his arm so he would look at her, then she thumbed silently toward the closed door of A-Hall not five yards from them on their right.

Christian squared his body off with the door and leaned forward in his spot. "What's that sound?"

The ground beneath Hannah felt like it was rumbling. She stood shoulder to shoulder with Christian, her eyes and ears tuned straight ahead.

"If we need to run, what's the plan?" Hannah whispered.

"I dunno. Lobby?" Christian scowled at her. "But what do you think we'll be running *from*?"

Then the yells and *whoops* and hollers grew with the rumbling coming from behind the closed door of A-Hall. Men's voices. Screaming. Excited. Like a rally. Stomping. One thousand feet with purpose.

"Christian?" she squeaked.

"Hannah … fucking run—"

The exploding burst of men, pumping fists and weapons over their head, who poured from the front door of A-Hall, like a dam had raptured, severed his sentence.

Hannah turned and tried to take off with such speed that she lost her balance and hit the ground hard. The charging horde of inmates, screaming and bumping into each other because too many of them crammed on the pathway between buildings, came at full speed like a freight train toward where Hannah lay on her side. Her shoulder throbbed from where she had landed on it.

She instinctively outstretched both arms and raised her feet, like a turtle on its back, to the oncoming rush of angry, screaming men. Then she noticed she could just faintly see through each one, the inmate behind each one now appearing as if it were on the other side of a glass of water.

Christian hooked an arm under one of her outstretched arms and spun her up and onto her feet.

Unorganized rows upon rows of shouting ethereal inmates streamed from A-Hall, most brandishing weapons. Each individual was a sepia color—somewhere between brownish gray and olive brown—and Hannah's immediate thought was how they all looked like they had stepped from a 1950s' gang movie. Their hairstyles, their tones, the way they wore their penitentiary-issued uniforms.

The apparitions bisected around Hannah and Christian, like a stream when encountering a large rock in its path, as they sprinted for the lobby. Hannah kept her arm entangled with Christian's so the flood wouldn't separate them.

The prisoners now had filled the pathway in front of them, running toward Death Row, as more and more still spilled from the front of A-Hall. The spirits ran past Hannah and Christian, seemingly noticing them enough to not run through them but also not caring about their presence.

"Start pushing through them to get to the lobby!" Hannah had to yell over the cheers and excited screams punctuating the air from the surging horde.

The wraiths seemed to be moving twice as fast, as if they were characters in a movie played at double speed. The front section of the tsunami of specters reached the steps of Housing Unit 3.

"They're heading to Death Row!"

"Good. We'll be alone in the lobby."

Hannah felt Christian keep trying to pull her toward the lobby door as it approached, but he kept bumping backward into her.

"What's wrong?" She still had to yell over the screams and hollers around them. It felt as if the sky itself was alive and raining wails.

"I can't get over there." Christian kept veering toward the lobby, but, even though the apparitions were translucent, Christian kept bouncing back to stay with the group.

Hannah felt the energy from the horde's movement keeping her and Christian going forward with the flow. "I'll push you." Hannah shoved Christian to give him more power, but his body bounced back into hers, and she ricocheted off one of the passing haunts to her left.

"Let's just stop and wait for them to pass," Christian suggested.

Hannah thought that was a solid plan, and they tried to slow down, but the energy from the cascading inmates marching toward Death Row was solid. They now had passed the back door to the lobby, and the flow of chanting and screaming inmates veered them around the bend and straight toward the front doors of Housing Unit 3.

Hannah surveyed all the pieces of broken chairs, wooden table legs, mops, brooms, and sledgehammers raised above their heads, pumping into the air as the inmates marched. She glanced behind her and saw plumes of smoke rising on the other side of A-Hall. "Christian, I think we're in the middle of the riot."

Christian side-eyed her. "Gee whiz, ya think?"

"It's a residual haunting," Hannah said introspectively as the tempest of ethereal rioters moved them closer to Death Row. "Their energy shouldn't be affecting us."

Almost as if the rioters wanted to prove her wrong, she felt someone arm-bar her from behind to keep her in line and moving forward. She glanced behind her at the never-ending flow of apparitions still pouring from the mouth of A-Hall. Hannah and Christian reached the steps of Death Row.

As she climbed, she scanned the yard. She ascertained at least a thousand, if not more, souls were charging Housing Unit 3, shoulder to shoulder, chest to back, weapons raised and fists pumping. Unseen buildings smoldered in the background somewhere.

"You know where we're going, right?" Christian whispered, the shoulders and arms of the spirits next to him keeping him locked into the center of the flow.

"We're going with them to kill that guy who snitched, aren't we?"

The moving mass of translucent rioters carried them through the front doors to Death Row, like they were leaves blowing in the wind. The cadence of screams from the rioters grew louder and became like an icepick through Hannah's skull as they squeezed through the front door with the swarm.

Hannah locked gazes with a man dressed in a guard uniform, his sepia-colored embodiment flickering, as if a hologram threatening to sputter out. She noted the fear in his eyes as the horde moved them toward him. She watched him panic, then throw a large brass keyring through the opening of the gate to keep the keys safe on the other side.

"Looks like that's exactly where we're going," Christian finally answered, after probably observing what Hannah had seen.

Hannah swallowed hard and tried to push her glasses up her nose with the back of her hand, but a rushing rioter bumped into her elbow, sending her frames lopsided. She frantically maneuvered her glasses to loop behind her ears, and, when the scene in front of her righted again, her heart exploded with realization.

The inmates would soon seize the guard room and would use the sledgehammers to crash through the wall to gain access to the cells. Then, stuck inside the swarm of palpable chaos, she and Christian would be unable to escape from accompanying these men forward to rip apart that man in protective custody—would be unable to escape witnessing cold-blooded murder.

Hannah grabbed Christian's hand, and he gave her an empathetic look. She knew he also was tracking what the next few minutes of their life would entail.

The guard who had thrown the keys turned his back to the rioters, to protect his face, but the inmates just redirected their trajectory toward the guards' room door. Hannah watched the denizen of rioters pile upon each other at the closed guards' door. Each inmate had been almost flattened atop each other, as if they were putty.

Hannah tried with one last-ditch effort to use brute force to fight her body backward toward the main entrance, but the stream of specters was too great, like a minnow trying to swim against a waterfall.

"Be strong," Christian said and smiled warmly at her.

"Is closing my eyes an option?"

He shrugged, with furrowed brows, then squeezed her hand in reassurance. "Do what you gotta do. I won't let you go."

As if a drain plug had been pulled in a sink full of water, a maelstrom of rioters bottlenecked into the guards' room, weapons raised, the men who brandished sledgehammers leading the charge.

Hannah and Christian flowed through the opening with the current. Hannah noticed the guards standing back, hands splayed outward in a surrender gesture, then saw a sepia-colored sledgehammer rise above an inmate's head and come down against the wall that separated the guards' room from the Death Row cells.

As the head of the tool struck the wall, and large chunks fell to the floor, the cheers and hollering intensified, now in galvanizing unison. With every blow against the wall, it was as if each fallen chunk became a symphonic conductor, signaling when the cheering should happen. The silence between each cheer dripped with violence and anger. It became cyclical: swing, strike, crash, cheer, silence … Swing, strike, crash, cheer, silence …

And each swing that chipped away another section of wall brought the mob closer to the other side of the cells. The ethereal horde moved as a single unit now with the sledgehammer, like disciplined rowers of a Viking ship. A flurry of rioters covered the guards' room from wall to wall, front to back. When the inmate with the sledgehammer recoiled the tool, every entity leaned backward with him, their sepia-colored bodies forcing Hannah and Christian to lean backward with the masses. Then the weapon-wielding inmate would throw his force forward to strike the growing hole, and the room would lean forward in sync. When the sledgehammer bounced off the wall, exposing more of a hole, the room would cheer, then fall silent for the next cycle.

Hannah glanced at Christian and shook her head, as if to say, *Stop the ride. I wanna get off.* She kept her gaze locked onto Christian's as they went through the next rotation of swing, strike, crash, cheer, silence. Then she noticed this cheer sounded different—more excited. Nefarious.

Hannah bit her bottom lip as she mustered the courage to look, already knowing the time was nye for the rioters to breech the wall, and then they would be off to the races again. To a horrific and gory endgame.

"You'd think Warden Big Boy wouldn't allow this behavior," Christian said with a half serious and a half-joking tone.

"Don't let go of my hand when we get through the wall. I'm gonna close my eyes," Hannah said just as the wall collapsed, exposing a hole that resembled more of a portal.

The rioters cheered. The plume of excited voices reminded her of the unified and determined death-or-glory cheers from *Braveheart* after Mel Gibson gave his famous motivational speech. And that comparison sent a shiver down her spine.

The screams slowly fell out of sync, and, instead of being one resounding voice, each individual voice became a soundscape of battle cries.

And through the gaping hole in the wall they went, storming down the corridor toward cell 18 like a tornado. Hannah closed her eyes so they were just slits—just enough where she could almost discern all the figures in front of them, her almost-touching eyelashes now resembling cell bars in her vision.

Christian squeezed Hannah's hand. "Here we go. Looks like we're going in with them."

Hannah clamped her eyes shut and scrunched her face for added protection so tightly that she thought her glasses would slide right off her nose and land on the floor, only to have a specter rioter trample them. She pursed her lips, which inclined her nose just enough to stop her glasses from falling any farther, the nosepieces resting uncomfortably on the tip.

The horde directed her feet to turn to the left, and she knew they were inside Donnell's cell. She flinched every time she heard the young man yelp. She flinched every time she heard another weapon—chairs, broomsticks, chair leg—strike the man's flesh.

Christian whispered, "Oh, God," and he squeezed her hand tighter. "Don't open your eyes."

She shook her head so fast that her long black hair slapped against her cheeks. Then the sounds of something sucking thick liquid filled the air. Gurgling and coughing replaced the man's screams. The loud snap of bones churned Hannah's stomach, followed by what sounded like soup being ladled into a bowl. A skull cracking and brain matter pouring out? A rib cracking and innards set free?

The distant ringing in her ears, which she had thought was just a result of all the screaming and yelling around her, grew louder. And louder. The ringing overpowered the sounds of the melee in the cell. She noticed red spots behind her eyelids. And the darkness of having her eyes closed grew darker still.

Hannah's heart pounded against her ribcage, ready to burst forth. Her breathing came in short bursts—even puffs would have been an improvement. She realized she had come to a junction; either she could let the growing panic attack have its way with her or she could go through the motions to stave it off.

The sound from a blunt object connecting with something hard and yet squishy on the floor decided it for her. The ringing in her ears engulfed her, and the growing spots behind her eyelids enveloped her.

"Halifax ...?" she pleaded, before the world went silent and black.

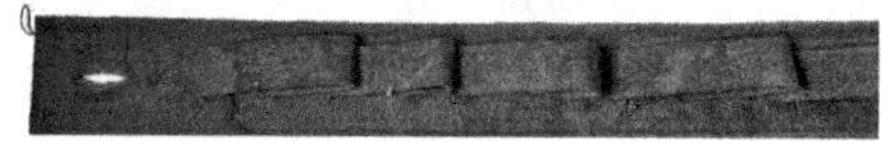

Silence. Complete silence. The ringing had been snuffed out. The screams and hollers from the rioters had been silenced. Then a voice. A single voice. Garbled. Way off in the distance. Could be a million miles away. Or down the hallway. Now closer. Familiar. Something shaking her shoulders. Christian's voice. Her name.

Hannah fluttered open her eyelids, saw Christian's face fill her vision. The images of the riot and the sounds of the desecration of that inmate flooded back, making her gasp and try to sit upright like a catapult.

Christian's hands slowed her abrasive movement, then carefully guided her into a sitting position. "Are you okay, Banana?" His eyes were glazed over, looking a thousand miles through her and not at her. His expression was robotic, stoic—shell-shocked, like a soldier who had just survived a mortar bombardment.

When all her faculties returned, she saw they were finally alone in the hallway of Death Row, his backpack on the floor next to where he squatted. She wrapped an arm around his neck and buried her face into it. She inhaled his essence, the sweat and dirt be damned. His skin pressed against her cheek, and her heart hiccupped. She realized she wouldn't want to see anyone else in the world after opening her eyes right now other than Christian.

"Is it over?" she whispered into his neck.

Hannah felt his body exhale and relax—but more in defeat than being content. "The riots seem to be, yes." He pulled her away from the crook of his neck to behold her face.

An overbearing feeling of resisting him almost made her close her eyes and dive back into that safe space against his body. Yet she refrained.

"There's still the matter of being stuck here until the morning crew opens up. And something more important. At least something more pressing."

"Oh?"

Christian scooted to the side so Hannah had a clear shot down the hallway—the hallway where the rioters had forced them down just moments before, the hallway where cell 18 lay at the end … and the memories of the sounds and images that her mind had created of the atrocities they had done to the inmate there.

Hannah's gaze shot back at Christian, still squatting next to her. "How did we get back here?"

"I–I don't know. When you passed out, everyone disappeared like a plug had been pulled, and we were back here at the start of the hallway. I don't remember moving."

Hannah rubbed the back of her head. "So, we just teleported? What? Fifty feet down the hallway? Did I hit my head? It hurts really bad. Maybe you hit your head too. That could explain it."

"No. I felt you start to go all Jell-O on me, and I caught you on the way down. A real knight in shining armor, I'd say." He winked and flashed her one his signature smiles that relayed a message to her that if she would just give him a chance … maybe even especially now after what they had endured together.

"So, what is more pressing?" she asked as she placed her hand on the floor to push to her feet.

Christian grabbed her elbow to help her rise. "You not gonna go all wobbly-weebly on me again, are you?"

Hannah snickered. "I think I'm good."

Christian scooped up his backpack and slung it around his shoulder, then pointed at a nearby cell. "What do you think, Banana? Leftover residual of Donnell? And, if so, why didn't he disappear with the rest of the chaos?"

Hannah squinted to see better down the hallway of cells. At the end of the corridor, supposedly right around cell 18, two legs were on the floor, sticking out of the cell and into the hallway.

"They look …" She swallowed hard, never expecting that these words would come from her mouth tonight. "Human."

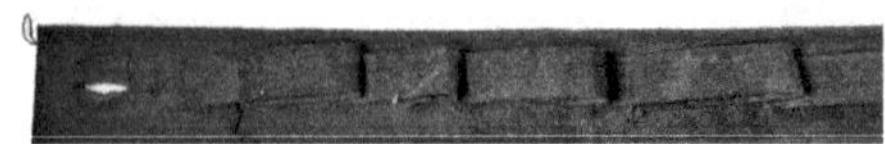

The silence that hung in the hallway between Hannah and Christian was thick enough to cut with a knife. Hannah tried to steady her breaths—inhale, pause, exhale … lather, rinse, repeat—but she remained more focused on the details of the legs and the feet sticking from the cell. She gasped and pushed her glasses up her nose when she discerned the fabric on the legs and the sneakers on the feet.

"Those sneakers are modern," she said as she bolted from her spot, her voice wavering with uncertainty and panic. She sprinted down the narrow row of cells. The fence to her right separated where the guards would walk—the same fence that the Creeper liked to use as vertical monkey bars.

"Hannah, wait!" Christian yelled and sprinted after her.

Cell by cell passed her on her left side—cavernous opening, wall, opening, wall, opening, wall. The sneakers got clearer as she approached. Female sneakers.

"What the …?" she muttered as she reached the cell, the sprawled body on the floor revealing more of itself. She heard Christian's panting right behind her, and she froze when the body became completely exposed to her.

"What the actual *fuck*?" he yelled, breaking her from her short reverie.

And the reality of what she saw hit her like a wrecking ball. Hannah screamed, then slapped a trembling hand to her mouth. Christian wrapped his arm around her shoulders and spun her from the body, her glasses going lopsided from the force of being pressed against his shirt.

"Who … Who is it?" Hannah asked. "Oh, God. Is it *real*?"

Christian pulled from her slightly and, with as much grace and confidence that she knew he was capable of, said, "Let me look. You stay here."

Hannah nodded and ran her fingers up and down the length of her right arm, trying to alleviate some anxiety.

Christian grabbed the corner of the entry to the cell and carefully, methodically inched his line of sight into the cell. "Holy fucking shit!" he yelled and quickly spun around so his back was against the wall next to the cell opening.

"What? What?" Hannah's pulse crescendoed into a drumline in her ears.

Christian placed his palms on his thighs as he bent forward, panting. "I don't want you to see …"

Hannah's gaze darted between Christian's face and the sneakers sticking from the opening of the cell, like the Wicked Witch of the West under the fallen house. "I–I don't need you to keep saving me." She regarded him with a soft expression so he would know what she was saying didn't come with any brashness but came from a place of appreciation.

"Okay. Maybe you can tell me what *you* see, because I have no clue what's going on."

Hannah took a deep breath, held it to steel herself, and stepped the few paces to look inside the cell. Her eyes widened as her brain tried to process what was happening in front of her. The guide's familiar reddish-purple dyed hair was the only thing she could see of the person lying on the floor. A black mass—a shadow figure—covered the woman's face completely, its elbows and knees higher than its body, like a spider.

"Is it him, Hannah?" Christian asked, his voice evidently shaky and on the verge of breaking. "Is it the …?"

"Creeper?" Hannah finished with a question.

Upon saying the shadow figure's nickname, the man—creature?—looked up and backward at Hannah over its inhumanly bent limb. It hissed, turned on the woman's face like a dial to face Hannah, and leaped from the cell.

Hannah screamed and jumped backward to give the Creeper space as it bounded down the woman's legs, jumped onto the fence that separated the cells from the guard's walkway, and scampered down the fence line like a spider, then disappeared around the corner.

Hannah looked back at Christian, drained of color, and whispered, "What the—?" The bells ringing somewhere in the void ahead of them made her pause. "That means it's gone, right? It rings the bells when it leaves. It did the last time."

"Beats the hell out of me." Christian gestured with his chin toward the woman's legs poking from the cell. "Do you want me to look first?"

Hannah wrung her hands, then crossed her arms. "I–I couldn't see her face. The Creeper completely covered it. I only know who it is by the hair."

Christian cocked his head in question.

"I think it's that guide Reese, who gave us the tour of this side of the building."

Christian moved forward with purpose but without discussing a plan with Hannah and stepped one pace into the cell. "Oh … Oh my … Fuck!"

Hannah placed a hand on Christian's shoulder and raised herself on her tiptoes to see better. Her throat constricted at the same time her stomach churned. "It's Reese," she whispered, trying to suppress the vomit from rising.

Where the Creeper had been on the tour guide's face was now bone and blood spurting, as if her heart still pumped.

"Was that thing … eating her?" Christian asked.

Hannah pivoted to face the floor—in case she vomited. "It certainly looks like it." Once she thought she had a bit of control over her gag reflex, she peeked around Christian's side. That *thing* had stripped Reese's face, from her hairline to her chin, but the skin on her ears remained.

"You okay?" he asked, eyeing her.

"Yep." She nodded quickly, trying to force herself to believe her own words.

"Banana?" he beseeched more forcefully.

"Yep?"

Christian laid a palm on his forehead and paced the hallway. "What the fuck is going on?" He circled like a tiger in a cage, back and forth, between Reese's legs and the cell on the far side. Then he stopped, frozen in time, his hand still on his forehead. "Oh no …"

Hannah skipped over Reese's legs—murmuring, "Sorry," to the half-eaten tour guide—to come alongside Christian and to peek into the next cell. Breaths heaved in and out of her chest. A shaky hand found Christian's forearm. Tears pricked the corners of her eyes, then didn't dam themselves as they stained her cheeks. "Christian? We. Need. To. Get. The. Fuck. Out. Of. Here."

Hannah surveyed the bodies stacked inside the cell, and she grew numb. Numb was the only way she could handle the scene in front of her. Two more dead tour guides. Limbs broken and left in unnatural angles. The firecracker-of-a-woman, Jenny, one eye open, one eye ripped from the socket. Lisa, lying on her stomach but her face looking ceilingward—her head turned a complete 180 degrees. They looked as if someone had haphazardly tossed them into the cell as an afterthought.

Christian stepped behind Hannah and squealed—the sound encompassing more fear than she had ever heard from him. "I don't know what's fucking real anymore! Are they residual too, like the riot? Or are these people really dead?"

Hannah felt the color drain from her body. "We just heard Jenny calling to empty the building a few minutes ago."

"Maybe none of this is real. Do you remember them being your tour guides on your birthday?"

"I was too shitfaced to remember anything!"

"Oh Christ, Hannah, just when we *need* you to remember something more important than what cell that stupid piece of fabric came from."

"I can help."

Hannah glared at Christian. "Was that your Casper-Capture?"

Christian yanked his phone from his pocket. "Yep."

"Take a drink."

Hannah side-eyed Christian. "You don't think he means—"

"You only saw the brimmed-hat dude when you drank."

Hannah shook her head to add as much denial to the situation as possible.

"Escape."

Christian's gaze hardened, and Hannah saw turmoil rising in his eyes, like a ship lost at sea.

"Don't want to stay."

Christian held his phone to Hannah's face so she could read the last few messages. "Your shadow man wants to help us get the fuck out of here."

"Good. I'm glad. Let's figure this out."

"I am innocent."

"No, Hannah. The time for figuring this out is long fucking gone."

"Vodka."

Hannah's gaze darted to Christian's phone in his hand.

"Banana, listen." Christian let his backpack fall to the floor, then took both her hands in his. "I will be here with you. Every step of the way. Take a few swallows. Give him just enough power to get us the fuck out of here. Then I will personally attend every and any AA meeting with you for the rest of your life. It's our way out."

Hannah remained silent, but her breaths came strong and forceful through her nostrils, like a bull ready to charge.

Christian bent down, unzipped the backpack, and removed the vodka bottle. He held it casually by his thigh. "Listen to the app. Maybe this is how we get out alive. Maybe this is how we get back to our families. Back to reality, Hannah! One more drink. That's it. Just one. One more conjuring of your shadow hat man. He said so himself. He'll lead us out. Back to the real world! Give him the strength to open the front *fucking door*!"

Hannah glared at the bottle resting by Christian's leg, as if it were a rattlesnake. She took a few steps backward—her line of sight of the murdered tour guides now blocked. "You've finally fucking snapped! You're a prick if you think that's how it works. Or that I would even entertain drinking that. *When* we get out of this, I don't ever want to see you again. You're dead to me." She spat on the floor at his feet. "*Dead* to me!" The back of her sneakers bumped into Reese's legs, and Hannah had to outstretch her arms to regain balance.

Christian's lips formed a taut line. His brows creased into a V shape. His eyes widened. He raised the bottle of vodka as he stepped toward her and shook it at her, like it was an extension of a pointing finger. "It won't have to end this way if you just give into temptation." He twisted the cap off the bottle.

Hannah heard the exact moment when the seal snapped free from the top—that all-too-familiar sound. She froze and went wide-eyed when she thought she saw the shimmering outline of a brimmed hat sitting snugly atop Christian's head. Then his eyelids fluttered, and his pupils turned gray.

Christian shook the vodka bottle so violently while he spoke that the liquid splashed to the floor—his voice sounding deeper, raspier and like it came through a distant radio. "I wouldn't even be here if you didn't have the fucking need to return that piece of *my* cell that you stole. I refuse to be trapped in these walls again. So take a fucking drink and keep that souvenir in your pocket, like the good girl you've always been for me over the years, so we can both get out of here." His gaze darted frantically up and down the hallway of cells. He reached for Hannah with his free hand.

Hannah recoiled and raised her hands to protect herself from Christian's fingers, which were now blurry and transposing between human digits and long skeletal shadows. "Anger fuels them, Christian. Please fight him. I–I can't lose you." She backed away, shaking her head rapidly, as if to say, *No, no, no, no, no …*

The air crackled with a menacing energy from somewhere close by; she could almost taste it. Hannah bit a cuticle off her thumb as she pondered how her brimmed-hat shadow figure seemed to now have control over Christian.

Hannah knew she had to suppress the boiling feeling of berating him for what he had just suggested to her. But she knew—his lifeless pupils confirming her suspicion—that it wasn't him thinking or speaking right now. Yet she had to try something as she watched Christian's head loll to the side, his far-off vacant stare shooting through her.

Hannah pinched the bridge of her nose to think, then grabbed both his hands, the neck of the bottle still secured in his grasp. The cool glass bottle that held her poison rested against her fingers and sent a wave of revolt through her stomach, bile threatening to spew from her mouth. "Halifax, look at me. Listen to me." She eyed the massacre of the tour guides beyond him, and a shadow grew from the floor against the back wall. "We gotta get the fuck out of this building."

Christian turned his head, zombielike—an ethereal gurgle coming from his lips—to glance behind him. Yet it wasn't *her* Christian who was looking; it might have been his body, but it wasn't his essence.

The warden had now crested over six feet tall against the back wall and still grew.

"Fuck. Big Boy," Hannah murmured, released one of Christian's hands, and used her grip on the other hand to pull him down the row of cells toward the front door of Death Row, abandoning Christian's backpack. Hannah couldn't help but notice how Christian felt like *dead weight* as she tugged him to possible freedom—his feet shuffling to keep up, as if he were now a medicated ghoul.

Hannah's glasses bounced down her nose with each footfall, and she pushed her frames up her nose with her free hand while she looked behind them. The warden had grown to its full seven-foot-tall height and slowly levitated down the corridor toward them. Hannah had a sinking thought that it didn't matter how fast *they* ran and how slowly the shadow figure moved. The warden would catch them regardless.

Hannah looked forward to their destination—hopefully to buy them a smidgen of time so they could formulate some semblance of a plan—and heard cell doors closing behind her.

Slide. And *slam!* Slide. And *slam!*

With each cell the warden passed, those bars slid closed. Hannah stole one last peek behind her and noticed the warden had left cell 18's door open—Reese's legs still half sprawled into the hallway, Christian's backpack lying on the floor like some exposed dirty secret.

No, she thought. The dirty secret was still clenched in his other hand. And her brimmed-hat shadow man had taken residency inside her friend and had tried to exploit her to get what he wanted. Had exploited her *friend* too.

Slide. And *slam!* Slide. And *slam!* More cell doors closed as the warden passed them.

A quick calculation in Hannah's head put the warden about three cells behind her and Christian. Too close to look back and confirm. Fear of the known drove her forward and kept her focus straight ahead.

She tugged Christian along as they reached the vestibule—his hand limp and body dragging behind her like a shambling sleepwalker. She surveyed the wall that led from the guards' room into Death Row—a wall now perfectly sealed, as if a sledgehammer hadn't smashed through it just a few minutes earlier. All patched back up, like it had been for more than the last half century.

Christian's hand ripped from her grip as they turned the corner to head down the stairs to freedom, and she spun around to see what had happened, her sneakers skidding to a halt. Christian's feet had been yanked from behind, and his chest and face smashed against the concrete. The vodka bottle struck the floor and shattered; shards of broken glass slid across the floor like hockey pucks.

"Christian!" Hannah screamed, bent forward, as something dragged him by the ankles backward into the emptiness of Death Row.

"Hannah! Fucking *run*!" he yelled now with pure clarity, freed from his tupor, and with his own lifeforce returning to his eyes; her brimmed-hat man had released his hold. Yet Christian still disappeared around the corner, his shirt rising on his chest from the backward force dragging him along.

His fingers futilely clawed at the concrete, trying to gain purchase. He screamed once—a full-faculty Christian scream—then his voice was severed, as if a plug had been pulled on the sound.

Hannah heard the floor scraping against his bare skin in the darkness—muffled by the *glug-glug-glugging* of the liquor draining from the broken bottle at her feet—as she dug her heels into the floor to propel her forward to make chase.

"Listen to him," came from her Casper-Capture app on her phone. She froze and yanked her phone from her back pocket.

"You won't survive if you follow."

"Hide."

"I can get us out."

Hannah didn't know how, but, deep down in the core of her being, she knew the messages were coming from her brimmed-hat man, and she crammed her phone into her jeans.

So, she listened. To both commands.

And ran to hide.

"Hannah … I'm sorry," came from her back pocket.

CHAPTER 13:
WOMEN'S UNIT (HOUSING UNIT 1)

The sound of her name coming from the app, originating from her shadow man for the first time, startled her as she flung open the doors to Death Row and burst forth down the pathway that connected the main buildings. Once crammed with angry rioters, now desolate and vacant. A hush of nothingness had descended upon the center yard area, reclaiming its silence.

As Hannah ran underneath the October moonlight, she contemplated which building to hide in. She didn't know how long she needed to hide, how long her brimmed-hat man required to implement whatever plan he was concocting. Her gaze darted between A-Hall to her right, where the throng of rioters had burst from, and the women's unit ahead of her. A quick weighing of her risk-to-benefit factors as she sprinted caused her to focus on the building in front of her, not because it was closer but because A-Hall was too open, too easy to see every walkway simultaneously—like shooting fish in a barrel. The women's unit was like a maze and a tower, all built into one, with ink-blotted openings that kept an imagination full of wraiths at bay.

Although she wondered if the warden knew where she was at all times regardless, and if he could materialize wherever he wanted. If that were the case, her decision between buildings would be moot.

But she didn't think her shadow man would have suggested that she hide if there wasn't *some* benefit to it. And right now, putting trust in the specter who had stalked her for the past seven years was the only option she had, if she wanted any chance to survive.

She crossed the distance to the sallyport and padded up the stairs three at a time, having to shove her glasses back up her nose from the vibrations of her footfalls. The darkness atop the stairs welcomed her with both hopes of sanctuary and yet a looming foreboding. The blackness swallowed her as she bounded onto the first floor. She sucked in her bottom lip as she crab-walked sideways, scouring the four rows of floors above her, contemplating which spot would be the best to hide. The best to become the smallest she could. The best to become invisible.

Hannah rounded the corner and thanked the moonlight for coming through the windows to help her see the staircases as they wound up, up, up into the towerlike building. She ran lightly up the steps on her tiptoes to minimize any unnecessary noise—any clue that would tip off the warden to her location.

She ascended the first flight. Not high enough. She grabbed the handrailing to spin herself onto the next set of stairs. Up another flight. And finally another. Until she landed on the highest walkway and looked over the railing. A wave of vertigo from the height made her step backward. She hoped this was high enough and far enough from Death

Row to buy her shadow figure whatever time he needed to implement a plan to get them out of there.

Hannah trotted down the walkway toward the center, thinking that hiding in a cell in the middle of the row would grant her a few added seconds of precious time to flee than hiding in a corner cell. She wanted to expunge the warden's element of surprise.

Hannah stood in front of a cell whose inmate had taken meticulous detail to paint the walls in a welcoming pattern of stenciled shapes. Not able to explain why, she felt compelled to pick this cell to hide in. She knew if the warden had the ability to conjure inside the cell, she would have no recourse of escape. But, if her brimmed-hat shadow figure had any workable solution for her predicament, then she would have a clear line of hearing from this vantage point, if someone came through the door below. She sat on the dusty cot, the floor littered with chunks of limestone and cement, and prayed that putting her faith in her brimmed-hat shadow figure right now would pay off.

For good luck, Hannah reached into her front right pocket and rubbed the piece of fabric, which had served as her shadow man's closet.

Hannah pulled her phone from her back pocket and switched the Casper-Capture app to Silent, where she would just have to keep checking the screen for any additional instructions in text format from her shadow figure. Then a blinking dot on the right corner of the screen caught her attention. She quickly checked for a signal, but the phone still read NO SERVICE, as if the device was eternally mocking her.

But she had new notifications. Her fingers worked slower than the hope bursting in her brain as she closed the ghost-hunting app and launched her text message icon.

Dollard: *Hey, babe. Where you at?*

Hannah checked the timestamp. Dollard had sent it a few hours ago. Hannah scrunched her face, pushed her glasses up her nose, and wondered why he had asked her that when he knew the hunt went until the middle of the night.

Dollard: *Please just let me know you're okay. The hotel staff says you never came back for your stuff. I'm calling the police.*

That one had come in just an hour ago. She glanced at the top of the screen again, still no service. Her hands trembled, sweat mixed with dirt staining her cheeks. She wiped the grime and moisture from her forehead. Then she noticed the voicemail alert symbol, which showed the number ninety-nine on the top right corner. Knowing that the icon couldn't count past ninety-nine, she whispered ever-so-quietly to herself, "Over one hundred voicemails? What in the …?"

She pressed the app icon and set the phone to give her the transcript of the voicemail message. That way it wouldn't play out loud, and she could read it silently instead. Her breath hitched in her chest as she scanned the words.

> *Hannah, it's been almost a year now. The police are now considering this a cold case. Your family is still going crazy. They're paying your phone bill in case you ever get to the phone. I–I don't know how much longer I'm supposed to hold on. To wait. I would never tell your parents this, but I–I gave up hope that you're still alive months ago. Too many stories of bad endings in the news. This will be my last message to you. I can't keep putting myself through the wringer every time I text or call, getting no answer. If you can*

hear these, Hannah, just know I love you. I'll always still hope for the best. Goodbye.

None of it made sense. She hoped Dollard was just playing a joke—thinking it would be funny to mess with her during a ghost hunt. Fucker never was any good at making appropriate jokes, she thought. And a feeling of disdain entombed her, with the image of her boyfriend taking shape in her mind's eye. Then her stomach fluttered with the memory of seeing two invisible hands drag Christian by his ankles into the blackness of Death Row.

Attempting to debunk Dollard's pitiful excuse for humor, she checked the time stamp again on his first texts. Yet now she focused on the date: October 31.

Hannah squealed and slapped her hand across her mouth, realizing that date would be tomorrow. And the hundred-plus voicemails from every friend and family member had all come in during a year that hadn't existed yet.

Hannah let the phone drop into her lap. She removed her glasses, set them next to her on the cot, and buried her face in her hands. Tears and snot leaked out without any apology. She sniffed deeply, but only one nostril cleared enough for her to breathe through it. Her fingers twitched against her clammy and dirt-marred face. Her chest heaved, and she tried to keep her sniveling to a minimum. But it was like the dam had burst open, flooding her brain with reality.

All the tour guides were dead. Christian was dead—she was sure of it. She was all alone and trapped on the bloodiest forty-seven acres in America, with a stolen memento in her pocket, hunted by a murderous shadow warden. And her cry almost morphed into a chuckle when she realized the absurdity that there was a good chance she had time traveled.

But she knew she hadn't time traveled. Something more diabolical was at work here. Maybe it was the warden fucking with her. Playing with her. Using her emotions and doctored texts and voicemails to get her to show herself, like how the guests used cat toys to coax the spirits into making contact. Maybe the warden was manipulating her phone to make her *think* she was going crazy …

Hannah took one good long inhale through her nose to clear her still-stuffed nostril and wiped the residual tears hanging from her eyelashes with the back of her hand. Nope, she thought. She would *not* allow the warden to mess with her like that.

"Plan failed, gaslighting asshole," she whispered and slapped her glasses back on her face. She unlocked her phone—still NO SERVICE across the top—and pressed the gear icon on the voicemail screen. She selected DELETE ALL and grinned when all ninety-nine notifications disappeared from the screen. "You gotta try harder than that, fucker."

"Hannah …?!"

She heard Christian's voice from the yard—the space between the main buildings. Hannah's heart leaped, and she rose from the cot so fast that she saw spots in her vision. Not wanting to pass out again, she paused to control her breathing and to convince herself to wait—to ensure this wasn't another of the warden's magic tricks to get her to come out.

Christian's voice carried from the outside of the building.

Hannah had to will herself not to reply, not to acknowledge him or to make her way down to flag him over just yet. Her gut told her to stay put.

Or maybe it was her brimmed-hat man helping her again. She quickly checked her phone for any further instructions on the app. It had not received any new communication since she had turned it off.

"Hannah! I'm hurt and scared. Where are you?"

She ran a hand along her belly to help squash the storm brewing in her stomach. The sound of Christian's voice, desperate and in need, quickened her pulse and accelerated her desire to protect him.

But she convinced herself that she needed more time before she did anything too brash that could jeopardize her own life. The fact that the warden had not materialized in her cell gave her hope that he didn't know where she was hiding.

"Come out and be cool, like Dano Zucko . . ." Christian's tone carried a tinge of taunting to it.

Hannah tapped her front teeth with two fingers as her brain quickly decoded the blunder of Christian's choice of words. Christian made that stupid *Grease* joke enough to where he would never mess up the main character's name. And the fact that Christian had nonchalantly confused the character's name with someone's real name who had just spent a few hours with them in here—*Dano* . . .

Hannah checked her phone again, an eerie pallor on her face from the glow of the screen in such a darkened atmosphere. The words, IT'S NOT HIM, scrawled across the app, a message from her shadow man, confirming she was already privy to Christian's subterfuge. One good thing about knowing someone as well as she knew Christian, the small tells would give him away.

She pulled the phone to her chest to hug it tightly—to help keep her emotions from spilling from her—and quietly lowered herself onto the cot again. She swallowed hard and prepared herself to ride out the wave of waiting patiently, until her shadow man gave the go-ahead to implement whatever plan he was formulating.

Christian's dissonate voice carried across the yard. "Hannah! I think I'm dying! I need you to come out here and help me!"

Hannah squeezed her eyelids shut as tightly as she could and pushed temptation into the abyss of her mind. She swallowed a small sob, and a single tear streaked her face.

Hannah crossed her legs and bounced her foot like a jackhammer as she stared at her phone, at the Casper-Capture app, waiting for the signal from her brimmed-hat man. Unconvinced the app was even working correctly anymore, she force-closed it, then relaunched it. Still no message.

The front door of the women's unit opened and slammed shut, and she held her breath. She scanned the room and contemplated sliding under the cot to give herself an added layer of protection if someone—some*thing*—just casually checked each cell. She debated executing that hiding plan or staying in her position. If Christian came this high, she could escape by running the opposite way and take refuge in one of the other buildings. A cat-and-mouse game that she needed to continuously win throughout the night to survive, but one that he only needed to win once to end her life.

Hannah strained her ears but could not hear any movement. No walking. No shuffling. Either that meant a disembodied warden was moving about like a shadow and she would have no idea when he landed on her floor or that whoever had entered stood motionless at the door. Maybe also listening for a movement or a sound.

Hannah remained frozen, controlling her breathing, which in turn controlled her heart rate. Keeping her panic at bay could be the difference between surviving the night or winding up like Reese, Lisa, and Jenny. Or worse.

The sound of something hard running slowly along the cell bars below wafted to the top floor. *Clink. Clink … Clink.*

Hannah frowned. *Someone dragging a sledgehammer across the bars as they walked to inevitably pummel her face*, she thought. The sound traveled away from her. Away from the staircase that would lead whoever was in here to the floors above them.

Christian's laugh from below filled the entire unit, masking the sound of the proverbial sledgehammer striking the bars for a moment. "I had to kill them all." His voice, deeper and tyrannical, felt as if it had come from the walls themselves and not from a single mouth below. "They failed at keeping all my inmates confined. Plus, they would have made you leave."

Clink. Clink … Clink.

"And I couldn't have *two* convicts escape my prison, now could I, *Hannaaaaaah* Ba Nan *Nah*?"

Hannah's breaths came in spurts. Remaining motionless and silent, while every fight-or-flight response went into overdrive in her body, proved to be a second-by-second struggle. Every fiber of her knew that wasn't the real Christian down there. It might be his body and his voice, but it was devoid of the man who she realized she loved—not a possession but an *otherness* of who he was.

"What kind of warden would that make me?" the Christian/warden-phantom continued. "A pitiful one, for sure. The first kill was hard—that little spitfire woman. I've been wanting to do that for *years*. The other two—well, fear can incapacitate even the ones who brag that they're the toughest. I killed them like plucking heads off dandelions. One. Two. Three. Pop. Pop. *Pop*!" His voice had hit the farthest point of the building from her, and she was still sure he was circling the bottom floor.

Hannah stared at the Casper-Capture app, every second feeling like an eternity. Looking for anything. Any sign that her shadow man was working on *something* to get her out of here. The screen remained blank.

"A soul leaving the body is like the finest moonshine, releasing the purest nodes of energy—energy I needed to hijack ole Halifax here."

Clink. Clink … Clink.

He had turned the corner and was working his way back to the staircase. "Energy ripe for the taking." He smacked his lips in delight.

The sound ricocheted off all the walls in her cell—or it came *from* the walls maybe.

"You fucking thief!" His voice rose so loud that it cracked, and his tone had deepened.

Hannah could feel his strife in her teeth.

"I despise *thieves*," he seethed.

Hannah focused on the sound of his footfalls and not on his voice to track his location. His voice sounded like he was making the walls talk, like the building was equipped with surround sound, so misleading her as to his position. But his steps pinpointed his whereabouts. And he had climbed the first few stairs.

"You belong here now too. By the power invested in me, I find you, *Hannaaaaaah* Ba Nan *Nah,* guilty of petty theft from the State of Missouri and of aiding and abetting an escaped convict! I hereby sentence you to an eternity right here in the women's unit."

Christian had hit the second level, and Hannah could not hear his sneakers shuffling anymore. He must have stopped to deliver the next part of his soliloquy.

"I could peel your skin like a fucking banana, Banana, if the mood strikes me, so it would behoove you to show yourself. Show yourself, and I'll ensure your transition is quick and painless, because I'm a rational warden. A fair warden. A *respectable* warden."

Footfalls climbed the second flight of stairs, and Hannah knew he had stopped again, probably trying to elicit some response from her. Maybe hope she made some sound, even just a cot creaking as she shifted her weight.

"If you want your friend to live, then turn yourself in. It's as easy as apple fucking pie."

Hannah glanced around her cell, at the walls behind her. Christian's voice oozed from their very stone material.

"A plea bargain, if you will. You for this groveling, spineless toy, who you have used as your pet and have kept around just to make you feel better about yourself. I almost snatched a two-for-one in Death Row just now, but your friend from cell 115 exited this mortal coil before I could commandeer both together. So now your *human* friend will just have to do."

Hannah's eyes widened, now knowing the cell number that had been the bane of her entire night. A little too late now. Hannah realized the Christian/warden-phantom had only revealed the cell number to taunt her of her failure. *What a colossal failure it had proved to be*, she thought.

"Both of you are pathetic. But I will release this boy-toy of yours. Hell, I'll personally escort him by the hand to the outside world and wave dismissively as he returns to his life. Just fucking show yourself, you bitch!" Christian hissed, like a snake.

In the solitude of her cell, Hannah closed her eyes and let memories of the past year with Christian flood her mind. The night when they had met—the day after she had been discharged from rehab. The first time he had smiled that signature smile at her, and the confusion it had brought her. His quick wit and humor, and how he had no qualms about teasing her. She remembered all the times he had made her laugh so hard that it hurt. The sparkle in his eyes when he would watch her laugh. The late-night phone calls and FaceTime. When he always would try to think of something else to say so she wouldn't hang up just yet …

"But it seems your accomplice with the stupid hat took a liking to you." Christian had reached the next floor. His voice still came from the walls around her, but it was louder. Closer. Like, if she touched the limestone, she would *feel* his voice.

"What do they call that? When the victim empathizes with their captor? *Hmm*? Anyone? Anyone?" Silence hung in the air for a while. "Stockholm Syndrome. Whoever down there on the first walkway just said that gets a prize. I will approve an extra day in the yard for you." He clapped his hands once and laughed maniacally. "But I need you to accept this trade—your sentencing in exchange for the release of this subpar vessel—and make yourself known."

Hannah remembered when Christian would tuck a wayward strand of hair behind her ear. The time when she had woken up from a nightmare about her mom dying, and she had called him at three in the morning. And he had answered, groggily, and spent an hour making everything okay enough so she could sleep the rest of the night …

"The problem, *Hannahhhh* Ba Nan *Nah,* is I haven't been able to see you for most of the night. And I don't like problems. I solve problems. I thought I got a glimpse of you during the bedlam of the riot. See? Chaos confuses them. It's a chink in their armor against me."

The memory of when he had shown up at her apartment the morning after she had to put her cat to sleep, and he had forced her to go to brunch with him. The silly messages he would send or pictures he would take that she knew were only meant for her to see. The night he had convinced her to let him make dinner for her after she and Dollard had gotten into a knock-out drag-down fight a few days prior and Dollard had stormed out, without contacting her for over a week, and while Christian finished cooking for her, he had accidentally flipped the pan with the entire entrée onto the floor from the stove—so he had taken her out for tacos at her favorite Mexican place …

"They riot every night." Christian traipsed up the next staircase.

One more and he would be on the same level as her.

"As if the riot will do any good. But I allow it, even if it exhausts me. Keeps them, shall we say, humble when they fail. Crestfallen. Easier to control."

How Christian had gifted her LEGO roses on Valentine's Day, because "LEGOs don't die." When she had gotten a flat tire one morning before the sun was up and had called him, he came out to change her tire on the side of the highway in his pajamas. And he had brought her a fresh coffee. Her favorite flavor too.

She realized those moments signified the pinnacle of her happiness and that Christian was her person. And why had she spent so much energy and time bucking against that idea? Was it because she *thought* she had a boyfriend who really cared? Who she had assumed was the right fit for her? Had that blinded her to Christian's version of Willy Wonka's golden ticket? When it had been right there for the taking all along?

Christian's chuckle emanated from the floor, ceiling, and walls surrounding Hannah. "Can't lie that I don't get *some* satisfaction in watching that snitch Donnell get his due every night. Sometimes it's the only thing I look forward to. Night after night, them smashing in his face with a sledgehammer."

She thought she heard Christian smack his lips, the same way he would do when he finished a plate of pancakes dripping with syrup, followed by the now-unmistakable sound of something heavy and metal running along the cell bars—the sledgehammer.

"But your accomplice from cell 115 had some powerful … friends in here. Friends who didn't partake in the riot. And they had pooled their energy during the riot to keep me from you. And they are still helping him right now. I can … *taste* them."

Christian's sneakers climbed the last set of stairs to reach the level where Hannah hid. "Don't you think it's a bit sick that they assume if they help you escape, they are escaping also? So fucking *delusional*."

Hannah checked the app again. No new message. She let her breathing get a bit deeper in preparation of needing to run or to fight.

And the idea of fighting Christian sent her into a tailspin. How could she ward off the man she loved? The man she knew loved her? If he found her in this cell and attacked, how could she violently defend herself? To possibly kill him, even if it meant she lived?

But she had to keep reminding herself that it *wasn't* the real Christian. The man she loved was not the same person as the despot creeping closer to find her.

"And I have a special place in the dungeon reserved for your friend from cell 115 when I get that closet strip back—when I get his soul back—for his indiscretions. An eternity behind a door that hasn't been opened in decades in the dungeon. But we know time works differently for us … haunts us differently than it does for the living. A night to you could be a year for us in here. A *year* of searching for you … Ba Nan *Nah*!"

Hannah removed the closet strip from her pocket and rubbed it between her fingers and immediately recalled the voicemail from Dollard: *It's been a year.* Maybe that wasn't a trick the warden was using against her.

Maybe all of this meant she—

A shadow figure gracefully stepped into the doorway of Hannah's cell, levitating a few inches above the floor. A female specter, whose skin resembled gray stone, like a weatherworn statue, filled the space. Hannah brought her knees to her chin and hugged her shins to pull her legs closer to her chest for protection. The full-bodied apparition didn't step into the cell as much as it glided, as if an invisible rope pulled her from somewhere inside the room.

The *schuw-schuw-schuw* of Christian's sneakers scrapping against each step of the next stairwell brought him closer to finding her. The sound of his ascent distracted Hannah for only a second. Then her shortness of breath became a reminder of the woman slowly floating toward her in the cell. Hannah scurried back on her palms and feet across the cot to wedge herself into the corner, thinking her own movements weren't much different from those of the Creeper on Death Row. Her sudden jerking backward caused her phone to slide off the cot, and it landed with a *clank!*

Hannah froze. The sound of her phone striking the cement seemed to reverberate through each hallway, bleeding from the crevices of each wall, then filtered down the stairwell. And she knew. She knew when she heard Christian stop walking.

But the sound that had revealed her hiding spot was only half her problem. The gray-skinned woman still hovered closer, dressed in gray prison garb that exuded a style from 150 years ago, as her whole being resembled a black-and-white photograph.

Hannah whimpered when her back hit the wall. She had nowhere else to go. She used the soles of her shoes to gain purchase against the mat and to slide her bottom so she was more in a laying position. She thought every inch might help if this uninvited guest had a predetermined limit that it could enter this cell.

Schuw-schuw-schuw. Christian's sneakers resumed their climb toward the top hallway. "That was pretty fucking loud, Hannah. Always the klutz. Always the goddamn one who makes a fucking mess of everything and everyone!"

Christian's voice seeped from the walls of Hannah's cell, but she knew it was not his words. Her gaze darted to the gray-skinned woman now hovering, motionless, in the middle of the cell. She spied her phone on the floor as Christian's footfalls reached the next landing and began their ascent to the floor below her.

The need to retrieve her phone from the floor to see if she was missing any advantageous instructions from her brimmed-hat man, the inmate from cell 115, overrode the fear that she would have to reach within inches of the gray-skinned apparition's prison shoes—overrode the fear that her movement might make more noise to help Christian, the *warden*, pinpoint her exact cell.

The realization that he already probably knew exactly where she was now sent a shiver up her spine, but it only got halfway before the shiver turned into a full-blown tidal wave. She spotted her cellmate standing in a silent vigil against the wall across from her, now staring at Hannah with eyes no longer there—eye sockets devoid of anything but an abyss of nothingness.

Hannah slowed her breathing, steadied her pulse, and closed her eyes. Her lips formed the words, but no sound came from her mouth. *God, grant me the serenity to accept the things I cannot change, the courage to change the things I can, and the wisdom to know the difference.*

With a burst of blind courage, Hannah opened her eyes, lunged forward, and swiped her phone off the floor, then scooted back into a defensive ball against the wall.

"*Haaaaaan-Nah.* Come out, come out, from the top floor."

Hannah studied the woman standing motionless and silent against the wall before Hannah could muster the shards of courage to check her Casper-Capture app for any messages from her brimmed-hat man.

Hannah's heart fluttered when the History tab showed unread messages. She clicked on the icon to read what she had missed: FOR COURAGE.

For courage? she wondered. A movement from the gray-skinned spirit standing in the cell startled Hannah, and she focused on the specter's outstretched hand—a rabbit's foot attached to a silver chain. The woman resumed being statuelike, her arm locked straight out, the parts of the chain that dangled through the spaces between her fingers still swaying from the movement.

"Parker's missing necklace from 3D," Hannah whispered mouselike. Hannah tried to meet the gray-skinned woman's gaze, but the apparition's empty eye sockets held nothing to discern. *I'm supposed to take it from you, aren't I?* she said more inside her head than aloud.

Hannah reread the message on the app: FOR COURAGE. She realized she would have to put blind faith in a shadow figure who had haunted her for the past seven years, put blind faith in a plan that she was a complete pawn in, but one that might be the only option for survival.

Christian's footfalls had turned the stairwell corner onto the final set of steps. "You fucking thief!" His tone was so venomous that she thought she heard spittle flying from his lips. "And you know, *Haaaaaaaanah* Ba Nan *Nah*. That you have stolen more than a stupid piece of fabric. Stolen more than one of my inmates." *Schuw-schuw-schuw* … "Stolen more than your own drunken years from yourself. Stolen more than this pathetic boy's heart. A heart I cannot *wait* to eat when I lock away for good both you and your friend from cell 115."

Then he growled so loudly that the venom coming from the walls inside her cell forced her to lean forward to create distance between herself and them.

"*No one* escapes from under my watch!"

Hannah's eyes widened when she realized he had reached the top step onto her floor and was sprinting down the skinny hallway toward her cell. She counted his steps in her head through her fatigue, realizing she could either freeze and accept her fate or—

Hannah snatched Parker's mislaid rabbit's foot from the gray-skinned figure, and as soon as the chain left the woman's hand, the apparition rose and beelined from the cell—or Hannah thought it looked more like that signature *whoosh* that the peekers made when they disappeared. Now alone in the cell, Parker's necklace dangling from her hand and Christian's steps coming like a freight train toward her from the left, Hannah almost dropped her phone when her Casper-Capture app filled the tiny cell with its voice.

"Front door is open. Used my last energy."

Hannah took a deep breath, squeezed the soft fur of the rabbit's foot, dug her heels into the dusty and plaster-strewn floor, and bolted from the cell. She hooked right onto the hallway and pushed her legs to move faster than she had ever before.

An animal's wail erupted from behind her on the hallway, and she shoved her glasses farther up her nose as she ran and chanced a glance behind her.

A fog or mistlike substance covered Christian's face. Hannah couldn't decipher his features, as if she were trying to look through a steamed bathroom mirror.

"She's a friend," came from her phone.

Hannah looked ahead to get her equilibrium just long enough to glance backward again. This time the image of the gray-skinned lady fluttered and blinked in and out of existence, like a hologram trying to find stability, as she fought back Christian—the warden.

Christian's scream morphed from human vocal cords into sludge. Murky. Guttural.

"Please get us both out," came the voice from the app.

Hannah reached the end of the walkway, and she spun to turn the corner to head down the length of another row of cells that would circumnavigate her to the staircase to bring her downstairs. To bring her to the lobby. To bring her to the hopefully unlocked front door.

To freedom.

Hannah's sneakers and panting as she ran became louder than Christian's choking and muddied wailing, and she swallowed hard when she realized she was leaving Christian behind. She was leaving her best friend, her everything, here alone to the mercy of the warden.

"No, Hannah Banana," she whispered to herself, "that is not Christian anymore."

She knew the real Christian—*her* Christian—was gone when Big Boy had yanked him backward into the shadows of Death Row. What was upstairs was just an empty vessel.

"Fucking whore!" Christian said, his voice no longer pregnant with anger, no longer wrestling with the gray-skinned lady—now free to pursue her. Hannah didn't know if Christian was referring to her or to the gray-skinned woman.

Hannah hit the first step and let momentum and gravity take her down, down, down. She heard Christian's sneakers reach the top step above her. As long as he matched her speed or went a hair slower, she could reach the bottom. And she was confident that she could outrace him on flat ground.

Hannah grabbed the railing on her left to whip herself around the corner to the next descending staircase. Christian's grunts and groans as he skipped downward stayed a beat behind her.

Hannah hit the next landing, spun herself onto the next set of steps, and her hand, wet from moisture and sweat, slipped from the metal railing. She stumbled and slammed against the wall, the collision making the sole of her sneaker miss the next stair, and both feet went airborne. Hannah's back smashed against the concrete steps, arms flailing to grab any part of the railing.

Christian chuckled behind her. His breath seemed to just tickle the hairs on the back of her neck.

Hannah regained control of her limbs and buckled her knees so her feet planted firmly on the step. Shins scraped, Hannah suppressed the burning pain under her jeans and remained focused on the bottom of the stairs.

Christian was less than an arm's reach away when she hit the bottom step and blasted through the sallyport door and through the lobby.

Hannah's huffs and puffs filled her ears as Christian's growl sounded less than a half step behind. She focused on the unobstructed glass front door—the cell bars now slid aside, her brimmed-hat man coming through on his promise to her. To *both* of them, she thought, as she felt the weight of the closet strip in her front right pocket with every lift of her leg.

Now ten yards from freedom, Hannah saw Christian's reflection in the glass doors ahead of her. His face was a void yet swirling within a whirlpool of moving maggots where the gray-skinned woman had accosted him. His clothes hung off him as if draped on a skeleton. His now long and boney fingers reached for her.

"He has no power outside," said the voice coming from her phone in back pocket.

The warden couldn't leave.

Christian couldn't leave.

But she could. And she could take her brimmed-hat friend with her.

On purpose this time.

For saving her life.

Hannah's sneakers dug into the Welcome mat that lay on the inside of the entryway, and she used both hands to push the bar that would open the door.

The door swung outward, and Christian's skeletal hand grazed her shoulder, sending a searing pain of a million flames through her back.

Hannah heard Christian scream through a maggot-filled maw as his arm broke the threshold that separated the inside of the penitentiary and the outside world. But his grip tightened like a vise, crushing her collar bone and shoulder blade and turning them into fine dust beneath her skin. She bellowed in pain as she tried to writhe free and looked behind her into the mass of swarming maggots where his face should be.

The Christian/Warden-phantom yanked Hannah backward, her left arm dangling loosely from her torso, with only tendons now to keep it in place.

Hannah backpedaled two steps, and her heel struck the interior Welcome mat. She felt the Christian/Warden-phantom reaching to grip her right shoulder and arm to yank her all the way back inside—perpetual obliteration of those bones inevitable.

With a mere second to act, Hannah made a decision.

She reached into her right front pocket with the remaining moment or two she had left before his viselike grip crushed her bones into dust inside her body. She pinched the closet strip and snatched it from its hiding place.

With the fabric balled into her fist, Hannah chucked it like a baseball toward the sidewalk.

Then her right arm and shoulder shattered into dust.

Her feet flew out front underneath her.

And the back of her skull landed on the lobby floor, her gaze pointing skyward through the open door at the twinkling stars now dimming to give way for dawn. Her glasses bounced off her face from the impact and skidded beyond her clarity of vision.

The last thing Hannah saw before the darkness consumed her was the missing face of swirling maggots coming down upon her.

And the last thing Hannah imagined before the Christian/Warden-phantom imprisoned her forever was her brimmed-hat friend's closet strip laying beyond the reaches of the warden on the sidewalk.

I've won. I freed him. Freed us both … she thought, finally finding solace.

Then nothingness.

CHAPTER 14:
INSIDE THE WARDEN'S MANSION

Sunlight fractured through the centuries'-old windowpanes inside one of the many sprawling rooms of the warden's mansion, the window sash climbing higher than anyone could reach without a ladder. The view of the massive limestone cathedral-like structure of Housing Unit 3 across the street filled only the bottom of the glass. The inmate-built wooden panels on the walls in this room still permeated a pleasant forestry scent. Traces of authority and dominance resided in these walls, even if the bottom floor now served as the penitentiary's museum and the top floors housed the segmented offices for the Jefferson City Tourism and Travel department.

Sheila stood silent, next to the construction crew foreman, looking over the few remaining buildings that comprised the bloodiest forty-seven acres in America. The wrecking ball at the end of the tall crane swung and collided with the side of the building that contained 3D.

Sheila shuddered and closed her eyes for a moment. Memories replayed behind her eyelids. For two decades, she had overseen the prison tours to the public—both historic tours and ghost hunts. She had memories of the delight from ghosthunters when they thought they had experienced something paranormal or otherworldly. Awe on the faces of the children during school field trips on the historic tours. People from all walks of life, from all over the world, getting a taste of the history and culture of Missouri that dated back centuries.

Shiela took a deep breath and stepped backward, her weight creaking the ancient wooden floor. But those images of delight and wonder always morphed with what they had found the morning after their last ghost hunt.

"You …" The foreman cleared his throat. "You okay there?"

Sheila opened her eyes to see the wrecking ball swinging backward, preparing to make another run at Death Row. She met the foreman's gaze, tears prickling at the corners of her eyes. "Today is the anniversary, Barker."

The man nodded solemnly.

"One year ago today was that vile ghost hunt, where we lost so much more than just the tours."

Barker put a reassuring hand on her shoulder. "We're doing the right thing, Shiela. Tearing it all down."

Sheila wiped away the tear threatening to spill down her cheek. "Oh, you don't have to tell me. Good fucking riddance."

Barker stared back out the window as the third strike from the wrecking ball finally sent Death Row crumbling to the ground in a plume of dust … and maybe something more. Secrets hidden. "Are you sleeping okay?"

Sheila shook her head, even though she knew he wasn't looking at her—fixated on the first of four buildings that would be no more after this week. "Not since the anniversary approached. I–I can't get their faces—what was done to their *bodies*—out of my mind. Those tour guides may have only worked for me, but they were family."

"And never any word on the missing girl?" Barker asked.

Sheila sniffed in deeply to compose herself and to stop some snot from leaking out. "I've kept in touch with Hannah's family. I even called her ex-boyfriend, Dollard, this morning. I thought they'd want to know that the first of the buildings were coming down today."

"And I'm sure it's harder on them today as well. It being the one-year mark and all."

Sheila silently nodded. "Dollard said he had just left the last voicemail this morning, to say his final goodbye to her, but doubted she would ever hear any of the messages he had left her. Told me that he couldn't put himself through the constant empty hopes anymore."

Barker flinched when the wrecking ball swung again, this time setting the housing unit side of the building to collapse on itself.

Sheila turned away and scanned the grandiose and ornate room, wallpapered with designs and fashions of a bygone era, and the space beyond where she stood. The ceilings were as high as a ballroom. The staircase as intricate as something on a luxury cruise liner from the Roaring Twenties. The ceiling as decorated and resplendent as a cathedral.

And behind her, through the warped windowpane, the history of almost two hundred years—of countless men and women—would fall within days.

"How did you end it with Hannah's family?" Barker asked, still looking across at the demolition.

"I told them that my thoughts would be with them for the rest of my life. And if I found any information that might lead to her whereabouts, they would be the first I would call."

Sheila folded her arms and let her vision go into a thousand-mile stare across the yard as her gaze landed on Housing Unit 4.

Barker stepped backward to stand alongside her. The two watched in silent brooding as the wrecking ball swung again, for good measure, that Housing Unit 3 would not try to get up and fight for life. "Can I ask you something, Shiela?"

"*Mmm-hmm.*"

Barker faced the curator of the property. "Do you think she's still alive?"

Sheila sighed heavily and stared at her feet. "We have found no trace of her. Anywhere. In any of the buildings or around the property. There are enough underground tunnels and hidden cells here where that asshole may have buried her."

"You still think her friend killed them all? And her?"

Shiela walked to the large oak dining room table and picked up her half-drunk cup of coffee. "Who else would have done it? I just don't know how he could have had enough strength to do what he did to their bodies."

"The tour guides?" Barker asked, pulling a piece of gum from his pocket.

Sheila turned and glared at Barker. "Jenny. Reese. And Lisa. Not just *the guides.*"

"I–I didn't mean any disrespect."

Sheila took a deep breath and ran a fingernail through her eyebrow. "No, no. I'm sorry. I'm just really on edge. It's the end of an era. One of the longest eras of American history. And we still have a missing girl. Police have filed it as a cold case now. They're convinced Christian was the murderer. They interviewed the other guests who were with Hannah and Christian during the ghost-hunting walkthrough, as well as the Get Haunted people. They all described Christian as jumpy and hostile. The two women who were part of their breakout group said, in their official statements, that it sounded like Hannah and Christian were arguing a lot during the tour."

"Didn't he get into a fistfight with one of the guys from the group?"

Sheila sighed. "Yes, and I think we kicked out the wrong person. Maybe everyone would still be alive and that young woman would be home safe with her family, if Duncan had thrown out Christian too. Or *only* threw out that fucker."

Barker stepped closer to the window to watch the wrecking ball come to rest, while the crew in the yard repositioned the crane toward Housing Unit 4. "Wait." He turned to face Sheila. "Didn't he steal something too?"

Sheila shook her head. "No, that was Hannah." Shiela reached high on a glorious mahogany bookcase that housed shopworn volumes of encyclopedias and drew down a long strip of fabric. "The morning staff saw this outside on the sidewalk before they found the bodies of the night guides in Death Row. When the police interviewed Get Haunted, Rob said Hannah had come that night to return it, thought she had brought some ghost home with her who was attached to it."

"And do you believe that?" Barker asked.

"I'm not quite sure I know what I believe anymore," Shiela answered in an eerie monotone.

Barker frowned. "If this theory is true, I wonder what will happen to all the haunts who are attached to all the items in the prison after we finish all the demolitions and move everything off the property."

"I'm trying *not* to think about that, to be honest." Sheila reached high again to stow the closet fabric from cell 115 back atop the bookshelf and turned and froze. Saliva filled her mouth as her pulse quickened.

"Everything all right?" Barker asked.

"*Huh*? Yeah, yeah. Fine," Shiela said, trying to blink away the image of a short man wearing a brimmed hat, standing in the doorway of her office.

"I heard something went missing from one of the guests on the night of the murders."

"Yep." Sheila took a sip of her coffee as she looked past Barker's shoulder toward A-Hall and the women's unit in the background, training her gaze ahead and not behind her where the brimmed-hat shadow figure had been standing. "Stole a necklace from that young man that he got into the fight with. The rabbit's foot was around Chistian's neck when we found him the next morning, all burned up in the gas chamber. Like Jenny used to say, *All tours end in the gas chamber*." Sheila stifled a sob at the memory of her deceased—no *murdered*; that fucker had slain her—tour guide.

No, not just a tour guide. A friend, Sheila thought.

Barker put his hands on his waist. "And you think he burned himself after killing Lisa, Reese, and Jenny? Like a mass murder-suicide? That's a horrific way to go."

Sheila set the cup on the long dining room table and furrowed her brows at the foreman, her face glum. "No. I think this place took matters into its own hands. And did what it does best. It rights its wrongs. Always."

The wrecking ball took its first swing into the side of A-Hall.

CHAPTER 15:
OUTSIDE OF MISSOURI STATE PENITENTIARY

Christian stopped the rental car in front of the ominous stone entrance to the bloodiest forty-seven acres in America. The two-glass front doors and an array of windows peered down at the roadway, judging its nightly tour of guests and choosing which of those guests the abandoned prison's disembodied inhabitants will play with tonight.

Christian leaned over Hannah, who sat in the passenger seat, to get a better view of the two sprawling castle-like towers on either side of the Missouri State Penitentiary entrance. Those towers stretched beyond his vision and looked as if they had suffered and had weathered their own arduous battles—internal and external—and had lost more than they had won.

"I told you that I don't want to talk about it anymore," Hannah said into the phone as Christian found an empty parking spot farther down the road from the prison.

"Looks like a full house. Did you see how many people were already lined up?" he asked.

After they had parked and positioned themselves at the end of the line, a short firecracker of woman walked the length of the crowd, reminding everyone to have their waivers signed before entry, to help expedite the process.

Hannah smiled at Christian and watched him shrug his backpack off his shoulder. She wondered what he could possibly have inside that raggedy old thing anyway. She figured it was really none of her business and slipped her hand into the front right pocket of her jeans to pinch the long piece of fabric that she had stolen from a cell seven years ago tonight.

Hannah only hoped that she could find the cell that she had swiped the piece of memorabilia from and could return it to its rightful owner, finally closing a long and tumultuous chapter of her life.

"Remind me what the different kind of haunts are, Banana," Christian said.

"*Intelligent* are ones that we can communicate with. *Residuals* are ones that are imprinted, like memories, usually traumatic, replaying over and over. I am most fascinated by residual hauntings, for sure!"

As the line filed toward the entrance of the lobby, Hannah and Christian smiled at each other, a bounce in her step that tonight would be good night and would provide an opportunity to right a wrong …

AUTHOR'S NOTE:
A STORY ABOUT THE STORY . . .
AND MY DIARY OF PARANORMAL EXPERIENCES WHILE WRITING THE NOVEL

Writing a novel about a ghost hunt gone wrong had never been on my radar as an author. Ever. I also never considered writing a novel where I based every character on a real person who had close ties to the source material. Funny how the universe can throw curveballs at you and put you somewhere you never expected to be.

I never imagined being in Missouri for eighteen weeks for job training, which was split into two phases. The first phase lasted ten weeks, with a three-week break back home, then the second phase was eight weeks long.

During the ten-week phase, a colleague mentioned that the Missouri State Penitentiary hosted overnight ghost hunts. I'm from Salem, MA. I love horror. I love ghosts. I love creepy buildings. Yet I had never done anything like this before. So, a group of us attended their five-hour overnight hunt.

After that initial five-hour hunt, I was so enamored with the experience that I immediately bought tickets for the following weekend's eight-hour ghost hunt. A caveat to this hunt, however, was that Get Haunted and the New England Society for Psychic Research (NESPR) were hosting it, bringing with them artifacts from Ed and Lorraine Warren's Occult Museum. (You might recognize those names as the demonologists whose real-life supernatural cases inspired *The Conjuring* & *Annabelle* film series.)

I attended the event with Parker and Christian (the irony that they become almost sworn enemies in my book is not lost on me) and some other colleagues. But this event also drew enthusiasts from all over the country who wanted to ghost hunt alongside Get Haunted or wanted to get close and personal with the Warrens' private collection.

Rob from Get Haunted separated the guests into groups and serendipitously combined Hannah and her friend Lizzy with me, Christian, Parker, and the rest of our crew. Later, during free roam, I met Taylor, whose middle name is Marie (as in both Taylor-Made Technology and the Marie character.) At some point—I think we were in 3D—a proverbial lightbulb went off over my head, and I thought, *I think there's a book here. I don't quite know what it is yet, but there's something …*

Later that week, I sent tour guide Jenny an unsolicited message on social media, explaining my idea. Her enthusiasm oozed from her reply, and she suggested that my barracks roommate, Heath, and I attend a history tour at the penitentiary the following Saturday morning, where we could gab more about my idea. It wasn't until I had the notion to write the entire novel inside the penitentiary—during the wee hours of the night, while ghost tours and hunts happened around me—that this project took on a life of its own. I must have said the right things to Jenny during Heath's and my visit, because she promised to discuss my proposal with her boss, Shiela.

And trust me, they vetted me before they gave me an answer.

And the answer was an excited and a resounding *Yes!*

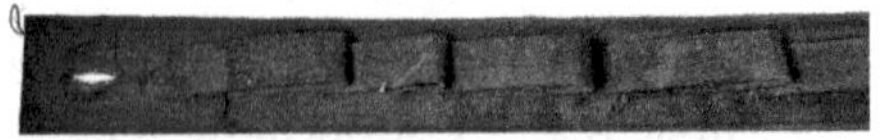

However, the yes came with some cans and can'ts, dos and don'ts. The rule that would prove most beneficial to the writing was Sheila's permission for me to stay unaccompanied in any of the open buildings of the Missouri State Penitentiary (MSP), as long as a staff member was on the property somewhere. Full access to write in any cell, in any accessible building. Alone. In the middle of the night. In the darkness.

On the first night, I decided to notate anything paranormal or unexplainable that happened to me. In the book's universe, my characters use Taylor-Made Technology's Casper-Capture app. I based this app on a similar real ghost-hunting app, which converts electromagnetic frequencies into words pulled from a database. I left the real app activated on my phone next to me whenever I wrote, wherever I was on the property. In my diary below, whenever I write, "and the app said ____," I am referencing what the real-life app conveyed on my phone.

While every character in this book is either a real MSP tour guide, a member of Get Haunted, or someone who I spent time with inside the penitentiary, I assigned different roles to some people to fill all spots. The three most notable changes are the real-life MSP tour guides Dano, Barker, and Duncan. I promoted Dano to the Coast Guard and made him a guest. Barker found a side hustle as a demolition team foreman. But the not-so-farfetched change was Duncan, who I reactivated from real-life police retirement to switch his tour guide shirt with his old Jefferson City PD uniform one last time.

Alisha is my younger sister who flew to Missouri from Salem, MA, to spend a weekend at MSP—the same weekend Hannah & Taylor (Marie) visited again to hang out while I wrote. Christian was the only character who I gave a full name. His fabricated last name, *Halifax*, exists purely as a private joke between me, Shiela, and Jenny.

And the identity of Hannah's boyfriend, Dollard, resides within my horror novel, *Welcome to Parkview.*

Before I let my diary loose on you, I want to reiterate how I could not have written this book without the MSP staff's hospitality, trust, and, most important, friendship while I "squatted" there for eight weekends, as well as the enthusiasm and welcoming support from the entire Get Haunted network. My gratitude is boundless toward Hannah, who remained an open book (pun intended) regarding her own sordid history and personal demons. Without her brutal honesty and specific details about her past while I outlined the novel, my protagonist's conflict and motivation would never exist.

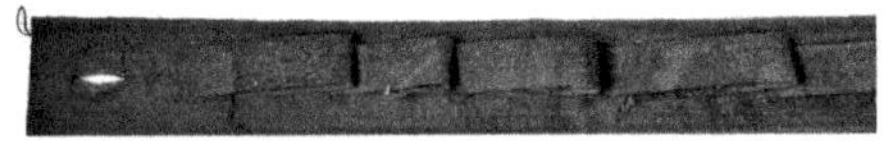

Night #1: I was sitting on the bench next to the payphones in A-Hall when I opened my laptop to begin the novel. I do not mention Hannah in the novel's first paragraph. However, in the second paragraph, I do. The moment I finished typing her name for the first time, the app on my phone said, "Hannah." Her name coming from a voice on my phone, while I was completely alone in A-Hall, within seconds of me typing it for the first time in the novel, blew my mind. I screenshotted Hannah's name in the app and texted it to her. I hadn't said her name out loud. How did it know I had typed her name? Who was watching and communicating? Goose bumps covered my body when I realized I probably wasn't alone in A-Hall.

Later I had three different guests (who weren't there together) show me their phones where their apps had said my name. I was in A-Hall writing, and another guest asked, "Who's Brian? My app keeps saying this name." Jenny had warned me that the peekers knew I was coming.

(1700 – 0300 = 10 hours)

Night #2: My app said, *"I remember you,"* multiple times after I arrived.

A daytime history tour guide, Lily, showed me her phone, where her app had said my name that morning before I had arrived.

Later, at dusk, while I wrote in A-Hall, the app asked, *"Who are you?"* I answered aloud, "You know who I am. I'm the one writing the book. Who are you?" The app replied, *"Forty-three."* I noticed cell 43 was directly in front of me, one row up. Of anything in the whole world it could've replied as an answer, it said the exact cell number across from me and up one walk, which I could plainly see inside the cell from where I sat. Then it said, *"Book."* I took it as maybe whoever resided in cell 43 was curious about the book? So, I wrote inside cell 43 for a while.

After I left the cell, I sat with Duncan and Adrienne (a cashier) in the center of A-Hall. The app said, *"Come up"* and *"Where did you go?"* … almost as if whoever occupied cell 43 didn't like that I had left, and they wanted me to come back inside to write.

Then it said, *"Christian,"* right after I had typed Christian's name.

(0900 – 1700 / 1900 – 0200 = 15 hours)

Night #3: The app asked what I was doing here again, and I would always answer, "You know what I'm doing here. I'm writing a book." This time the app said, *"Horror."* Then asked, *"Where are you from?"* I said, "Salem, Massachusetts," and it replied, *"Ritual. Witch."*

While I silently debated which character would sit in the gas chamber chair first for the Estes Method scene in chapter five, my app said, *"Marie."* This was now the third time the app knew a character's name, and this time I wasn't even typing; I was mentally deciding which character I wanted to use in the scene.

I began writing tonight with a fully charged laptop battery, which usually gives me two days' worth of work time. My laptop ran out of battery within four hours. I actually watched the percentage count down. MSP has countless stories of guests trying to take photos with their phones, but the phones power down due to depleted batteries.

(1700 – 0200 = 9 hours)

Night #4: An indie film director will be shooting a movie titled *Vincent Said Violence* at MSP tomorrow morning, and my app said, *"Movie,"* twice and kept saying, *"Screen."*

I was writing the first scene where Duncan escorts the group to the next location, and my app said his real first name.

Trevor from Get Haunted visited MSP to hang out while I wrote and to attend the overnight ghost hunt. We were in A-Hall, just the two of us, before the ghost hunt started. I was sitting at my writing desk across from cell 43, and Trevor was sitting on the blue bench (which was a church pew from the old chapel) next to the payphones. From nowhere, he yelled, "Brian, what the fuck is that?!" and stood from the bench.

I looked down A-Hall toward the stairs that led to the dungeon and saw a black mass, low to the ground, skitter across the hall. I rose and asked him what he had seen. I wanted to hear his description before I told him what I had seen, for corroboration. Trevor said he saw a peeker standing outside a cell and behind one of the movie projectors by the stairs to the dungeon, then it lowered itself and crawled across the floor—imagine the Creeper from Death Row.

Later in the night, during the ghost hunt, Trevor went with me to 3D so I could write down there (as that was one of two places I would never go by myself). Two women were at the end of the horseshoe by the shower—where the warden appears behind Dano in the book. I asked one of them to take a picture of me and Trevor, and, right after she did, my app said, *"Katherine."* I asked the two women if that name meant anything to them, since I didn't have a character in my book named Katherine, and they gasped. Both of their middle names were Katherine! And spelled with a *K*, just like the app had transcribed.

I sat in the metal chair at the end of 3D, and after I wrote when Hannah calls Christian a "real Danny Zucko," my app said, *"Funny."*

(0800 – 1600 / 1900 – 0200 = 15 hours)

Night #5: I was sitting by myself at my writing desk across from cell 43 in A-Hall, and I kept seeing peekers from all the different walkways going in and out of cells in my peripheral vision, along with hearing shuffling sounds right above me. Occasionally I would hear loud bangs from the cells, like a cell door had slammed shut. I was the only one in A-Hall, as all the staff were in the office, and the doors hadn't opened yet to the public.

I stood from my writing desk to go to the office for a cup of coffee, and my app said, *"Don't leave."*

When I returned to A-Hall and sat at my writing desk, I heard my first disembodied voice whisper something. I couldn't decipher the words, but it sounded like someone had their lips right against my ear. I flinched and looked around, and my app said, *"Watching you."*

Then I heard someone dragging something in the dungeon, and my app said, *"Under."* Then a loud burst of noise came from the dungeon, like an elongated cough. When I told Jenny about this later, she said the inmates sometimes had to carry their own foot lockers. That dragging noise sounded like someone dragging a heavy object backward, take a few steps, then drag it toward them, then step backward, then drag again, etc.

Still alone in A-Hall, now with the sun setting, hearing the dragging sound, the coughing, the whisper in my ear, the shuffling from above, the cell door slamming, and seeing the peekers doing what they do best, my nerves had reached the point where I needed music or something to settle my anxiety. I put Johnny Cash on Shuffle on my phone, and I asked aloud if it was okay if I played music, and the app said, *"Phone."*

The first tour of the night entered A-Hall, so I paused the music. When the tour left A-Hall, I asked, "If you want me to keep playing music, make a noise." Nothing happened. A-Hall remained silent. I asked a second time, and two loud bangs came from above on one of the walkways. I was completely alone. I hit Play on the Johnny Cash playlist again, and the app said, *"Singing,"* and *"Sing,"* back-to-back.

I was finishing a scene where Duncan delivers guests to a new location, and my app said the real Duncan's first name three times in a row. If you know anything about these apps, they very rarely repeat anything in succession—never mind someone's name three times!

Then the app asked, *"Why is he here?"* I replied, "I'm writing a book." And the app replied, *"Annoying,"* then, *"Go away."* I asked, "Who wants me to go away?" And the app replied, *"Nine."* Here we go again; cell 9 was directly across from me on the bottom level.

(1700 – 0200 = 9 hours)

Night #6: While alone and before guests were allowed inside for the ghost hunt, I played Johnny Cash again in A-Hall, across from cell 43, while I wrote the scene where Hannah sees the brimmed-hat man in front of that cell; yes, I picked that cell for the book because it seemed to keep talking to me. The app said, *"Singing / Elderly / Horror,"* in rapid succession—"singing" and "elderly" referencing Johnny Cash, and "horror" referencing the book? And the peekers were peeking again.

I entered cell 42 to write—next door to my ghostly friend in 43—and the app said, *"William. Forty-two."* Had someone named William stayed in cell 42? I didn't have a character in the book named William, and I was all alone in A-Hall. And the app had said the name and the cell number in the same burst.

Many MSP guides claim that sometimes something throws pebbles at them while they give tours. Something kept skipping small rocks across the floor from farther down the row of cells at me while I wrote at my desk. I watched one skitter and stop right before my chair.

Again, the app said Duncan's real-life first name while writing a scene that involved him.

I had been using the term "grated door" to describe the section of fence in 3D that separates the ending portion of the corridor, but I didn't like the way it sounded. As I stared at my screen, contemplating what would be a better term, my app said, *"Gate,"* which made perfect sense. The timing and the word choices of the app couldn't be coincidences, especially going back to night #1, where it had said Hannah's name after I had typed it for the first time.

The overnight ghost hunt had begun, so guests roamed the buildings. One amateur ghost-hunting troop invited me to write in 3D while they investigated. Again, 3D and the dungeon were the only two places on the property where I would not go by myself but were my two favorite places on the property to work. So I never said no to an opportunity to write there.

When we got down to 3D, I sat on the infamous metal chair at the end of the horseshoe, while the small team set up their gear: a handful of Rem Pods, several cat balls, K2 meters, a device that would change color based on yes or no questions, and phone apps that registered frequencies. I mentioned how the peekers had responded to music in A-Hall, so one of the guests played some '50s and '60s doo-wop. All their Rem Pods, K2s, and other devices blinked to the beat of the music. When she changed songs on her phone, the devices changed their flashing to match the new beat. The guests said they had never seen anything like it.

As I told them about an incident in 3D involving Big Boy and the tour guide Marianne during a ghost hunt, one of the guest's app said, *"Marianne, ha-ha-ha."* It actually said her name and laughed! They had a device that, when you asked a question, if the light turned green, the spirit was answering yes, and if the light turned red, the spirit was answering no. We asked if whoever was down in 3D liked Marianne, and the device glowed green. We asked if they thought it was funny about what had happened to her, and it glowed green. We asked if we should call Marianne down to 3D now, and it glowed green.

I knew Marianne was with Jenny somewhere on the property, so I called Jenny's phone and told her to send Marianne to 3D. About five minutes later, Marianne turned the corner at the end of the corridor to approach us, and all the Rem Pods flashed excitedly.

I left 3D to return to A-Hall, and another guest was heading into the dungeon and asked if I wanted to go with her to write while she sat down there. We chose the In-Your-Face cell, and she stood in the middle of the room, while I sat in the metal chair in the corner. After a bit, her app said, *"Can you feel it?"*

She asked me, "What do you think that means? Feel what?" Then something pulled her ponytail so hard that it yanked her head to the side. Next we heard what sounded like fingernails tapping from left to right on the walls behind my head.

I had started accompanying the staff at the end of each night to do a sweep of the buildings to ensure no guests were inside, to shut off the lights, and to lock the doors. Jenny and I were clearing Housing Unit 1, and we walked through a patch of heavy perfume hanging in the air. The building was empty; the guests had been gone for a while. Jenny said it was common for guests and the staff to smell a strong perfume odor in the women's unit. We both smelled it, and it was so strong that I almost choked on it. Then it vanished.

(0900 – 1700 / 1900 – 0300 = 16 hours)

Night #7: I was sitting at my writing desk alone in A-Hall, before any guests were allowed inside, and my app said, *"Over here,"* twice back-to-back. I looked up and saw a peeker dip into cell 44 right above me, then another peeker disappeared into the back left corner.

Later Lisa and Dano brought their ghost tour into A-Hall, and while Lisa gave her speech about the building, we heard two extremely loud crashes at the end of the hall from inside a cell near the staircase to the dungeon. Lisa called out, asking if anyone was there. Of course no one was there. I had been the only person inside the building until the tour had entered a few moments ago. Dano and I approached the back of A-Hall, calling out into the darkness to see if someone—or something—would answer. To be on the safe side, Lisa did a head count of the guests, and everyone was accounted for. Dano and I scanned each cell with our flashlights to no avail. When we turned to head back to the group, we saw all the guests standing, on edge, watching us.

We never found anything that could have made that loud of a noise.

Toward the end of the night, I was alone in A-Hall again, sitting in the dark at my writing desk, and my app said, *"Twenty-eight."* Cell 28 was the cell that my writing desk sat directly beside, less than three feet from its entrance. Any time the app said a number, it was always a cell that I could see from where I sat, and the numbers were getting closer to my location …

(1700 – 0200 = 9 hours)

Night #8: When I arrived in A-Hall and sat at my writing desk, before any tours started, I put my music on Shuffle. The first song my phone played was by the band Mudvayne. The first message to come across my app was, *"Horrible."* I laughed and changed the music to Johnny Cash.

After a bit, I went to use the Porta Potty outside A-Hall and left my laptop on my writing desk. When I returned, the writing program I use had been shut down. I have been using this program since 2017. This novel is the eighth book I have written using this specific program. It has never shut down before. You must complete multiple steps and click on numerous tabs to close it. Was someone or something messing with my laptop again?

I went into cell 43 again to write and took a photo from inside the cell, looking down at my writing space, to get the vantage point of whatever had been watching me from here. As soon as I took the photo, the app said, *"I see you."* I replied, "I don't see you. Are you in here with me?" The app said, *"There's three. Haunted."*

I sat on the cot to write and heard voices speaking softly below and banging sounds. I heard a male voice so clear that I got up and exited the cell because I thought Mike, the tour guide, had entered A-Hall prematurely with his group. Nope. A-Hall was still empty.

I left MSP to have dinner with Jenny, and when I returned and sat at my writing desk in A-Hall, the app said, *"You're back."*

Before I wrote more of the novel, I added to the thanks list. When I wrote Fred's name, the app said, *"Fred."* Then it said, *"Forty-one,"* which was another cell right above me. I looked up at the cell's entryway, and the app said, *"Behind you."* A breeze blew on my neck, then it said, *"Scream."*

(0800 – 1600 / 1900 – 0200 = 15 hours)

Night #9: My younger sister Alisha flew in from Salem, MA, for the weekend. I entered A-Hall by myself before the guests arrived and sat at my writing desk, while Alisha finished acclimating herself with the property. I started playing Johnny Cash, and my app said, *"Turn it off."*

A few seconds before Alisha entered A-Hall, my app asked, *"Who is she?"* I didn't know Alisha was about to open the door to the building, so I asked, "Who is who?" The app replied, *"In front of you,"* as Alisha opened the metal door to A-Hall.

I stopped the music to chat with Alisha and to give her a brief tour, and the app said, *"Sing."* I asked, "Do you want me to play Johnny Cash again?" The app replied, *"Forty-six,"* which was the cell we were standing in front of.

After I gave Alisha a brief tour, I returned to my writing desk to work on the book, and the app asked, *"What is this? Horror?"*

(1900 – 0200 = 7 hours)

Night #10: Real-life characters graced tonight's ghost hunt. My sister Alisha was still here, and Hannah and her friend Lizzy were driving from Iowa, and Taylor (Marie) and her friend Victoria were coming in from Kansas City. Hannah was bringing a doll that doubled as a Rem Pod to use during the hunt.

I was in A-Hall alone, standing at my writing desk and waiting for everyone to arrive, and I heard a disembodied male voice by the dungeon staircase say, "Sit down!"

Alisha came into A-Hall to wait with me, and her app kept saying, *"Knots,"* repeatedly. (Yes, it was spelled *knots* on the screen, but it's the phonetic of the word that will mean something to people who know why that is significant). Right before Hannah and Lizzy arrived, Alisha's app said, *"Abigail."* That name meant nothing to us at the time, until later, when Hannah introduced us to her Rem Pod doll that she had named … you guessed it, Abigail!

I was in A-Hall writing, while Alisha joined Jenny's ghost tour to learn more about the buildings. Alisha and Jenny told me the following accounts of events later that night: They were on the first floor of Housing Unit 1 (the women's unit), and the guests stood against the wall, facing the row of cells. One guest, named Jennifer Tissot—at the time a stranger to us (she gave me permission to retell this story and to share the photo)—raised her phone and casually snapped a photo of the cell in front of her. She gasped and showed the picture to Alisha and Jenny. Ms. Tissot did not have time to doctor or edit the photo from the time she had taken it until when she showed people. The detail in the fingers extending between the cell bars is astonishing. Of course, after Jenny forwarded that photo to me, I spent less time writing the book in A-Hall and put a new writing seat dead center in the entranceway of that cell!

During the overnight ghost hunt, after Jenny had shared that photo with the rest of the staff, we as a group—Jenny, Barker, Alisha, Hannah, Lizzy, Taylor (Marie), Victoria, Dano, and I—went to the women's unit. I wanted to write in that specific cell, and they would investigate with all the ghost-hunting equipment. On the walk up the sallyport, Alisha felt something push her from behind, and she tripped up the stairs. Nobody in our group had touched her. She fell hard enough to cut her shin.

While they set up the Rem Pods in the hallway outside the cell, Dano sat on the cot inside the cell, and I sat on the chair that I had placed where the hands had been in the photo. Hannah placed Abigail in the cell next to us. I wrote, and everyone remained quiet, and I heard a groan/roar in the corner of the room that did *not* come from Dano, where I jumped from my chair so fast that I almost catapulted my laptop.

Later, in A-Hall, Hannah, Lizzy, Alisha, Dano, and I went into cell 36, where inmates had brutally stabbed a prisoner to death decades ago. I sat on the cot to write while they used the apps and Rem Pods to capture any activity. Using the Seer function of the app, I got an image of a man with stab marks covering his face on my phone.

Right before the hunt ended, Hannah, Lizzy, Alisha, and I were in the women's unit, where I wanted to finish a chapter. Hannah asked where my sister had gone, so I climbed the staircase to look for her on the upper floors—the same staircase the Christian/Warden-phantom climbs at the end of the book. I found Alisha, white as a ghost (pun intended), staring down the stairwell. She said she had been climbing the stairs and had heard someone behind her, so she turned to see if it was one of us, but a tall shadow figure of a man, a full apparition—short brown hair, blue button-down shirt and pants, and black boots; however his face was too "shady to make out"—was directly behind her, climbing the stairs too. Then he vanished.

(0900 – 1700 / 1900 – 0600 = 19 hours)

Night #11: When I entered A-Hall and sat at my writing spot, the app said, *"You're back."* Instead of writing, I needed to outline how alcohol would play a part in Christian's possession/transformation at the end. While I was working through different scenarios with the vodka bottle in his backpack, the app said, *"Beer. Gin."*

And the peekers were peeking tonight. I felt like they were trying to recreate the opening sequence of *The Muppet Show*, where all the Muppets have their own box. It seemed every time I looked anywhere on the walks, I would see one or two pop in and out.

I wanted to buy the main tour guides a gift for being so hospitable toward me during my stay, so I perused some websites for something regarding the film *Creepshow* for Lisa. I found a Jordy Verill Christmas tree ornament and a tee-shirt and couldn't decide between the two. The app said, *"Ornament."* I know much of this diary has been listing what the app said, but you need to understand how specific and beyond coincidence the words and their timing were. I don't just mean saying some of the characters' names when I typed them (which is bizarre all on its own), but to have it say something like *ornament* when I was shopping for an ornament, when the app had never said that word ever before, was mind-blowing.

I spotted a peeker on the second walkway, and I shone the red LED flashlight onto the entryway of the cell from my writing spot, and the app said, *"Don't."*

Then Lisa—who I had been shopping for—texted me from the office to inform me of something happening in the office, and my app said, *"Ornament,"* again.

In between two ghost tours, I went to the catwalk that started at cell 43 above my writing desk and extended to the opposite side of A-Hall. I sat, dangling my legs over the edge to write, and the app said, *"Be careful."*

I didn't need to mention him yet, but a bat lived in A-Hall during the entire eight weekends I was there. Reese lovingly named him Barney the Bat. He would hang out in the rafters, chirping away after sunset or dive-bombing guests during tours and hunts. Sharing space with Barney the Bat had become so normal to me when I was in A-Hall that I would forget he was there. As I focused on writing, my app said, *"Beside you,"* and a second later, Barney the Bat chirped right next to me as he swooped and almost hit my head. I ducked, and the app said, *"You're listening."*

I need to explain the backstory of cell 20 so this diary entry makes sense. On that Get Haunted overnight ghost hunt when I had been a guest, I met Wade, a NESPR member and one of the curators of the Warren Occult Museum. When I announced that I would be writing this book inside MSP, Wade told me to ensure I spent time in cell 20 but that the entity in there was a bit shy, so I would have to introduce myself. It was night eleven, and I had yet to sit in that cell to write. I mentioned this to Barker, and he said he had seen a shadow figure coming in and out of cell 20 multiple times this year. So I decided that tonight I would spend the rest of the time inside cell 20 to write.

I sat in the old penitentiary barber chair that rests in the back corner of cell 20 to work. Barker accompanied me, and when he sat next to me on a bench, we got visible goose bumps for no explanation. I apologized aloud for not writing in here earlier. Barker asked aloud if whoever occupied this cell wanted me to write in here tonight. My app went crazy, saying, *"It's time!"* at least two dozen times, like a needle stuck on a record player. In all the years Barker had been using the app, he said he had never heard the same phrase spoken this many times in a row.

MSP employs a uniformed Jefferson City Police Officer every night (hence why I moved Duncan from tour guide back to cop, which was what he had retired from in real life). A female cop, Officer Jensen, was on duty tonight and sat in cell 20 with me and Barker. My app continued to spit out, *"It's time!"* almost like it was stuck.

Officer Jensen and I chatted about Jefferson City while we sat in the cell. As she described the city's nightlife and some bars and clubs she used to visit, my app stopped saying, *"It's time,"* and spit out, *"Whore!"* Then it returned to saying, *"It's time,"* again. We guessed that, at this point, the app had said *It's time* upward to fifty-or-so times. When we stopped acknowledging it, the app played music, and a voice sang, *"It's time …*

It takes a lot to rattle Barker, but we left the cell because we just needed a break from the onslaught of the app repeating the same phrase. When we left, the app went silent.

Barker, Officer Jensen, and I returned to cell 20 a few hours later so I could write in that barber chair again and could take my obligatory nightly photo. As I sat in the chair, my laptop open, waiting for Barker to snap the photo, something touched my left ear hard enough to push down the top of it, and I jumped. My app immediately said, *"Twenty."* While I was glad it didn't said, *"It's time,"* again, having it say the number of the cell we were inside, when something had just pushed on my ear, frazzled me even more.

I resumed writing in the barber chair, while Officer Jensen sat next to me, and Barker sat across from me on the floor. They talked while I wrote, and Officer Jensen said something was touching her leg. Barker and I saw a black mass covering and obscuring the bottom of her right leg, like her leg wasn't there. She asked for the mass to go somewhere else, and Barker and I watched this black shape move from her leg, toward the far wall, and disappear under the sink. Afraid to look down, Officer Jensen asked if it was gone, because she couldn't feel it anymore. The three of us remained silent for a moment, then I closed my laptop, and we left cell 20 for the night.

Barker, Officer Jensen, and I relocated to Housing Unit 1 so I could sit in the entryway of the cell where Ms. Tissot had taken the photo of the apparition's hands. Jenny was already in that hallway with some other guests, also investigating that spot. Barker's app said a number, which didn't seem to correlate with any of the cells, so Jenny asked if that number meant anything to anyone. Barker said it was his age. Then his app said, *"Apologize."* He asked who needed to apologize, and his app said his full name. First and last. Everyone freaked out because no one had ever heard someone's full name before.

A guest entered the cell next to the one where Ms. Tissot had photographed the hands, and the guest's app said, *"Abigail."* The guest asked if anyone knew an Abigail, and I realized the guest was in the same cell where Hannah had put her Abigail Rem Pod doll the previous weekend.

After the hunt ended and the guests left, I accompanied Barker on the nightly sweep of clearing and locking the buildings. On the way up the dungeon staircase into A-Hall, something touched my elbow hard enough for me to flinch and to swipe at it.

(0900 – 1500 / 1700 – 0200 = 15 hours)

Night #12: I sat at my writing desk in A-Hall, and the app started with, *"It's time!"* again. At this point, I contemplated changing the name of the novel to *It's Time!*

While it is common to see peekers from the corner of your eye in A-Hall or to just get a glimpse of one for under a second, I watched a shadow figure exit a cell on the third floor to my right, walk a handful of cells toward me, then dip into a cell and disappear.

From my writing desk, I asked, "Do you want me to come back to cell 20 to write?" And my app said, *"It's time!"* again.

Guides Kathy and Lily brought a tour into A-Hall while I was writing. As I told Lily about the activity last night, her app said, *"Book,"* twice.

Rob from Get Haunted texted me a series of questions for me to answer in the dungeon, while I was alone. Remember how the dungeon and 3D were the two locations on the property I refused to go by myself. But, for the sake of authenticity, I steeled myself, put on a brave face, and entered the dungeon's cave-type darkness alone. While I walked through the horseshoe of the corridor toward the back cell, my red LED flashlight kept flickering on and off. It had never done that before.

I sat in the In-Your-Face cell to record the answers to Rob's interview questions on a selfie video, and, beyond my phone, the doorway to the corridor darkened. There is dark, then there is *MSP dungeon dark*. It looked like something had draped a black curtain over the entryway—like how the warden had done to Hannah and Christian in the book.

My red LED flashlight operated normally while I recorded the video, then flashed on and off again only during my walk through the dungeon corridor to leave. When I returned topside to A-Hall, my flashlight resumed normal steadiness.

Later, during the ghost hunt, I sat in the barber chair in cell 20 once more to write, and my app started again with, *"It's time!"* It was crazy how the app only said it when I was inside that cell or just outside its doorway.

I was discussing Hannah with someone while I was still writing in cell 20, and the app said, *"You met her here,"* then, *"Bookstores."*

(0800 – 1600 / 1900 – 0200 = 15 hours)

Night #13: I spent most of the day writing in A-Hall and in cell 20. The app said, *"It's time,"* in such repetition that I lost count. We were certainly in the hundreds at this point.

I relocated to write in cell 48 during sunlight hours, and when I was sitting on the cot, a shadow figure of a man walked past the door and disappeared.

(1200 – 1700 / 1900 – 2300 = 9 hours)

Night #14: A few things happened simultaneously when I reached my writing desk in A-Hall. I opened my laptop, launched the writing program I use, and stepped into the center of the hall to write a text to Hannah. The moment I hit Send, one of the cell doors sounded like someone had slammed it closed, echoing the loudest *BANG* through the hall. I was in there alone. Only the staff were on the premises, and I had just left them in the office.

I activated the ghost-translator app to hear if anything was trying to communicate, and a burst of voices came through the app, followed by the sound of a cell door closing again somewhere above me. As the cell door banged, the chapter of the warden attacking Hannah and draining her smartwatch in 3D launched on my laptop. I was not near my laptop nor touching it. I could see the screen from where I stood. The writing program I use separates each chapter into different tabs. I had the program currently on the chapter I was working on. For a previous chapter to launch in the program, someone or something must physically click on that tab.

After I took my obligatory nightly photo, the app said, *"Photo."* I sent this photo to my friend and fellow author Marissa D'Angelo, and when she replied, the app said, *"Photo,"* again simultaneously as the text alert sounded.

As I wrote, the app said, *"Behind you."* I didn't look up from my laptop but asked, "What's behind me?" The app replied, *"Twenty-eight."* My writing desk was directly to the left of cell 28 so close that I could touch the entryway. Then something fell or dropped inside cell 28 so loudly that I flinched, thinking a part of the ceiling had collapsed. I was alone and in complete darkness in A-Hall, save for the glow of the laptop screen. I braved a look into the neighboring cell but did not see anything out of place.

I was in the dungeon with Barker, writing in the In-Your-Face cell. Barker went into the hallway because we heard the metal door of the dungeon's entrance slam shut. I continued writing and heard Barker speaking to someone as he reapproached the cell. Whoever he was talking to stopped in the entranceway to the In-Your-Face cell; I could see their outline in the archway. Then Dano entered the cell with Barker from around the corner, and whoever had been standing in the entranceway was gone. They had both been in the hallway while talking. Neither of them had been standing in the entranceway in front of me. And we were the only three in the dungeon.

I haven't discussed doppelgängers yet nor did I include this phenomenon in the novel. Almost every MSP staff member, as well as some uniformed Jefferson City Police Officers and tour guests, have experienced paranormal doppelgängers. We know very little about their origin or why they exist, but, if you ever visit MSP for a tour or a hunt, ask any of the guides about these stories. They love to tell them!

These occurrences revolve around a replica of someone who is somewhere else on the property. They tend to not interact with people and seem almost preprogrammed in their movements. Unlike shadow figures, doppelgänger features are defined and clear. Everyone has their level of skepticism for the unknown. Doppelgängers, while I believed the staff's firsthand stories, were one level of paranormal occurrences I just couldn't wrap my head around. Until I saw one …

Dano and I were sitting in the In-Your-Face cell in the dungeon while I wrote, and we heard someone approaching the end of the corridor horseshoe. We both looked up, expecting a guest to enter the cell and to hang out with us, which was common during ghost hunts—the dungeon is a fan favorite! Instead, we watched a guest, who we remembered from Jenny's security briefing at the start of the night, walk past the doorway. His face, hair, backward baseball hat, height, etc. were perfectly clear and visible.

If you remember from the novel, when I described the dungeon's layout, the In-Your-Face cell was the last open cell in the horseshoe before the dead end, but after the cell was the sealed door that had never been opened. Guests sometimes want to try to see inside or to take pictures of the mystery door, so it wasn't completely weird that the man powerwalked past the In-Your-Face cell toward the end of the corridor.

Seconds later, Barker and Lisa arrived at the cell. Dano asked if a guest was at the end of the corridor. They said no. It would have been impossible for someone *not* to be there, based on how soon Lisa and Barker had arrived and how Dano and I had not seen the guest walk back past the cell door. So, where had he gone? Dano was convinced we had just experienced a doppelgänger. My skepticism still lay heavy.

Until …

Dano and I went on a mission to find the guest. And we did. With his female counterpart. On a different part of the property. And we asked him about it. He had not been in the dungeon yet that night. And he had not left his female companion's sight. But Dano and I saw him—100 percent.

And he must have disappeared somewhere at the end of that corridor. I was now a believer in this phenomenon.

Milestone: I finished the first draft of the novel just after midnight inside cell 115. When I knew I only had a few pages left to write, I went to cell 115 specifically to pay homage to our brimmed-hat shadow man. I finished the last chapter while sitting on his cot, underneath where Hannah had snatched his closet strip years prior.

(1700 – 0200 = 9 hours)

Night #15: After I finish the first draft of a novel, I export it from the writing program I use into a document to work on the second draft. After I arrived, I went into cell 20 to export the book and to begin work on the second draft. I was sitting in the barber chair while I began the export, and a shadow figure passed the doorway three times. I was alone in A-Hall; the staff were in the office, and guests had not been let onto the property yet.

I got an error message from my writing program that none of the files (each chapter had its own file) were in the correct supported format for exporting. I had to copy and paste each chapter individually into a new document. Again, I have been using this writing program since 2017, starting with *Moonlight City Drive* and through my next six published novels, and I have never had this issue.

Later, while I worked on the second draft on a cot in cell 43, the app said, *"I'm leaving."* I asked who was leaving, and it said, *"Forty-three."* Remember, this cell had perfect visibility of my writing desk below, so I said, "I thought we were buddies." And my app fired off, *"Leave. Stalker. Turn it off … He won't leave."*

Dano and I were sitting inside cell 20, and we saw a shadow figure outside the cell, looking in at us, then it disappeared. We mentioned the Get Haunted/NESPR event where they had brought the Shadow Doll from the Warren Occult Museum, and the app said, *"The doll."*

I was in the women's unit with a Tracer Light (a device that works like a Rem Pod, but the lights travel up and down a runwaylike strip instead of flashing on a circular object), working on the second draft in the doorway of the cell where Ms. Tissot took the photo of the hands. The Tracer Light turned red, and a breeze blew from inside that cell behind me and into the hallway. The cells have no windows.

A guest entered the cell and used the app where the energies can show us images. On her phone was an image of a woman holding up her hands.

I was describing the cell that had the Disney Magic Kingdom castle painted on its toilet on the fourth floor—the floor where Hannah hides at the end of the book—to two guests, and the app said, *"Mansion,"* then *"Hannah."*

In A-Hall, I sat in one of the rows of metal folding chairs to write, and someone was playing music on their phone. They turned it off, and someone else's app, from the other side of A-Hall, said, *"The music."*

A guest exited cell 23, all excited about something and wanting to get our attention. I walked the length of A-Hall, and she told me and Dano that the doctor's coat that hung inside the cell was swinging by itself. Cell 23 has a bunch of medical gear on display, along with the white doctor's scrub hanging on a coatrack. It was not moving when we entered, but she showed me a video she had taken of it. As we reviewed the video, movement caught our eye, and we watched the coat swing, as if someone was moving it back and forth. No one was in an arm's length of it, and no windows were open. Then someone's app said, *"Heart attack."*

Toward the end of the night at the gas chamber, Lisa was describing the mass graves of prisoners in the corner of the parking lot to the guests. A guest asked why we couldn't investigate or ghost hunt the gravesites. Lisa explained why MSP does not encourage it, and the app said, *"Thank you for your respect."*

(0800 – 1600 / 1900 – 0600 = 19 hours)

Night #16: When I reached my writing desk in A-Hall, I announced to the empty building, sans Barney the Bat, that this was my last weekend here. My app said, *"Don't leave."*

I was working on the second draft at my writing desk and texted Hannah about something funny that had happened, and she replied in text, *That's hilarious.* I resumed working on the second draft, and the app said, *"Hannah. You are funny."*

During the scene in 3D where everyone gets sucked into the cells, I was rewriting Alisha's dialogue, and my app said, *"Sister."*

(1700 – 0300 = 10hrs)

Night #17: My final night had arrived. This night was also MSP's special event, titled appropriately enough, "These Walls Still Talk." I hunkered down in cell 48 to hopefully finish the second draft—and the last draft before I send the novel to my wonderful editor. I typed the word "closet" simultaneously as the app said, *"Closet,"* when I was reworking the scene where Hannah hid in the women's unit. When I was rearranging the scene where the warden needs Christian's energy to hunt Hannah at the climax, the app said, *"Am I ghost?"* then *"No energy."*

It was time for the first tour to enter A-Hall, and the app said, *"They're here,"* when guides Randy and Fred opened the front door.

Later, while I sat at my writing desk in A-Hall, I heard sounds that resembled someone pulling a cluster of empty soda cans along the walkway above me.

I went to cell 115 in A-Hall to finish the second draft, except the final chapter, and somewhere below I heard something hitting the cell bars, loud—almost like how the Christian/Warden-phantom ran the sledgehammer along the bars at the end of the novel.

Milestone: A few minutes past 3:00 p.m., I finished the second draft. I typed the final word while sitting in one of the gas chamber chairs, because, as Jenny preaches: *All tours (and now books) end in the gas chamber.*

Now I could enjoy the "These Walls Still Talk" event tonight without having a book to work on. The first thing I did was stand at my writing desk, look up at cell 43, and say farewell to whoever had been in there watching me for the past eight weekends. As soon as I finished my goodbye, something touched my left hand with enough pressure that I flinched. No one was in the building—except Barney the Bat, and he was chirping away in the rafters.

Tonight was special because it marked the twentieth anniversary of MSP closing its doors as a functioning penitentiary, hence the event. At the stroke of midnight, the on-duty guides—Jenny, Lisa, Reese, Barker, Duncan—had organized a rave in A-Hall, complete with glow sticks and music. The hundred-or-so guests lined the four walkways of the building where I had spent the past eight weekends writing, usually alone. To watch the guests wave all their glow sticks to the beat, covering every walkway and catwalk of the building on my final night, was a sight to behold. And a tad emotional.

But all things must come to an end. After the event ended, the staff asked me to do a final walkthrough of the women's unit to check for any wayward guests before we locked the front doors. As I climbed the stairwell—the same one the Christian/Warden-phantom climbed to hunt Hannah—at the exact spot where Alisha had seen the full-figured shadow figure during her visit, I saw this gray smoky mist rise from the floor to the ceiling. *Gray* … Wasn't the woman who resided in this unit a gray-skinned lady in my book? Maybe she was saying goodbye. Or maybe she was ensuring I was kept safe from the warden, who may have been just around the corner, lurking in the shadows and waiting for his moment to strike …

I want to mention something nonparanormal that happened tonight, because it hit close to home with scenes in the novel. What does Jenny say is the number one rule? Do *not* close any of the cell doors. Over one thousand doors are on the property, and the staff only have a handful of keys at best. What is another major rule to attend a ghost hunt? No alcohol. That means no arriving drunk nor drinking on the property. And what happens if this occurs? The uniformed Jefferson City Police Officer will escort them off the property.

Well, on my final night at MSP, on the night I finished the novel, on the night they had a special event named, "These Walls Still Talk," we got the trifecta. A guest, who had arrived drunk, locked his wife in a cell as a joke, and the on-duty officer escorted them off the property. Sometimes reality follows fiction, as in my storyline, where Hannah had arrived drunk on her twenty-first birthday, and the shadow warden had closed cells on guests, and Officer Duncan had escorted Heath, Parker, and Dano off the property. And here we were, on my final night in MSP, and I witnessed all three moments that I had already written, in a finished work of fiction, just happen to real humans simultaneously.

Sometimes you just can't make this shit up …

(0900 – 1700 / 1800 – 0300 = 22 hours)

Total time inside = 214 hours

… I need a nap.

I did not fabricate a single building, cell number, or location for the book, so if you visit the Missouri State Penitentiary for their daytime history tours or their nighttime ghost tours/hunts, ensure you say hello to the shadow warden in 3D, the Creeper in Death Row, my writing buddy in cell 43, the gray-skinned lady in Housing Unit 1, the tuggers in the dungeon, and all the peekers in A-Hall. But most important, take a moment to visit cell 115 in A-Hall to pay your respects to our escaped inmate with the brimmed hat. You'll find he has a solitary bolt screwed into the wall above his cot to the left of the window, with no closet strip hanging from it anymore …

I would like to thank and acknowledge the rest of the tour guides and new friends who I didn't have enough characters for; I didn't want this to turn into the ensemble of Victor Hugo's Les Miserables.

MSP staff: Marianne, Kathy, Fred, Les, Mike, Ashley (both of them), Randy, De'Nel, Adrienne, and Sgt. Glass (who informed me that the inmates called those strips of fabric that hang in all the cells that Hannah stole "*closets*").

Additional friends who I wish I had enough places in the book for, who had firsthand experiences with me at the penitentiary: Lizzy, Victoria, Bennett, Bryan, Gonzales, Polk, and Moore. (They know who they are.)

And last but certainly not least, Barney the Bat—sometimes the only carbon-based lifeform inside A-Hall / Housing Unit 4 with me while I wrote at night.

Jenny's mantra in the book and in real life rings true, "All tours end in the gas chamber," because this was where my journey writing this book ended also, as I said goodbye to the penitentiary and its staff from the gas chamber, after their "These Walls Still Talk" event.

… Is it synchronicity that I finished the final version of this Author's Note & Diary on Halloween, October 31—a celebration of the dead?

… And keeping with the milestones coincidentally happening on important days, (I finished the book on the night of MSP's twentieth anniversary of closing the prison, during their "These Walls Still Talk" event. Then I finished the Author's Note on Halloween), now I finished the final proofread, before it goes to my editor, on December 1—which is my birthday.

… And I finished implementing my editor's notes and suggestions, completely coincidentally, on my son Everett's sixteenth birthday: February 11.

Is it serendipity or coincidence? Does it garner a gasp or an eyeroll? A good argument for both, I think. And that balance between skepticism and belief—and the drive to keep finding answers yet loving when new questions arise—is what fuels this amazing community. Thank you for going on this ride with me.

But is the ride over …?

Cast of Characters & Writing Moments

Rob from Get Haunted
in the Dungeon

Sara's doppelgänger
(from Get Haunted) in Death Row

Me & Trevor from Get Haunted down in 3D

Me & Jenny in the lobby

Me & Reese at the sallyport into the Women's Unit

Lisa in the lobby

Me & Dano on the steps
to Death Row/HU3

Me & Barker in cell 20
in A-Hall

Me & Duncan in the lobby

Me & Shiela on the walkway
to A-Hall behind us

Lily in A-Hall

Me & Hannah outside the front doors of MSP

Christian in Death Row
when something touched him

Me & Taylor Marie in A-Hall

Me & Alisha at the stairs to the Dungeon in A-Hall

Me & Heath in the Gas Chamber

Parker in A-Hall

Me writing in cell 43
in A-Hall

Me writing down in 3D

Me writing in Death Row

Ms. Tissot's photo of the ghost hands in HU1

<-- Me writing in that cell

Writing desk from 4-walk in A-Hall

Me writing in the Dungeon's "In Your Face" cell

Me in cell 115 in A-Hall
finishing the first draft

Typing the last word in
the Gas Chamber

www.ingramcontent.com/pod-product-compliance
Lightning Source LLC
LaVergne TN
LVHW092100120725
815787LV00004B/19

* 9 7 8 1 9 6 0 8 5 5 0 9 1 *